There was a sluggishne[...]
was a thick feeling, lik[...]
been shuttered for year[...]
ergies together, but they seemed to resist, to follow his desires with only the greatest reluctance.

Khadgar's face grew stern as he tried to pull more of the power of the room, the energies, into himself. This was a simple spell. If anything, it should be easier in this spellroom, where such castings would be commonplace. Suddenly the young mage was swamped with the thick, fetid feel of the magic. It fell upon him in a thick blanket, crushing the spell and driving him physically to his knees. Despite himself, he cried out.

Medivh was at his side at once, helping the young mage to his feet. "There, there," he said. "I didn't expect you to succeed even that well. Good try."

"What is it?" managed Khadgar, suddenly able to breathe again. "It was like nothing I've felt before."

"That's good news for you, then," said Medivh. "The magic has been twisted here, a result of what happened earlier."

"You mean like a haunting?" said Khadgar. "Even in Karazhan, I never . . ."

"No, not like that," said Medivh. "Something much worse. The two dead mages here were summoning demons. It's that taint that you feel. A demon was here."

WARCRAFT®

THE LAST GUARDIAN

JEFF GRUBB

POCKET BOOKS
New York London Toronto Sydney Singapore

The sale of this book without its cover is unauthorized. If you purchased this book without a cover, you should be aware that it was reported to the publisher as "unsold and destroyed." Neither the author nor the publisher has received payment for the sale of this "stripped book."

This book is a work of fiction. Names, characters, places and incidents are products of the author's imagination or are used fictitiously. Any resemblance to actual events or locales or persons living or dead is entirely coincidental.

An *Original* Publication of POCKET BOOKS

POCKET BOOKS, a division of Simon & Schuster, Inc.
1230 Avenue of the Americas, New York, NY 10020

Copyright © 2002 by Blizzard Entertainment. All rights reserved. Warcraft and Blizzard Entertainment are trademarks or registered trademarks of Blizzard Entertainment in the U.S. and/or other countries. All other trademarks are the property of their respective owners.

All rights reserved, including the right to reproduce this book or portions thereof in any form whatsoever.
For information address Pocket Books, 1230 Avenue of the Americas, New York, NY 10020

ISBN: 0-671-04151-7

First Pocket Books printing December 2002

10 9 8 7 6 5 4 3 2 1

POCKET and colophon are registered trademarks of Simon & Schuster, Inc.

For information regarding special discounts for bulk purchases, please contact Simon & Schuster Special Sales at 1-800-456-6798 or business@simonandschuster.com

Cover art by Sam Didier

Printed in the U.S.A.

To Chris Metzen,
Who Kept the Vision

THE LAST GUARDIAN

PROLOGUE
The Lonely Tower

The larger of the two moons had risen first this evening, and now hung pregnant and silver-white against a clear, star-dappled sky. Beneath the lambent moon the peaks of the Redridge Mountains strained for the sky. In the daylight the sun picked out hues of magenta and rust among the great granite peaks, but in the moonlight they were reduced to tall, proud ghosts. To the west lay the Forest of Elwynn, its heavy canopy of greatoaks and satinwoods running from the foothills to the sea. To the east, the bleak swamp of the Black Morass spread out, a land of marshes and low hills, bayous and backwaters, failed settlements and lurking danger. A shadow passed briefly across the moon, a raven-sized shadow, bearing for a hole in the heart of the mountain.

Here a chunk had been pulled from the fastness of

the Redridge Range, leaving behind a circular vale. Once it might have been the site of some primeval celestial impact or the memory of an earth-shaking explosion, but the aeons had worn the bowl-shaped crater into a series of steep-edged, rounded hillocks which were now cradled by the steeped mountains surrounding them. None of the ancient trees of Elwynn could reach its altitude, and the interior of the ringed hills was barren save for weeds and tangled vines.

At the center of the ringed hills lay a bare tor, as bald as the pate of a Kul Tiras merchant lord. Indeed the very way the hillock rose steeply, than gentled to a near-level slope at its apex, was similar in shape to a human skull. Many had noted it over the years, though only a few had been sufficiently brave, or powerful, or tactless to mention it to the property's owner.

At the flattened peak of the tor rose an ancient tower, a thick, massive protrusion of white stone and dark mortar, a man-made eruption that shot effortlessly into the sky, scaling higher than the surrounding hills, lit like a beacon by the moonlight. There was a low wall at the base of the tower surrounding a bailey, and within those walls the tumbledown remains of a stable and a smithy, but the tower itself dominated all within the ringed hills.

Once this place was called Karazhan. Once it was home of the last of the mysterious and secretive Guardians of Tirisfal. Once it was a living place. Now it was simply abandoned and timelost.

There was silence upon the tower but not a stillness.

In the night's embrace quiet shapes flitted from window to window, and phantoms danced along the balconies and parapets. Less than ghosts, but more than memories, these were nothing less than pieces of the past that had become unstuck from the flow of time. These shadows of the past had been pried loose by the madness of the tower's owner, and were now condemned to play out their histories again and again, in the silence of the abandoned tower. Condemned to play but denied of any audience to appreciate them.

Then in the silence, there was the soft scrape of a booted foot against stone, then another. A flash of movement beneath the lambent moon, a shadow against the white stone, a flutter of a tattered, red-hued cloak in the cool night air. A figure walked along the topmost parapet, on the crenellated uppermost spire that years before had served as an observatory.

The parapet door into the observatory screeched open on ancient hinges, then stopped, frozen by rust and the passage of time. The cloaked figure paused a moment, then placed a finger on the hinge, and muttered a few choice words. The door swung open silently, the hinges made as if new. The trespasser allowed himself a smile.

The observatory was empty now, what tools that remained smashed and abandoned. The trespassing figure, almost as silent as a ghost himself, picked up a crushed astrolabe, its scale twisted in some now-forgotten rage.

Now it is merely a heavy piece of gold, inert and useless in his hands.

There was other movement in the observatory, and the trespasser looked up. Now a ghostly figure stood nearby, near one of the many windows. The ghost/non-ghost was an broad-shouldered man, hair and beard once dark but now going to a premature gray at the edges. The figure was one of the shards of the past, unglued and now repeating its task, regardless of whether it had observers or not. For the moment, the dark-haired man held the astrolabe, the unbroken twin to the one in the trespasser's hands, and fiddled with a small knob along one side. A moment, a check, and a twitch of the knob. His dark brows furrowed over ghostly green eyes. A second moment, another check, and another twitch. Finally, the tall, imposing figure sighed deeply and placed the astrolabe on a table that was no longer there, and vanished.

The trespasser nodded. Such hauntings were common even in the days when Karazhan was inhabited, though now, stripped of the control (and the madness) of their master, they had become more brazen. Yet these shards of the past belonged here, while he did not. He was the interloper, not they.

The trespasser crossed the room to its staircase leading down, while behind him the older man flickered back into the view and repeated his action, sighting his astrolabe on a planet that had long since moved to other parts of the sky.

The trespasser moved down through the tower,

crossing levels to reach other stairs and other hallways. No door was shut to him, even those locked and bolted, or sealed by rust and age. A few words, a touch, a gesture and the fetters flew loose, the rust dissolved into ruddy piles, the hinges restored. In one or two places ancient wards still glowed, potent despite their age. He paused before them for a moment, considering, reflecting, searching his memory for the correct counter-sign. He spoke the correct word, made the correct motion with his hands, shattered the weak magic that remained, and passed on.

As he moved through the tower, the phantoms of the past grew more agitated and more active. Now with a potential audience, it seemed that these pieces of the past wished to play themselves out, if only to be made free of this place. Any sound they once possessed had long-since eroded away, leaving only their images moving through the halls.

The interloper passed an ancient butler in dark livery, the frail old man shuffling slowly down the empty hallway, carrying a silver tray and wearing a set of horse-blinders. The interloper passed through the library, where a green-fleshed young woman stood with her back to him, pouring over an ancient tome. He passed through a banquet hall, at one end a group of musicians playing soundlessly, dancers twirling in a gavotte. At the other end a great city burned, its flames beating ineffectively against the stone walls and rotting tapestries. The trespasser moved through the silent flames, but his face grew drawn and tense as he witnessed once more the mighty city of Stormwind burn around him.

In one room three young men sat around a table and told now-unknown lies. Metal mugs were scattered on the table's surface as well as beneath it. The trespasser stood watching this image for a long time, until a phantom taverness brought another round. Then he shook his head and pressed on.

He reached nearly the ground level, and stepped out on a low balcony that hung precariously to the wall, like a wasps' nest over the main entrance. There, in the wide space before the tower, between the main entrance and a now-collapsed stables across the bailey, stood a single ghostly image, lonely and separated. It did not move like the others, but rather stood there, waiting, tentative. A piece of the past that had not been released. A piece that was waiting for him.

The immobile image was of a young man with a skunk stripe of white running through his dark, untidy head of hair. The straggling fragments of a beard, newly grown, clung to his face. A battered rucksack lay at the youth's feet, and he held a red-sealed letter with a deathlike grip.

This was well and truly no ghost, the trespasser knew, though the owner of this image may yet be dead, fallen in combat beneath a foreign sun. This was a memory, a shard of the past, trapped like an insect in amber, waiting for its release. Waiting for his arrival.

The trespasser sat on the stonework ledge of the balcony and looked out, beyond the bailey, beyond the hillock, and beyond the ringed hills. There was silence in the moonlight, as the mountains themselves seemed to be holding their breath, waiting for him.

The trespasser lifted a hand and intoned a series of chanted words. Softly came the rhymes and rhythms the first time, then louder, and finally louder still, shattering the calm. In the distance wolves picked up his chant and cast it back in howling counterpoint.

And the image of the ghostly youth, its feet seemingly trapped in mud, took a deep breath, hoisted his rucksack of secrets to his shoulder, and slogged his way toward the main entrance of Medivh's Tower.

ONE
Karazhan

Khadgar clutched the crimson-sealed letter of introduction and desperately tried to remember his own name. He had ridden for days, accompanying various caravans, and finally making the journey alone to Karazhan through the vast, overgrown, woods of Elwynn. Then the long climb into the heights of the mountains, to this serene, empty, lonely place. Even the air felt cold and apart. Now, sore and tired, the scruffy-bearded young man stood in the gathering dusk of the courtyard, petrified of what he now must do.

Introduce himself to the most powerful mage of Azeroth.

An honor, the scholars of the Kirin Tor had said. An opportunity, they insisted, that was not to be missed. Khadgar's sage mentors, a conclave of influential scholars and sorcerers, told him they had been trying to insinuate a sympathetic ear in the tower of Karazhan for years. The Kirin Tor wanted to learn what knowledge the most powerful wizard in the land had hidden away in his library. They wanted to know what research he favored. And most of all they wanted this maverick mage to start planning for his legacy, wanted to know when the great and powerful Medivh planned to train an heir.

The Great Medivh and the Kirin Tor had been at loggerheads on these and other matters for years, apparently, and only now did he relent to some of their entreaties. Only now would he take on an apprentice. Whether it was from a softening of the wizard's reportedly hard heart, or mere diplomatic concession, or a feeling of the mage's own creeping mortality, it did not matter to Khadgar's masters. The simple truth was that this powerful independent (and to Khadgar, mysterious) wizard had asked for an assistant, and the Kirin Tor, which ruled over the magical kingdom of Dalaran, were more than happy to comply.

So the youth Khadgar was selected and shuttled off with a list of directions, orders, counter-orders, requests, suggestions, advice, and other demands from his sorcerous masters. Ask Medivh about his mother's battles with demons, asked Guzbah, his first instructor. Find out all you can about elven history from his library, requested Lady Delth. Check his volumes for any bestiaries, commanded Alonda, who was convinced that there was a fifth species of troll as yet unrecorded in her own volumes. Be direct, forthright, and honest, advised Norlan the Chief Artificer—the Great Magus Medivh seemed to value those traits. Be diligent and do what you're told. Don't slouch. Always seem interested. Stand up straight. And above all, keep your ears and eyes open.

The ambitions of the Kirin Tor did not bother Khadgar horribly—his upbringing in Dalaran and his early apprenticeship to the conclave made it clear to him that his mentors were insatiably curious about magic in all its forms. Their continual accumulation, cataloging, and definition of magic were imprinted on young students at an early age, and Khadgar was no different than most.

Indeed, he realized, his own curiosity may have accounted for his current plight. His own nocturnal wanderings through the halls of the Violet Citadel of Dalaran had uncovered more than a few secrets that the conclave would rather not have noised about. The Chief Artificer's fondness for flamewine, for example, or Lady Delth's preference for young cavaliers a slender fraction of her age, or Korrigan the Librarian's secret collection of pamphlets describing (in lurid fashion) the practices of historical demon-worshipers.

And there was something about one of the great sages of Dalaran, venerable Arrexis, one of the gray eminences that even the others respected. He had disappeared, or died, or something horrible had happened, and the others chose to make no mention of it, even to the point of excising Arrexis's name from the volumes and not speaking of him again. But Khadgar had found out, nonetheless. Khadgar had a way of finding the necessary reference, making the needed connection, or talking to the right person at the right time. It was a gift and may yet prove to be a curse.

Any one of these discoveries could have resulted in his drawing this prestigious (and for all the planning and warnings, potentially fatal) assignment. Perhaps they thought young Khadgar was a little *too* good at ferreting out secrets—easier for the conclave to send him somewhere where his curiosity would do some good for the Kirin Tor. Or at least put him far enough away so he wasn't finding things out about the other natives of the Violet Citadel.

And Khadgar, through his relentless eavesdropping, had heard *that* theory as well.

So Khadgar set out with a rucksack filled with notes, a heart filled with secrets, and a head filled with strong demands and useless advice. In the final week before leaving Dalaran, he had heard from nearly every member of the conclave, each of whom was interested in something about Medivh. For a wizard living on the butt-end of nowhere, surrounded by trees and ominous peaks, the members of the Kirin Tor were extremely curious about him. Urgent, even.

Taking a deep breath (and in doing so reminding himself that he still was too close to the stables), Khadgar strode forward toward the tower itself, his feet feeling like he was pulling his pack-pony along by his ankles.

The main entrance yawned like a cavern's mouth, without gate or portcullis. That made sense, for what army would fight its way through the Forest of Elwynn to top the rounded walls of the crater, all to fight the Magus Medivh himself? There was no record of anyone or anything even attempting to besiege Karazhan.

The shadowed entrance was tall enough to let an elephant in full livery pass beneath. Overhanging it slightly was a wide balcony with a balustrade of white stone. From that perch one would be level with the surrounding hills and gain a view of the mountains beyond. There was a flicker of motion along the balustrade, a bit of movement that Khadgar *felt* more than actually witnessed. A robed figure, perhaps, moving back along the balcony into the tower itself. Was he being watched even now? Was there no one to greet him, or was he expected to brave the tower on his own?

"You are the New Young Man?" said a soft, almost sepulchral voice, and Khadgar, his head still craned upward, nearly jumped out of his skin. He wheeled to see a stooped, thin figure emerge out of the shadows of the entranceway.

The stooped thing looked marginally human, and for a moment Khadgar wondered if Medivh was mutating forest animals to work as his servants. This one looked like a hairless weasel, its long face was framed by what looked like a pair of black rectangles.

Khadgar didn't remember making any response, but

the weasel person stepped farther from the shadows, and repeated itself.

"You are the New Young Man?" it said. Each word was enunciated with its own breath, encapsulated in its own little box, capitalized and separate from the others. It stepped from the shadows fully and revealed itself as nothing more or less threatening than a whip-slender elderly man in dark worsted livery. A servant—human, but a servant. It, or rather he, was still wearing black rectangles on the sides of his head, like a set of earmuffs, that extended forward to his most prominent nose.

The youth realized that he was staring at the old man, "Khadgar," he said, then after a moment presented the tightly held letter of introduction. "Of Dalaran. Khadgar of Dalaran, in the kingdom of Lordaeron. I was sent by the Kirin Tor. From the Violet Citadel. I am Khadgar of the Kirin Tor. From the Violet Citadel. Of Dalaran. In Lordaeron." He felt like he was casting conversational stones into a great, empty well, hoping that the old man would respond to any of them.

"Of course you are, Khadgar," said the old man. "Of the Kirin Tor. Of the Violet Citadel. Of Dalaran. Of Lordaeron." The servant took the proffered letter as if the document were a live reptile and, after smoothing out its crumpled edges, tucked it inside his livery vest without opening it. After carrying and protecting it for so many miles, Khadgar felt a pain of loss. The letter of introduction represented his future, and he was loath to see it disappear, even for a moment.

"The Kirin Tor sent me to assist Medivh. Lord Medivh. The Wizard Medivh. Medivh of Karazhan," Khadgar realized he was but a half-step from collapsing into a full-fledged babble, and with a definitive effort tightly clamped his mouth shut.

"I'm sure they did," said the servant. "Send you, that is." He appraised the seal on the letter, and a thin hand dipped into his waistcoat, pulling out a set of black rectangles bound by a thin band of metal. "Blinders?"

Khadgar blinked. "No. I mean, no thank you."

"Moroes," said the servant.

Khadgar shook his head.

"I am Moroes," the servant said. "Steward of the Tower. Castellan to Medivh. Blinders?" Again he raised the black rectangles, twins to those that framed his narrow face.

"No thank you . . . Moroes," said Khadgar, his face twisted in curiosity.

The servant turned and motioned that Khadgar follow with a weak wave of the arm.

Khadgar picked up his rucksack and had to lope forward to catch up with the servant. For all his supposed fragility the steward moved at a good clip.

"Are you alone in the tower?" Khadgar ventured as they started climbing a curved set of wide, low stairs. The stone dipped in the center, worn by myriad feet of passing servants and guests.

"Eh?" responded the servant.

"Are you alone?" repeated Khadgar, wondering if he

would be reduced to speaking as Moroes spoke in order to be understood. "Do you live here by yourself?"

"The Magus is here," responded Moroes in a wheezing voice that sounded as faint and as fatal as grave dust.

"Yes, of course," said Khadgar.

"Wouldn't be much point for you to be here if he wasn't," continued the steward. "Here, that is." Khadgar wondered if the old man's voice sounded that way because it was not used that often.

"Of course," agreed Khadgar. "Anyone else?"

"You, now," continued Moroes. "More work to take care of two than one. Not that I was consulted."

"So just you and the Wizard, then, normally?" said Khadgar, wondering if the steward had been hired (or created) for his taciturn nature.

"And Cook," said Moroes, "Though Cook doesn't talk much. Thank you for asking, though."

Khadgar tried to restrain himself from rolling his eyes, but failed. He hoped that the blinders on either side of the steward's face kept the servant from seeing his response.

They reached a level spot, a cross-hallway lit by torches. Moroes crossed immediately to another set of saddle-worn, curving stairs opposite them. Khadgar paused for a moment to examine the torches. He raised a hand mere inches from the flickering flame, but felt no heat. Khadgar wondered if the cold flame was common throughout the tower. In Dalaran they used phosphorescent crystals, which beamed with a steady, constant glow, though his research spoke of reflective mirrors, elemental spirits bound within lanterns, and in one case, huge captive fireflies. Yet these flames seemed to be frozen in place.

Moroes, half-mounted up the next staircase, slowly turned and let out a gasping cough. Khadgar hurried to catch up. Apparently the blinders did not limit the old steward that much.

"Why the blinders?" Khadgar asked.

"Eh?" replied Moroes.

Khadgar touched the side of his head. "The blinders. Why?"

Moroes twisted his face in what Khadgar could only assume was a smile. "Magic's strong here. Strong, and wrong, sometimes. You see . . . things . . . around here. Unless you're careful. I'm careful. Other visitors, the ones before you, they were less careful. They're gone now."

Khadgar thought of the phantom he may or may not have seen on the overhanging balcony, and nodded.

"Cook has a set of rose-quartz lenses," added Moroes. "Swears by them." He paused for a moment, then added, "Cook is a bit foolish that way."

Khadgar hoped that Moroes would be more chatty once he was warmed up. "So, you've been in the Magus's household for long?"

"Eh?" said Moroes again.

"You've been with Medivh long?" Khadgar said, hoping to keep the impatience out of his voice.

"Ayep," said the steward. "Long enough. Too long. Seems like years. Time's like that here." The weathered steward let his voice trail off and the two climbed in silence.

"What do you know about him?" ventured Khadgar, finally. "The Magus, I mean."

"Question is," said Moroes, pulling open yet another door to reveal yet another staircase up. "What do *you* know?"

Khadgar's own research in the matter was surprisingly unproductive, and his results were frustratingly sparse. Despite access to the Violet Citadel's Grand Library (and surreptitious access to a few private libraries and secret collections), there was precious little on this great and powerful Medivh. This was doubly odd, since every elder mage in Dalaran seemed to hold Medivh in awe, and wanted one thing or another from him. Some favor, some boon, some bit of information.

Medivh was apparently a young man, as wizards went. He was merely in his forties, and for a grand bulk of that time seemed to have made no impact whatsoever on his surroundings. This was a surprise to Khadgar. Most of the tales he had heard and read described independent wizards as being extremely showy, fearless in dabbling in secrets man was not meant to know, and usually dead, crippled, or damned from messing with powers and energies beyond their ken. Most of the lessons he had learned as a child about non-Dalaran mages always ended in the same fashion—without restraint, control, and thought, the wild, untrained, and self-taught wizards always came to a bad end (sometimes, though not often, destroying a large amount of the surrounding countryside with them).

The fact that Medivh had failed to bring a castle down on top of himself, or disperse his atoms across the Twisting Nether, or summon a dragon without knowing how to control that dragon, indicated either great restraint or great power. From the fuss that the scholars had made about his appointment, and the list of instructions he had received, Khadgar decided on the latter.

Yet for all his research, he could not figure out why. Nothing indicated any great research of this Medivh's, any major discovery, nor any ground-shaking achievement, that would account for obvious awe in which the Kirin Tor held this independent mage. No huge wars, great conquests, or known mighty battles. The bards were noticeably sketchy when it came to the matters involving Medivh, and otherwise diligent heralds nodded when it came time to discuss his accomplishments.

And yet, realized Khadgar, there was something important here, something that created in the scholars a mixture of fear, respect, and envy. The Kirin Tor held no other spellcasters as their equals for magical knowledge, indeed often sought to hinder those wizards who did not hold allegiance to the Violet Citadel. And yet they kowtowed to Medivh. Why?

Khadgar had only the smallest bits—a bit on his parentage (Guzbah was particularly interested in Medivh's mother), some margin notes in a grimoire invoking his name, and mention of the occasional visit to Dalaran. All these visits were within the past five years, and apparently Medivh met only with elder mages, such as the now-missing Arrexis.

To sum up, Khadgar knew previous little of this supposedly great mage he was assigned to work for. And as he considered knowledge to be his armor and sword, he felt woefully underequipped for the coming encounter.

Aloud, he said, "Not much."

"Eh?" responded Moroes, half-turning on the staircase.

"I said I don't know much," said Khadgar, louder than he meant to. His voice bounced off the bare walls of the stairway. It was curved now, and Khadgar was wondering if the tower was truly as high as it seemed. Already his thighs were aching from the climb.

"Of course you don't," said Moroes. "Know, that is. Young people never know much. That's what makes them young, I suppose."

"I mean," said Khadgar, irritated. He paused and took a deep breath. "I mean, I don't know much about Medivh. You asked."

Moroes held for a moment, his foot poised on the next step, "I suppose I did," he said at last.

"What *is* he like?" asked Khadgar, his voice almost pleading.

"Like everyone else, I suppose," said Moroes. "Has his druthers. Has his moods. Good days and bad. Like everybody else."

"Puts his pants on one leg at a time," said Khadgar, sighing.

"No. He levitates into them," said Moroes. The old servant looked at Khadgar, and the youth caught the slightest tug of a smile along the old man's face. "One more set of stairs."

The final set of stairs curled tightly, and Khadgar guessed that they had to be near the tower's highest spire. The old servant led the way.

The stairway opened up on a small circular room, surrounded by a wide parapet. As Khadgar had surmised, they were at the topmost tip of the tower, with a large observatory. The walls and ceilings were pierced by crystalline windows, clear and unfogged. In the time of their climb, night had fallen fully, and the sky was dark and strewn with stars.

The observatory itself was dim, lit by a few torches of the same, unwavering light as found elsewhere. Yet these were hooded, their lamps banked for observing the night sky. An unlit brazier sat in the middle of the room in preparation for later, as the temperature would drop toward morning.

Several large curved tables spread around the outer wall of the observatory, decked with all manner of devices. Silver levels and golden astrolabes acted as paperweights for foolscap, or as bookmarks keeping ancient texts open to certain pages. A half-disassembled model, showing planetary movement through the celestial vault, sat on one table, fine wires and additional beads laid out among the delicate tools next to it. Notebooks lay stacked against one wall, and others were in crates jammed beneath the tables. A map of the continent was stretched on a frame, showing the southern lands of Azeroth and Khadgar's own Lordaeron, as well as the reclusive dwarven and elven kingdoms of Khaz Modan and Quel'Thalas. Numerous small pins bedecked the map, constellations that only Medivh could decipher.

And Medivh was there, for to Khadgar it could be no other. He was a man of middling years, his hair long and bound in a ponytail in the back. In his youth his hair had likely been ebon black, but now it was already turning gray at the temples and along the beard. Khadgar knew that this happened to many mages, from the stress of the magical energies they wielded.

Medivh was dressed in robes simple for a mage—well cut and fitted to his large frame. A short tabard, unadorned by decoration, hung to his waist, over trousers tucked into oversize boots. A heavy maroon cloak hung from his broad shoulders, the hood pulled back.

As Khadgar's eyes adjusted to the darkness, he realized that he was wrong about the wizard's clothing being unadorned. Instead, it was laced with silver filigree, of such a delicate nature that it was invisible at first blush. Looking at the mage's back, Khadgar realized he was looking at the stylized face of some ancient demon-legend. He blinked, and in that time the tracery transformed itself into a coiled dragon, and then into a night sky.

Medivh had his back to the old servant and the young man, ignoring them entirely. He was standing at one of the tables, a golden astrolabe in one hand, a notebook in the other. He seemed lost in thought, and Khadgar wondered if this was one of the "things" that Moroes had warned him about.

Khadgar cleared his throat and took a step forward, but Moroes raised a hand. Khadgar froze in place, as surely as if transfixed with a magical spell.

Instead the old servant walked quietly to one side of the master mage, waiting for Medivh to recognize his presence. A minute passed. A second minute. Then a period that Khadgar swore was an eternity.

Finally, the robed figure set down his astrolabe, and made three quick jots in the notebook. He closed the book with sharp snap, and looked over at Moroes.

Seeing his face for the first time, Khadgar thought that Medivh was much older than his supposed forty-plus years. The face was deeply lined and worn. Khadgar wondered what magics Medivh wielded that wrote such a deep history on his face.

Moroes dipped into his vest and brought out the crumpled letter of introduction, the crimson seal now bloodred in the steady, unflickering torchlight. Medivh turned and regarded the youth.

The mage's eyes were deeply set beneath his dark, heavy brows, but Khadgar was aware at once of the power within. Something danced and flickered within those deep green eyes, something powerful, and perhaps uncontrolled. Something dangerous. The master mage glanced at him, and in a moment Khadgar felt that the wizard had taken in his sum total of existence and found it no more intriguing than that of a beetle or flea.

Medivh looked away from Khadgar and at the still-sealed letter of introduction. Khadgar felt himself relax almost immediately, as if a large and hungry predator had stalked past him without giving him a second look.

His relief was short-lived. Medivh did not open the letter. Instead his brows furrowed only slightly, and the parchment burst into flames with an explosive rush of air. The flames clustered at the far end of the document from where Medivh held it, and flickered with an intense, blue flame.

When Medivh spoke his voice was both deep and amused.

"So," said Medivh, oblivious to the fact he was holding Khadgar's future burning in his hand. "It seems our young spy has arrived at last."

TWO
Interview with the Magus

"Is something wrong?" asked Medivh, and Khadgar suddenly felt himself under the master mage's gaze again. He felt like a beetle again, but this time one that had inadvertently crawled across a bug-collector's work desk. The flames had already consumed half the letter of introduction, and the wax seal was already melting, dripping onto the observatory's flagstones.

Khadgar was aware that his eyes were wide, his face bloodless and pale, and his mouth hanging open. He tried to force the air out of his body, but all his managed was a strangled, hissing sound.

The dark, heavy brows pursed in a bemused glance. "Are you ill? Moroes, is this lad ill?"

"Winded, perhaps," said Moroes in a level tone. "Was a long climb up."

Finally Khadgar managed to gather his senses about him sufficiently to say, "The letter!"

"Ah," said Medivh. "Yes. Thank you, I had almost forgotten." He walked over to the brazier and dropped the burning parchment on top of the coals. The blue ball of flame rose spectacularly to about shoulder height, and them diminished into a normal-looking flame, filling the room with a warm, reddish glow. Of the letter of introduction, with its parchment and crimson seal inscribed with the symbol of the Kirin Tor, there was no sign.

"But you didn't read it!" said Khadgar, then caught himself, "I mean, sir, with respect . . ."

The master mage chuckled and settled himself into a large chair made of canvas and dark carved wood. The brazier lit his face, pulling out the deep lines formed into a smile. Despite this, Khadgar could not relax.

Medivh leaned forward in his chair and said, " 'Oh Great and Respected Magus Medivh, Master Mage of Karazhan, I bring you the greetings of the Kirin Tor, most learned and puissant of the magical academies, guilds, and societies, advisors to the kings, teachers of the learned, revealers of secrets.' They continue on in that fashion for some ways, puffing themselves up more with every sentence. How am I doing so far?"

"I couldn't say," said Khadgar, "I was instructed—"

"Not to open the letter," finished Medivh. "But you did, anyway."

The master mage raised his eyes to regard the young man, and Khadgar's breath caught in his throat. Something flickered in Medivh's eyes, and Khadgar wondered if the master mage had the power to cast spells without anyone noticing.

Khadgar slowly nodded, steeling himself for the response.

Medivh chuckled loudly, "When?"

"On the . . . on the voyage from Lordaeron to Kul Tiras," said Khadgar, unsure if what he said would amuse or irritate his potential mentor. "We were becalmed for two days and . . ."

"Curiosity got the better of you," finished Medivh again. He smiled, and it was a clean white smile beneath the graying beard. "I probably would have opened it the moment I got out of sight of Dalaran's Violet Citadel."

Khadgar took a deep breath and said, "I considered that, but I believed they had divination spells in operation, at least at that range."

"And you wanted to be far from any spell or message recalling you for opening the letter. And you patched it back together well enough to fool a cursory examination, sure that I would likely break the seal straightaway and not notice your tampering." Medivh allowed himself a chuckle, but drew his face into a tight, focused knot. "How did I do that?" he asked.

Khadgar blinked. "Do what, sir?"

"Know what was in the letter?" said Medivh, the sides of his mouth tugging down. "The letter I just burned says that I will find the young man Khadgar most impressive in his deduction and intelligence. Impress me."

Khadgar looked at Medivh, and the jovial smile of a few seconds before had evaporated. The smiling face was now that of some primitive stone god, judgmental and unforgiving. The eyes that had been tinged with mirth earlier now seemed to be barely concealing some hidden fury. The brows knitted together like the rising thunderhead of a storm.

Khadgar stammered for a moment, then said, "You read my mind."

"Possible," said Medivh. "But incorrect. You're a stew of nerves right now, and that gets in the way of mind reading. One wrong."

"You've gotten this sort of letter before," said Khadgar. "From the Kirin Tor. You know what kind of letters are written."

"Also possible," said the master mage. "As I *have* received such letters and they *do* tend to be overweening in their self-congratulatory tone. But you know the exact wording as well as I do. A good try, and the most obvious, but also incorrect. Two wrong."

Khadgar's mouth formed into a tight line. His mind raised and his heart thundered in his chest. "Sympathy," he said at last.

Medivh's eyes remained unreadable, and his voice level. "Explain."

Khadgar took a deep breath. "One of the magical laws. When someone handles an item, they leave a part of their own magical aura or vibration attached to the item. As auras vary with individuals, it is possible to connect to one by affecting the other. In this way a lock of hair may be used in a love charm, or a coin may be tracked back to its original owner."

Medivh's eyes narrowed slightly, and he dragged a finger across his bearded chin. "Continue."

Khadgar stopped for a moment, feeling the weight of Medivh's eyes pressing in on him. That was what he knew from lectures. He was halfway there. But how did Medivh use it to figure out . . . .

"The more someone uses an item, the stronger the resonance," said Khadgar quickly. "So therefore an item that experiences a lot of handling or attention will have a stronger sympathy." The words were coming together tighter and more rapidly now. "So a document which someone had written has more aura to it than a blank piece of parchment, and the person is concentrating on what they are writing, so . . ." Khadgar let his thoughts catch up for a moment. "You were mind reading, but not my mind—the mind of the scribe who wrote the letter at the time he was writing it—you picked up his thoughts reinforcing the words."

"Without having to physically open the document," said Medivh, and the light danced within his eyes again. "So how would this trick be useful to a scholar?"

Khadgar blinked for a moment, and looked away from the master mage, seeking to avoid his piercing glance. "You could read books without having to read books."

"Very valuable for a researcher," said Medivh. "You belong to a community of scholars. Why don't you do that?"

"Because . . . because . . ." Khadgar thought of old Korrigan, who could find anything in the library, even the smallest marginal notation. "I think we do, but for older members of the conclave."

Medivh nodded. "And that is because . . ."

Khadgar thought for a moment, then shook his head.

"Who would write if all the knowledge could be sucked out with a mental twist and a burst of magic?" suggested Medivh. He smiled, and Khadgar realized he had been holding his breath. "You're not bad. Not bad at all. You know your counterspells?"

"To the fifth roster," said Khadgar.

"Can you power a mystic bolt?" asked Medivh, quickly.

"One or two, but it's draining," answered the younger man, suddenly feeling that the conversation had taken a serious turn once more.

"And your primary elementals?"

"Strongest in flame, but I know them all."

"Nature magic?" asked Medivh. "Ripening, culling, harvesting? Can you take a seed and pull the youth from it until it becomes a flower?"

"No, sir. I was trained in a city."

"Can you make a homunculus?"

"Doctrine frowns on it, but I understand the principles involved," said Khadgar, "If you're curious . . ."

Medivh's eyes lit up for a moment, and he said, "You sailed here from Lordaeron? What type of boat?"

Khadgar felt thrown for a moment by the sudden change of discussion. "Yes. Um . . . A Tirassian windrunner, the *Gracious Breeze,*" he replied.

"Out of Kul Tiras," concluded Medivh. "Human crew?"

"Yes."

"You spoke with the crew at all?" Again, Khadgar felt himself sliding once more from conversation to interrogation.

"A little," said Khadgar. "I think I amused them with my accent."

"The crews of the Kul Tiras ships are easily amused," said Medivh. "Any nonhumans in the crew?"

"No, sir," said Khadgar. "The Tirassians told stories of fish men. They called them Murlocs. Are they real?"

"They are," said the Magus. "What other races have you encountered? Other than variations of humans."

"Some gnomes were at Dalaran once," said Khadgar. "And I've met dwarven artificers at the Violet Citadel. I know dragons from the legends; I saw the dragon's skull in one of the academies once."

"What about trolls, or goblins?" said Medivh.

"Trolls," said Khadgar. "Four known varieties of trolls. There may be a fifth."

"That would be the bushwah Alonda teaches," muttered Medivh, but motioned for Khadgar to continue.

"Trolls are savage, larger than humans. Very tall and wiry, with elongated features. Um . . ." He thought for a moment. "Tribal organization. Almost completely removed from civilized lands, almost extinct in Lordaeron."

"Goblins?"

"Much smaller, more the size of dwarves. Just as inventive, but in a destructive fashion. Fearless. I have read that as a race they are insane."

"Only the smart ones," said Medivh. "You know about demons?"

"Of course, sir," said Khadgar quickly. "I mean from the legends, sir. And I know the proper abjurations and protections. All mages of Dalaran are taught so from our first day of training."

"But you've never summoned one," said Medivh. "Or been present when someone else did so."

Khadgar blinked, wondering if this was a trick question. "No sir. I wouldn't even think of it."

"I do not doubt that you wouldn't," said the Magus, and there was the faintest edge in his voice. "Think of it, that is. Do you know what a Guardian is?"

"A Guardian?" Khadgar suddenly felt the conversation take yet another left-hand turn. "A watchman? A guard? Perhaps another race? Is it a type of monster? Perhaps a protector against monsters?"

Medivh smiled, now, and shook his head. "Don't worry. You're not *supposed* to know. It's part of the trick." Then he looked up and said, "So. What do you know about *me?*"

Khadgar shot a glance toward Moroes the Castellan, and suddenly realized that the servant has vanished, fading back into the shadows. The young man stammered for a moment. "The mages of the Kirin Tor hold you in high regard," he managed at last, diplomatically.

"Obviously," said Medivh brusquely.

"You are a powerful independent mage, supposedly an advisor to King Llane of Azeroth."

"We go back," said Medivh, nodding at the youth.

"Beyond that . . ." Khadgar hesitated, wondering if the mage truly could read his mind.

"Yes?"

"Nothing specific to justify the high esteem . . ." said Khadgar.

"And fear," put in Medivh.

"And *envy,*" finished Khadgar, feeling suddenly put upon by the questions, unsure about how to answer. He quickly added, "Nothing specific to explain directly the high *respect* the Kirin Tor holds you in."

"It's supposed to be that way," snapped Medivh peevishly, rubbing his hands over the brazier. "It's supposed to be that way." Khadgar could not believe how the master mage could possibly be cold. He himself felt nervous sweat drip down his back.

At length, Medivh looked up, and the brewing storm was in his eyes again. "But what do you know about *me?*"

"Nothing, sir," said Khadgar.

"Nothing?" Medivh's voice raised and seemed to reverberate across the observatory. "Nothing? You came all this way for nothing? You didn't even bother to check? Perhaps I was just an excuse for your masters to get you out of their hair, hoping you'd die en route. It wouldn't be the first time someone tried that."

"There wasn't that much to check. You haven't done that much," responded Khadgar hotly, then took a deep breath, realizing whom he was speaking with, and what he was saying. "I mean, not much that I could find out, I mean . . ."

He expected an outburst from the older mage, but Medivh just chuckled. "And what *did* you find out?" he asked.

Khadgar sighed, and said, "You come from a spell-caster heritage. Your father was a mage of Azeroth, one Nielas Aran. You mother was Aegwynn, which may be a title as opposed to a name, one that goes back at least eight hundred years. You grew up in Azeroth and know King Llane and Lord Lothar from your childhood. Beyond that . . ." Khadgar let his voice trail off. "Nothing."

Medivh looked into the brazier and nodded, "Well, that *is* something. More than most people can find out."

"And your name means 'Keeper of Secrets'," Khadgar added. "In High Elven. I found that out as well."

"All too true," said Medivh, looking suddenly tired.

He stared into the brazier for a while. "Aegwynn is not a title," he said at length. "It is merely my mother's name."

"Then there were several Aegwynns, probably a family name," suggested Khadgar.

"Only one," said Medivh, somberly.

Khadgar gave a nervous laugh. "But that would make her . . ."

"Over seven hundred fifty years old when I was born," said Medivh, with a surprising snort. "She is much older than that. I was a late child in her life. Which may be one reason the Kirin Tor is interested in what I keep in my library. Which is why they sent you to find out."

"Sir," said Khadgar, as sternly as he could manage. "To be honest, every mage save the highest in the Kirin Tor wants me to find out *something* from you. I will accommodate them as best as I am able, but if there is material that you want to keep restricted or hidden, I will fully understand. . . ."

"If I thought that, you would not have gotten through the forest to reach here," said Medivh, suddenly serious. "I need someone to sort and organize the library, for starters, then we work on the alchemical laboratories. Yes, you'll do nicely. You see, I know the meaning of your name just as you know mine. Moroes!"

"Here, sir," said the servant, suddenly manifesting out of the shadows. Despite himself, Khadgar jumped.

"Take the lad down to his quarters and make sure he eats something. It's been a long day for him."

"Of course, sir," said Moroes.

"One question, Master," said Khadgar, catching himself. "I mean, Lord Magus, sir."

"Call me Medivh for now. I also answer to Keeper of Secrets and a few other names, not all of them known."

"What do you mean when you say you know my name?" asked Khadgar.

Medivh smiled, and the rooms suddenly seemed warm and cozy again. "You don't speak dwarven," he observed.

Khadgar shook his head.

"My name means 'Keeper of Secrets' in High Elven. Your name means 'Trust' in the old dwarven language. So I will hold you to your name, young Khadgar. Young Trust."

Moroes saw the young man to his quarters halfway down the tower, explaining in that ghostly, definitive voice as he shuffled down the stairs. Meals in Medivh's Tower were simple fare—porridge and sausages for breakfast, a cold lunch, and a large, hearty dinner, usually a stew or a roast served with vegetables. Cook would retire after the evening meals, but there were always leftovers in the cold room. Medivh kept hours that could be charitably described as "erratic" and Moroes and Cook had long since learned how to accommodate him with a minimal amount of hardship on their parts.

Moroes informed young Khadgar that, as an assistant instead of a servant, he would not have that luxury. He would be expected to be available to help the master mage whenever he deemed necessary.

"I'd expect that, as an apprentice," said Khadgar.

Moroes turned in midstep (they were walking along an upper gallery overlooking what seemed to be a reception hall or ballroom). "Not an apprentice yet, Lad," wheezed Moroes. "Not by half."

"But Medivh said . . ."

"You could sort out the library," said Moroes. "Assistant work, not apprentice's. Others have been assistants. None became apprentices."

Khadgar's brow furrowed, and he felt the warmth of a blush on his face. He had not expected there to be a level *before* apprentice in the mage's hierarchy. "How long before . . ."

"Couldn't say, really," gasped the servant. "None have ever made it that far."

Khadgar thought of two questions at once, hesitated, then asked, "How many other 'assistants' have there been?"

Moroes looked out over the gallery railing, and his eyes grew unfocused. Khadgar wondered if the servant was thinking or had been derailed by the question. The gallery below was sparsely furnished with a heavy central table and chairs. It was surprisingly uncluttered, and Khadgar surmised that Medivh did not hold many banquets.

"Dozens," said Moroes at last. "At least. Most of

them from Azeroth. An elfling. No, two elflings. You're the first from the Kirin Tor."

"Dozens," repeated Khadgar, his heart sinking as he wondered how many times Medivh had welcomed a young would-be mage into his service.

He asked the other question. "How long did they last?"

Moroes snorted this time, and said, "Days. Sometimes hours. One elf didn't even make it up the tower stairs." He tapped the blinders at the side of his wizened head. "They *see* things, you know."

Khadgar thought of the figure at the main gate and just nodded.

At last they arrived at Khadgar's quarters, in a side passage not far from the banquet hall. "Tidy yourself up," said Moroes, handing Khadgar the lantern. "The jakes is at the end of the hall. There's a pot beneath the bed. Come down to the kitchen. Cook will have something warm for you."

Khadgar's room was a narrow wedge of the tower, more suitable to the contemplations of a cloistered monk than a mage. A narrow bed along one wall, and an equally narrow desk along the other with a bare shelf above. A standing closet for clothes. Khadgar tossed his rucksack into the closet without opening it, and walked over to the thin window.

The window was a slim slice of leaded glass, mounted vertically on a pivot in the center. Khadgar pushed on one half and it slowly pushed open, the solidifying oil in the bottom mount oozing as the window rotated.

The view was from still high up the tower's side, and the rounded hills that surrounded the tower were gray and bare in the light of the twin moons. From this height it was obvious to Khadgar that the hills had once been a crater, worn and weathered by the passage of the years. Had some mountain been pulled from this spot, like a rotted tooth? Or maybe the ring of hills had not risen at all, but rather the rest of the surrounding mountains had risen faster, leaving only this place of power rooted in its spot.

Khadgar wondered if Medivh's mother was here when the land rose, or sank, or was struck by a piece of the sky. Eight hundred years was long even by the standards of a wizard. After two hundred years, most of the old object lessons taught, most human mages were deathly thin and frail. To be seven hundred fifty years old and bear a child! Khadgar shook his head, and wondered if Medivh was having him on.

Khadgar shed his traveling cloak and visited the facilities at the hall's end. They were spartan, but included a pitcher of cold water and a washbasin and a good, untarnished mirror. Khadgar thought of using a minor spell to heat the water, then decided merely to tough it out.

The water was bracing, and Khadgar felt better as he changed into less-dusty togs—a comfortable shirt that reached nearly to his knees and a set of sturdy pants.

His working gear. He pulled a narrow eating knife from his sack and, after a moment's thought, slid it into the inside sleeve of one boot.

He stepped back out into the hallway, and realized that he had no clear idea where the kitchen was. There had been no cooking shed out by the stables, so whatever arrangements were likely within the tower. Probably on or near the ground level, with a pump from the well. With a clear path to the banquet hall, whether or not the hall was commonly used.

Khadgar found the gallery above the banquet hall easily enough, but had to search to find the staircase, narrow and twisting in on itself, leading to it. From the banquet hall itself he had a choice of exits. Khadgar chose the most likely one and ended up in dead-end hallway with empty rooms on all sides, similar to his own. A second choice brought a similar result.

The third led the young man into the heart of a battle.

He did not expect it. One moment he was striding down a set of low flagstone steps, wondering if he needed a map or a bell or a hunting horn to navigate the tower. The next moment the roof above him opened up into a brilliant sky the color of fresh blood, and he was surrounded by men in armor, armed for battle.

Khadgar stepped back, but the hallway had vanished behind him, only leaving an uneven, barren landscape unlike any he was familiar with. The men were shouting and pointing, but their voices, despite the fact that they were right next to Khadgar, were indistinct and muddied, like they were talking to him from underwater.

A dream? thought Khadgar. Perhaps he had laid down for a moment and fallen asleep, and all this was some night terror brought on by his own concerns. But no, he could almost feel the heat of the dying, corpulent sun on his flesh, and the breeze and shouting men moved around him.

It was as if he had become unstuck from the rest of the world, occupied his own small island, with only the most tenuous of connections to the reality around him. As if he had become a ghost.

Indeed, the soldiers ignored him as if he were a spirit. Khadgar reached out to grab one on the shoulder, and to his own relief his hand did not pass through the battered shoulder plate. There was resistance, but only of the most amorphous sort—he could feel the solidity of the armor, and if he concentrated, feel the rough ridges of the dimpled metal.

These men had fought, Khadgar realized, both hard and recently. Only one man in three was without some form of rude bandage, bloodstained badges of war sticking out from beneath dirty armor and damaged helms. Their weapons were notched as well, and spattered with dried crimson. He had fallen into a battlefield.

Khadgar examined their position. They were atop a small hillock, a mere fold in the undulating plains that seemed to surround them. What vegetation existed had been chopped down and formed into crude battlements, now guarded by grim-faced men. This was no safe redoubt, no castle or fort. They had chosen this spot to fight only because there was no other available to them.

The soldiers parted as their apparent leader, a great, white-bearded man with broad shoulders, pushed his way through. His armor was a battered as any, but consisted of a breastplate bolted over a crimson set of scholar's robes, of the type that would not have been out of place in the halls of the Kirin Tor. The hem, sleeves, and vest of these crimson robes were inscribed with runes of power—some of which Khadgar recognized, but others which seemed alien to him. The leader's snowy beard reached almost to his waist, obscuring the armor beneath, and he wore a red skullcap with a single golden gem on the brow. He held a gem-tipped staff in one hand, and a dark red sword in the other.

The leader was bellowing at the soldiers, in a voice that sounded to Khadgar like the raging sea itself. The warriors seemed to know what he was saying, though, for they formed themselves up neatly along the barricades, others filling gaps along the line.

The snow-bearded commander brushed past Khadgar, and despite himself the youth stumbled back, out of the way. The commander should not have noticed him, no more than any of the blood-spattered warriors had.

Yet the commander did. His voice dropped for a moment, he stammered, his foot landed badly on the uneven soil of the rocky hilltop and he almost stumbled. Yet instead he turned and regarded Khadgar.

Yes, he looked at Khadgar, and it was clear to the would-be apprentice that the ancient mage-warrior saw him and saw him clearly. The commander's eyes looked deeply into Khadgar's own, and for a moment Khadgar felt as he had under Medivh's own withering glare earlier. Yet, if anything, this was more intense. Khadgar looked into the eyes of the commander.

And what he saw there made him gasp. Despite himself, he turned away, breaking the locked gaze with the mage-warrior.

When Khadgar looked up again, the commander was nodding at him. It was a brief, almost dismissive nod, and the old man's mouth was a tight frown. Then the snow-bearded leader was off again, bellowing at the warriors, entreating them to defend themselves.

Khadgar wanted to go after him, to chase him down and find out how he could see him when others did not, and what he could tell him, but there was a cry around him, a muddy cry of tired men called into duty one last time. Swords and spears were raised to a sky the shade of curdled blood, and arms pointed toward the nearby ridges, where flooding had stripped out patterns of purple against the rust-colored soil.

Khadgar looked where the men were pointing, and a wave of green and black topped the nearest ridge.

Khadgar thought it was some river, or an arcane and colorful mudflow, but he realized that the wave was an advancing army. Black was the color of their armor, and green was the color of their flesh.

They were nightmare creatures, mockeries of human form. Their jade-fleshed faces were dominated by heavy underslung jaws lined with fanged teeth, their noses flat and snuffling like a dog's, and their eyes small, bloody, and filled with hate. Their ebon weapons and ornate armor shone in the eternally dying sun of this world, and as they topped the rise they let out a bellow that rocked the ground beneath them.

The soldiers around him let out a cry of their own, and as the green creatures closed the distance between the hill they let out volley after volley of red-fletched arrows. The front line of the monstrous creatures stumbled and fell, and were immediately trampled by those who came behind. Another volley and another rank of the inhuman monsters toppled, yet their failing was subsumed by the advancing tide of the mass that followed.

To Khadgar's right there were flashes as lightning danced along the surface of the earth, and the monstrosities screamed as the flesh was boiled from their bones. Khadgar thought of the warrior-mage commander, but also realized that these bolts only thinned the charging hordes by the merest fraction.

And then the green-fleshed monstrosities were on top of them, the wave of ebon and jade smashing against the rude palisade. The felled timbers were no more than twigs in the path of this storm, and Khadgar could feel the line buckle. One of the soldiers nearest him toppled, impaled by a great dark spear. In the warrior's place there was a nightmare of green flesh and black armor, howling as it swept down upon him.

Despite himself, Khadgar backed two steps, then turned to run.

And almost slammed into Moroes, who was standing in the archway.

"You," wheezed Moroes calmly, "were late. Might have gotten lost."

Khadgar wheeled again in place, and saw that behind him was not a world of crimson skies and green monstrosities, but an abandoned sitting room, its fireplace empty and its chairs covered with drop cloths. The air smelled of dust only recently disturbed.

"I was . . ." gasped Khadgar. "I saw . . . I was . . ."

"Misplaced?" suggested Moroes.

Khadgar gulped, looked about, then nodded mutely.

"Late supper is ready," groaned Moroes. "Don't get misplaced, again, now."

And the dark-clad servant turned and glided quietly out of the room.

Khadgar took one last look at the dead-end passage he had stumbled into. There were no mystic archways or magical doorways. The vision (if vision it was) had ended with a suddenness only to be equaled by its beginning.

There were no soldiers. No creatures with green

flesh. No army about to collapse. There was only a memory that scared Khadgar to his core. It was real. It had felt real. It had felt true.

It was not the monsters or the bloodshed that had frightened him. It was the mage-warrior, the snow-haired commander that seemed to be able to see him. That seemed to have looked into the heart of him, and found him wanting.

And worst of all, the white-bearded figure in armor and robes had Khadgar's eyes. The face was aged, the hair snow-white, the manner powerful, yet the commander had the same eyes that Khadgar had seen in the untarnished mirror just moments (lifetimes?) before.

Khadgar left the sitting room, and wondered if it would not be too late to get a set of blinders.

THREE
Settling In

"We'll start you off slow," said the elder wizard from across the table. "Take stock of the library. Figure out how you are going to organize it."

Khadgar nodded over the porridge and sausages. The bulk of the breakfast conversation was about Dalaran in general. What was popular in Dalaran and what were the fashions in Lordaeron. What they were arguing about in the halls of the Kirin Tor. Khadgar mentioned that the current philosophical question when he left was whether when you created a flame by magic, you called it into being or summoned it from some parallel existence.

Medivh huffed over his breakfast. "Fools. They wouldn't know an alternate dimension if it came up and bit them on the . . . . So what do you think?"

"I think . . ." And Khadgar, suddenly realizing he

was once again on the spot. "I think that it may be something else entirely."

"Excellent," said Medivh, smiling. "When given a choice between two, choose the third. Of course you meant to say that when you create fire, all you are doing is concentrating the inherent nature of fire contained in the surrounding area into one location, calling it into being?"

"Oh yes," said Khadgar, then adding, "had I thought about it. For a while. Like a few years."

"Good," said Medivh, dabbing at his beard with a napkin. "You've a quick mind and an honest appraisal of yourself. Let's see how you do with the library. Moroes will show you the way."

The library occupied two levels, and was situated about a third of the way up the tower itself. The staircase along this part of the tower hugged the outside edge of the citadel, leaving a large chamber two floors high. A wrought iron platform created an upper gallery on the second level. The room's narrow windows were covered with interwoven rods of iron, reducing what natural light the room had to little more than that of a hooded torch. On the great oak tables of the first level, crystalline globes covered with a thick patina of dust glowed with a blue-gray luster.

The room itself was a disaster area. Books were scattered opened to random pages, scrolls were unspooled over chairs, and a thin layer of dusty foolscap covered everything like the leaves on the forest floor. The more ancient tomes, still chained to the bookshelves, had been unshelved, and hung from their links like prisoners in some dungeon cell.

Khadgar surveyed the damage and let out a deep sigh. "Start me off slow," he said.

"I could have your gear packed in a hour," said Moroes from the hallway. The servant would not enter the library proper.

Khadgar picked up a piece of parchment at his feet. One side was a demand from the Kirin Tor for the master mage to respond to their most recent missive. The other side was marked with a dark crimson smear that Khadgar assumed at first was blood but realized was nothing more than the melted wax seal.

"No," said Khadgar, patting his small pouch of scribe tools. "It's just more of a challenge than I first anticipated."

"Heard that before," said Moroes.

Khadgar turned to ask about his comment, but the servant was already gone from the doorway.

With the care of a burglar, Khadgar picked his way through the debris. It was as if a battle had erupted in the library. Spines were broken, covers were half-torn, pages were folded over upon themselves, signatures had been pulled from the bindings entirely. And this was for those books that were still mostly whole. More portfolios had been pulled from their covers, and the dust on the tables covered a layer of papers and correspondences. Some of these were open, but some were noticeably still unread, their knowledge contained beneath their wax seals.

"The Magus does not need an assistant," muttered Khadgar, clearing a space at the end of one table and pulling out a chair. "He needs a housekeeper." He shot a glance at the doorway to make sure that the castellan was well and truly gone.

Khadgar sat down and the chair rocked severely. He stood up again, and saw that the uneven legs had shifted off a thick tome with a metallic cover. The front cover was ornate, and the page edges clad in silver.

Khadgar opened the text, and as he did so he felt something shift within the book, like a slider moving down a metal rod or a drop of mercury moving through a glass pipe. Something metallic unwound within the spine of the tome.

The book began to tick.

Quickly Khadgar closed the cover, and the book silenced itself with a sharp whirr and a snap, its mechanism resetting. The young man delicately set the volume back on the table.

That was when he noticed the scorch marks on the chair he was using, and the floor beneath it.

"I can see why you go through so many assistants," said Khadgar, slowly wandering through the room.

The situation did not improve. Books were hanging open over the arms of chairs and metal railings. The correspondence grew deeper as he moved farther into the room. Something had made a nest in one corner of the bookshelf, and as Khadgar pulled it from the shelf, a small shrew's skull toppled out, crumbling when it struck the floor. The upper level was little more than storage, books not even reaching the shelves, just piled in higher stacks, foothills leading to mountains leading to unattainable peaks.

And there was one bare spot, but this one looked like someone had started a fire in a desperate attempt to reduce the amount of paper present. Khadgar examined the area and shook his head—something else burned here as well, for there were bits of fabric, probably from a scholar's robe.

Khadgar shook his head and went back to where he had left his scribe's tools. He spilled out a thin wooden pen with a handful of metal nibs, a stone for sharpening and shaping the nibs, a knife with a flexible blade for scraping parchment, a block of octopus ink, a small dish in which to melt the ink, a collection of thin, flat keys, a magnifying lens, and what looked at first glance like a metallic cricket.

He picked up the cricket, turned it on its back, and using a specially-fashioned pen nib, wound it up. A gift from Guzbah upon Khadgar completing his first training as a scribe, it had proved invaluable in the youth's perambulations among the halls of the Kirin Tor. Within was contained a simple but effective spell that warned when a trap was in the offing.

As soon as he had wound it one revolution, the metallic cricket let out a high-pitched squeal. Khadgar, surprised, almost dropped the detecting insect. Then he realized that the device was merely warning about the intensity of the potential danger.

Khadgar looked at the piled volumes around him, and muttered a low curse. He retreated to the doorway, and finished winding the cricket. Then he brought the first book he had picked up, the ticking one, over to the doorway.

The cricket warbled slightly. Khadgar set the trapped book to one side of the doorway. He picked up another volume and brought it over. The cricket was silent.

Khadgar held his breath, hoped that the cricket was enchanted to handle all forms of traps, magical and otherwise, and opened the book. It was a treatise written in a soft feminine hand on the politics of the elves from three hundred years back.

Khadgar set the handwritten volume to the other side of the doorway, and went back for another book.

"I know you," said Medivh, the next morning, over sausage and porridge.

"Khadgar, sir," said the youth.

"The new assistant," said the older mage. "Of course. Forgive, but the memory is not everything it once was. Too much going on, I'm afraid."

"Anything you need aid with, sir?" asked Khadgar.

The elder man seemed to think about it for a moment, then said, "The library, Young Trust. How are things in the library?"

"Good," said Khadgar. "Very good. I'm busy sorting the books and papers."

"Ah, by subject? Author?" asked the master mage.

Fatal and non-fatal, thought Khadgar. "I'm thinking by subject. Many are anonymous."

"Hmmmfph," said Medivh. "Never trust anything that a man will not set his reputation and name upon. Carry on, then. Tell me, what is opinion of the Kirin Tor mages about King Llane? Do they ever mention him?"

The work proceeded with glacial slowness, but Medivh did not seem to be aware of the time involved. Indeed, he seemed to start each morning with being mildly and pleasantly surprised that Khadgar was still with them, and after a short summary of the progress the conversation would switch into a new direction.

"Speaking of libraries," he would say. "What is the Kirin Tor's librarian, Korrigan, up to?"

"How do people in Lordaeron feel about elves? Have any ever been seen there, in living memory?"

"Are there any legends of bull-headed men in the halls of the Violet Citadel?"

And one morning, about week into Khadgar's stay, Medivh was not present at all.

"Gone," said Moroes simply when asked.

"Gone where?" asked Khadgar.

The old castellan shrugged, and Khadgar could almost hear the bones clatter within his form. "He's not one to say."

"What's he doing?" pressed Khadgar.

"Not one to say."

"When will he be back?"

"Not one to say."

"He would leave me alone in his tower?" asked Khadgar. "Unsupervised, with all his mystic texts?"

"Could come stand guard over you," volunteered Moroes. "If that's what you want."

Khadgar shook his head, but said, "Moroes?"

"Ayep, young sir?"

"These visions . . ." started the younger man.

"Blinders?" suggested the servant.

Khadgar shook his head again. "Do they show the future or the past?"

"Both, when I've noticed, but I usually don't," said Moroes. "Notice, that is."

"And the ones of the future, do they come true?" said the young man.

Moroes let out what Khadgar could only assume was a deep sigh, a bone-rattling exhalation. "In my experience, yes, young sir. In one vision Cook saw me break a piece of crystal, so she hid them away. Months passed, and finally the Master asked for that piece of crystal. She removed it from its hiding place, and within two minutes I had broken it. Completely unintentionally." He sighed again. "She got her rose quartz lenses the next day. Will there be anything else?"

Khadgar said no, but was troubled as he climbed the staircase to the library level. He had gone as far as he had dared so far in his organization, and Medivh's sudden disappearance left him high and dry, without further direction.

The young would-be apprentice entered the library. On one side of the room were those volumes (and remains of volumes) that the cricket had determined were "safe," while the other half of the room was filled with the (generally more complete) volumes that were noted as being trapped.

The great tables were covered with loose pages and unopened correspondence, laid out in two semiregular heaps. The shelves were entirely bare, the chains hanging empty of their prisoners.

Khadgar could sort through the papers, but better to restock the shelves with the books. But most of the volumes were untitled, or if titled, their covers so barely worn, scuffed, and torn as to be illegible. The only way to determine contents would be to open the books.

Which would set off the trapped ones. Khadgar looked at the scorched mark on the floor and shook his head.

Then he started looking, first among the trapped volumes, then among the untrapped ones, until he found what he was looking for. A book marked with the symbol of the key.

It was locked, a thick metal band holding it closed, secured by a lock. Nowhere in his searches had Khadgar come across a real key, though that did not surprise him, given the organization of the room. The binding was strong, and the cover itself was a metal plate bound in red leather.

Khadgar pulled the flat pieces of keys from his pouch, but they were all insufficient for the large lock. Finally, using the tip of his scraping knife, Khadgar managed to thread the sliver of metal through the lock, and it gave a satisfying "click" as he drove it home.

Khadgar looked at the cricket he kept on the table, and it was still silent.

Holding his breath, the young mage opened the heavy volume. The sour smell of decayed paper rose to his nostrils.

"Of Trapes and Lockes," he said aloud, wrapping his mouth around the archaic script and over-vowelled words. "Beeing a Treateese on the Nature of Securing Devicees."

Khadgar pulled up a chair (slightly lower as he had sawed off the three long legs to balance it) and began to read.

Medivh was gone a full two weeks, and by that time, Khadgar had claimed the library as his own. Each morning he rose for breakfast, gave Moroes a perfunctory update as to his progress (which the castellan, as well as Cook never gave any indication of curiosity about), then buried himself away within the vault. Lunch and supper were brought to him, and he often worked into the night by the soft bluish light from the glowing balls.

He adjusted to the nature of the tower as well. There were often images that hung at the corner of his eye, just a twinkling of a figure in a tattered cloak that would evaporate when he turned to look at it. A half-finished word that drifted on the air. A sudden coldness as if a door or window had been left open, or a sudden change of pressure, as if a hidden entrance had suddenly appeared. Sometimes the tower groaned in the wind, the ancient stones shifting on each other after centuries of construction.

Slowly, he learned the nature, if not the exact contents, of the books that were within the library, foiling the traps that were placed around the most valuable tomes. His research served him well in the last case. He soon became as expert at foiling spell mechanisms and weighted traps as he had been with locked doors and hidden secrets in Dalaran. The trick for most of them was to convince the locking mechanism (whether magical or mechanical in nature) that the lock had not been foiled when in reality it had been. Determining what set the particular trap off, whether it was weight, or a shifting bit of metal or even exposure to the sun or fresh air, was half the battle to defeating it.

There were books that were beyond him, whose locks foiled even his modified picks and dexterous knife. Those went to the highest level, toward the back, and Khadgar resolved to find out what was within them, either on his own or by threading the knowledge out of Medivh.

He doubted the latter, and wondered if the master mage had used the library as anything else than a dumping ground for inherited texts and old letters. Most mages of the Kirin Tor had at least some semblance of order to their archives, with their most valuable tomes hidden away. But Medivh had everything in a hodgepodge, as if he didn't really need it.

Except as a test, thought Khadgar. A test to keep would-be apprentices at bay.

Now the books were on the shelves, the most valuable (and unreadable) ones secured with chains on the upper level, while the more common military histories, almanacs, and diaries were on the lower floor. Here were the scrolls as well, ranging from mundane listing of items bought and sold in Stormwind to recordings of epic poems. The last were particularly interesting since a few of them were about Aegwynn, Medivh's claimed mother.

If she lived over eight hundred years, she must have been a powerful mage indeed, thought Khadgar. More information about her would likely be in the protected books in the back. So far these tomes had resisted every common entreaty and physical attempt to sidestep their locks and traps, and the detecting cricket practically mewled in horror whenever he attempted to unlock them.

Still, there was more than enough to do, with categorizing the loose pieces, reassembling those volumes which age had almost destroyed, and sorting (or at least reading) most of the correspondence. Some of the later was in elven script, and even more of it, from a variety of sources, was in some sort of cipher. The latter type came with a variety of seals upon it, from both Azeroth, Khaz Modan, and Lordaeron, as well as places that Khadgar could not locate in the atlas. A large group communicated in cipher with each other, and with Medivh himself.

There were several ancient grimoires on codes, most of them dealing with letter replacement and cant. Nothing compared to the code used in these ciphers. Perhaps they used a combination of methods to create their own.

As a result, Khadgar had the grimoires on codes, along with primers in elven and dwarven languages, open on the table the evening that Medivh suddenly returned to the tower.

Khadgar didn't hear him as much as felt his sudden presence, the way the air changes as a storm front bears across the farmland. The young mage turned in his chair and there was Medivh, his broad shoulders filling the doorway, his robes billowing behind him of their own volition.

"Sir, I . . ." started Khadgar, smiling and half-rising from his chair. Then he saw that the master mage's hair was in disarray, and his lambent green eyes were wide and angry.

"Thief!" shouted Medivh, pointing at Khadgar. "Interloper!" The elder mage pointed at the younger and began to intone a string of alien syllables, words not crafted for the human throat.

Despite himself, Khadgar raised a hand and wove a symbol of protection in the air in front of him, but he might as well have been making a rude hand gesture for all the effect it had on Medivh's spell. A wall of solidified air slammed into the younger man, bowling over both him and the chair he sat in. The grimoires and primers went skating along the surface of the table like boats caught in a sudden squall, and the notes danced away, spinning.

Surprised, Khadgar was driven back, slammed into one of the bookshelves behind him. The shelf itself rocked from the force of the blow, and the youth was afraid it would topple, spoiling his hard work. The bookcase held its position, though the pressure on Khadgar's chest from the force of the attack intensified.

"Who are you?" thundered Medivh. "What are you doing here?"

The young mage struggled against the weight on his chest and managed to speak, "Khadgar," he gasped. "Assistant. Cleaning library. Your orders." Part of his mind wondered if this was why Moroes spoke in such a shorthand fashion.

Medivh blinked at Khadgar's words, and straightened like a man who had just been woken from a deep sleep. He twisted his hand slightly, and at once the wave of solidified air evaporated. Khadgar dropped to his knees, gasping for air.

Medivh crossed to him and helped him to his feet. "I am sorry, lad," he began. "I had forgotten you were still here. I assumed you were a thief."

"A thief that insisted on leaving a room neater than he found it," said Khadgar. It hurt a little when he breathed.

"Yes," said Medivh, looking around the room, and nodding, despite the disruption his own attack had caused. "Yes. I don't believe anyone else had ever gotten this far before."

"I've sorted by type," said Khadgar, still bent over and grasping his knees. "Histories, including epic poems, to your right. Natural sciences on your left. Legendary material in the center, with languages and reference books. The more powerful material—alchemic notes, spell descriptions, and theory go on the balcony, along with some books I could not identify that seem fairly powerful. You're going to have to look at those yourself."

"Yes," said Medivh, now ignoring the youth and scanning the room. "Excellent. An excellent job. Very good." He looked around, seeming like a man just getting his bearings again. "Very good indeed. You've done well. Now come along."

The master mage bolted for the door, pulled himself up short, then turned. "Are you coming?"

Khadgar felt as if he had been hit by another mystic bolt. "Coming? Where are we going?"

"To the top," said Medivh curtly. "Come now or we'll be too late. Time is of the essence!"

For an older man Medivh moved swiftly up the stairs, covering them two at a time at a brisk pace.

"What's at the top?" gasped Khadgar, finally catching up at a landing near the top.

"Transport," snapped Medivh, then hesitated for a moment. He turned in place and his shoulders dropped. For a moment it looked like the fire had burned out of his eyes. "I must apologize. For back there."

"Sir?" said Khadgar, his mind now spinning with this new transformation.

"My memory is not what it once was, Young Trust," said the Magus. "I should have remembered you were in the tower. With everything, I assumed you must have been a . . ."

"Sir?" interrupted Khadgar. "Time is of the essence?"

"Time," said Medivh, then he nodded, and the intensity returned to his face. "Yes, it is. Come on, don't lollygag!" And with that the older man was up on his feet and taking the steps two at a time.

Khadgar realized that the haunted tower and the disorganized library were not the only reason people left Medivh's employ, and hastened after him.

The aged castellan was waiting for them in the tower observatory.

"Moroes," thundered Medivh as he arrived at the top of the tower. "The golden whistle, if you please."

"Ayep," said the servant, producing a thin cylinder. Dwarven runes were carved along the cylinder's side, reflecting in the lamplight of the room. "Already took the liberty, sir. They're here."

"They?" started Khadgar. There was the rustle of great wings overhead. Medivh headed for the ramparts, and Khadgar looked up.

Great birds descended from the sky, their wings luminescent in the moonlight. No, not birds, Khadgar realized—gryphons. They had the bodies of great cats, but their heads and front claws were those of sea eagles, and their wings were golden.

Medivh held out a bit and bridle. "Hitch yours up, and we'll go."

Khadgar eyed the great beast. The nearest gryphon let out a shrieking cry and pawed the flagstones with its clawed forelegs.

"I've never . . ." started the young man. "I don't know . . ."

Medivh frowned. "Don't they teach anything among the Kirin Tor? I don't have time for this." He raised a finger and muttered a few words, touching Khadgar's forehead.

Khadgar stumbled back, shouting in surprise. The elder mage's touch felt as if he were driving a hot iron into his brain.

Medivh said, "Now you *do* know. Set the bit and bridle, now."

Khadgar touched his forehead, and let out a surprised gasp. He *did* know now, how to properly harness a gryphon, and to ride one as well, both with saddle and, in the dwarven style, without. He knew how to bank, how to force a hover, and most of all, how to prepare for a sudden landing.

Khadgar harnessed his gryphon, aware that his head throbbed slightly, as if the knowledge now within had to jostle that already within his skull to make room.

"Ready? Follow!" said Medivh, not asking for a response.

The pair launched themselves into the air, the great beasts straining and beating the air to allow them to rise. The great creatures could take armored dwarves aloft, but a human in robes approached their limits.

Khadgar expertly banked his swooping gryphon and followed Medivh as the elder mage swooped down over the dark treetops. The pain in his head spread from the point where Medivh had touched him, and now his forehead felt heavy and his thoughts muzzy. Still, he concentrated and matched the master mage's motions exactly, as if he had been flying gryphons all his life.

The younger mage tried to catch up with Medivh, to ask where they were going, and what their goal was, but he could not overtake him. Even if he had, Khadgar realized, the rushing wind would drown out all but the greatest shouts. So he followed as the mountains loomed above them, as they winged eastward.

How long they flew Khadgar could not say, He may have dozed fitfully on gryphon-back, but hands held the reins firm, and the gryphon kept pace with its brother-creature. Only when Medivh suddenly jinked his gryphon to the right did Khadgar shake himself out of his slumber (if slumber it was) and followed the master mage as his course turned south. Khadgar's headache, the likely product of the spell, had almost completely dissipated, leaving only a ragged ache as a reminder.

They had cleared the mountain range and Khadgar now realized they were flying over open land. Beneath them the moonlight was shattered and reflected in myriad pools. A large marsh or swamp, Khadgar thought. It had to be early in the morning now, the horizon on their right just starting to lighten with the eventual promise of day.

Medivh dropped low and raised both hands over his head. Incanting from gryphon-back, Khadgar realized, and though his mind assured him that he knew how to do this, steering the great beast with his knees, he felt in his heart that he could never be comfortable in such a maneuver.

The creatures dropped farther, and Medivh was suddenly bathed in a ball of light, both limning him clearly and catching Khadgar's gryphon as a trailing shadow. Beneath them, the young mage saw an armed encampment on a low rise that jutted from the surrounding swamp. They passed low over the camp, and beneath him Khadgar could hear shouts and the clatter of armor and weapons being hastily grabbed. What was Medivh doing?

They passed over the encampment, and Medivh

pulled into a high, banking turn, Khadgar following him move for move. They returned over the camp, and it was brighter now—the campfires that had previously been banked were now fed fresh fuel, and blazed in the night. Khadgar saw it was a large patrol, perhaps even a company. The commander's tent was large and ornate, and Khadgar recognized the banner of Azeroth flapping overhead.

Allies, then, for Medivh was supposedly closely connected to both King Llane of Azeroth and Lothar, the kingdom's Knight Champion. Khadgar expected Medivh to land, but instead the mage kicked the sides of his mount, pulling the gryphon's head up. The beast's great wings beat the dark air and they climbed again, this time rocketing north. Khadgar had no choice but to follow, as Medivh's light dimmed and the master mage took the reins again.

Over the marshlands again, and Khadgar saw a thin ribbon beneath, too straight for a river, too wide for an irrigation ditch. A road, then, plowed through the swamp, connecting bits of dry land that rose out of the fen.

Then the land rose to another ridge, another dry spot, and another encampment. There were also flames in this encampment, but they were not the bright, contained ones of the army's forces. These were scattered throughout the clearing, and as they neared, Khadgar realized they were wagons set alight, their contents strewn out among the dark human forms that were tossed like children's dolls on the sandy ground of the campsite.

As before, Medivh passed over the campsite, then wheeled high in the air, banking to make a return pass. Khadgar followed, the young mage himself leaning over the side of his mount to get a better look. It looked like a caravan that had been looted and set ablaze, but the goods themselves were scattered on the ground. Wouldn't bandits take the booty and the wagons? Were there any survivors?

The answer to the last question came with a shout and a volley of arrows that arched up from the brush surrounding the site.

The lead gryphon let out a shriek as Medivh effortlessly pulled back on the reins, banking the creature clear of the flight of arrows. Khadgar attempted the same maneuver, the warm, false, comforting memory in his head telling him that this was the correct way to turn. But unlike Medivh, Khadgar was riding too far forward on his mount, and he had insufficient pull on his reins.

The gryphon banked, but not enough to avoid all the arrows. A barbed arrow pierced the feathers of the right wing, and the great beast let out a bleating scream, jerking in flight and desperately attempting to beat its wings to get above the arrows.

Khadgar was off-balance, and was unable to compensate. In a heartbeat his hands slipped loose of the reins, and his knees slipped up from the sides of the gryphon. No longer under tight control, the gryphon bucked, throwing Khadgar entirely free of its back.

Khadgar lashed out to grab the reins. The leather lines whipped at his fingertips and then were gone into the night, along with his mount.

And Khadgar plummeted toward the armed darkness below.

FOUR
Battle and Aftermath

The air rushed out of Khadgar's lungs as he struck the ground. The earth was gritty beneath his fingers, and he realized he must have landed on a low dune of sandy debris collected along one side of the ridge.

Uneasily the young mage rose to his feet. From the air the ridge looked like a forest fire. From the ground it looked like an opening to hell itself.

The wagons were almost completely consumed by fire now, their contents scattered and blazing along the ridge. Bolts of cloth had been unwound in the dirt, barrels staved and leaking, and food despoiled and mashed into the earth. Around him were bodies as well, human forms dressed in light armor. There was an occasional gleam of a helmet or a sword. Those would be the caravan guards, who failed their task.

Khadgar shrugged a painful shoulder, but it felt bruised as opposed to broken. Even given the sand, he should have landed harder. He shook his head, hard. Whatever ache was left from Medivh's spell was outweighed by greater aches elsewhere.

There was movement among the wreckage, and Khadgar crouched. Voices barked back and forth in an unfamiliar tongue, a language to Khadgar's ears both guttural and blasphemous. They were searching for him. They had seen him topple from his mount and now they were searching for him. As he watched, stooped figures shambled through the wreckage, forming hunched silhouettes where they passed before the flames.

Something tickled the back of Khadgar's brain, but he could not place it. Instead he started to back out of the clearing, hoping the darkness would keep him hidden from the creatures.

Such was not to be. Behind him, a branch snapped or a booted foot found a chuckhole covered by leaves, or leather armor was tangled briefly in some brush. In any event, Khadgar knew he was not alone, and he turned at once to see . . .

A monstrosity from his vision. A mockery of humanity in green and black.

It was not as large as the creature of his vision, nor as wide, but it was still a nightmare creature. Its heavy jaw was dominated by fangs that jutted upward, its other features small and sinister. For the first time

Khadgar realized it had large, upright ears. It probably heard him before it saw him.

Its armor was dark, but it was leather and not the metal of his dream. The creature bore a torch in one hand that caught the deep features of its face, making it all the more monstrous. In its other hand the creature carried a spear decorated with a string of small white objects. With a start Khadgar realized the objects were human ears, trophies of the massacre around them.

All this came to Khadgar in an instant, in the moment's meeting of man and monster. The beast pointed the grisly-decorated spear at the youth and let out a bellowing challenge.

The challenge was cut short as the young mage muttered a word of power, raised a hand, and unleashed a small bolt of power through the creature's midsection. The beast slumped in on itself, its bellow cut short.

One part of his mind was stunned by what he had just done, the other knew that he had seen what these creatures could do, in the vision in Karazhan.

The creature had warned the other members of its unit, and now there were war-howls in return around the encampment. Two, four, a dozen such travesties, all converging on his location. Worse yet, there were other howls from the swamp itself.

Khadgar knew he did not have the power to repulse all of them. Summoning the mystic bolt was enough to weaken him. Another would put him in dire danger of fainting. Perhaps he should try to flee?

But these monsters probably knew the dark fen that surrounded them better than he did. If he kept to the sandy ridge, they would find him. If he fled into the swamp, not even Medivh would be able to locate him.

Khadgar looked up into the sky, but there was no sign of either the Magus or the gryphons. Had Medivh landed somewhere, and was sneaking up on the monsters? Or had he returned to the human force to the south, to bring them here?

Or, thought Khadgar grimly, had Medivh's quicksilver mood changed once again and he had forgotten he had someone with him on this flight?

Khadgar looked quickly out into the darkness, then back toward the site of the ambush itself. There were more shadows moving around the fire, and more howling.

Khadgar picked up the grisly trophy-spear, and strode purposely toward the fire. He might not be able to fire off more than a mystic bolt or two, but the monsters didn't know that.

Perhaps they were as dumb as they looked. And as inexperienced with wizards as he was with them.

He did surprise them, for what it was worth. The last thing they expected was their prey, the victim they had unseated from its flying mount, suddenly to manifest at the edge of the campfire's light, bearing the trophy-spear of one of their guards.

Khadgar tossed the spear sideways on the fire, and it sent up a shower of sparks as it landed.

The young mage summoned a bit of flame, a small ball, and held it in his hand. He hoped that it limned his features as seriously as the torch had lit the guard's. It had better.

"Leave this place," Khadgar bellowed, praying that his strained voice would not crack. "Leave this place or die."

One of the larger brutes took two steps forward and Khadgar muttered a word of power. The mystic energies congealed around his flaming hand and blasted the green nonhuman full in the face. The brute had enough time to raise a clawed hand to its ruined features before it toppled.

"Flee," shouted Khadgar, trying to pitch his voice as deeply as he could, "Flee or face the same fate." His stomach felt like ice, and he tried not to stare at the burning creature.

A spear launched out of the darkness, and with the last of his energy Khadgar summoned a bit of air, just enough to push it clearly aside. As he did he felt faint. That was the last he could do. He was well and truly tapped out. It would be a good time for his bluff to work.

The surrounding creatures, about a dozen visible, took a step back, then another. One more shout, Khadgar reckoned, and they would flee back into the swamp, and give him enough time to flee himself. He had already decided he would flee south, toward the army encampment.

Instead there was a high, cackling laugh that froze

Khadgar's blood. The ranks of the green warriors parted and another figure shambled forward. It was thinner and more hunched than the others, and wore a robe the color of curdled blood. The color of the sky of Khadgar's vision. Its features were as green and misshapened as the others, but this one has a gleam of feral intelligence in its eyes.

It held out its hand, palm upward, and took a dagger and pierced its palm with the tip. Reddish blood pooled in the clawed palm.

The robed beast spoke a word that Khadgar had never heard, a word that hurt the ears, and the blood burst into flame.

"Human wants to play?" said the robed monster, roughly matching the human language. "Wants to play at spells? Nothgrin can play!"

"Leave now," tried Khadgar. "Leave now or die!"

But the young mage's voice wavered now, and the robed mockery merely laughed. Khadgar scanned the area around him, looking for the best place to run, wondering if he could grab one of the guard's swords laying on ground. He wondered if this Nothgrin was bluffing as much as Khadgar had been.

Nothgrin took a step toward Khadgar, and two of the brutes to the spellcaster's right suddenly screamed and burst into flame. It happened with a suddenness that shocked everyone, including Khadgar. Nothgrin wheeled toward the immolated creatures, to see two more join them, bursting into flame like dry sticks.

They screamed as well, their knees buckling, and they toppled to the ground.

In the place where the creatures had been now stood Medivh. He seemed to glow of his own volition, diminishing the main fire, the burning wagons, and the burning corpses on the ground, sucking their light into himself. He seemed radiant and relaxed. He smiled at the collected creatures, and it was a savage, brutal smile.

"My apprentice told you to leave," said Medivh, "You should have followed his orders."

One of the beasts let out a bellow, and the rogue magus silenced it with a wave of his hand. Something hard and invisible struck the beast square in the face, and there was a shattering crack as its head came loose of its body and rolled backward, striking the ground only moments before the creature's body struck the sand.

The rest of the creatures staggered backward a step, then fled entirely into the night. Only the leader, the robed Nothgrin, held its ground, and its overwide jaw flapped open in surprise.

"Nothgrin knows you, human," he hissed. "You are the one. . . ."

Anything else the creature said disappeared in a scream as Medivh waved a hand and the creature was pulled off its feet by a burst of air and fire. It was swept upward, screaming, until at last its lungs collapsed from the stress and remains of its burned body drifted down like black snowflakes.

Khadgar looked at Medivh, and the wizard had a

toothy, self-satisfied smile. The smile faded when he looked at Khadgar's ashen face.

"Are you all right, lad?" he asked.

"Fine," said Khadgar, feeling the weight of his exhaustion sweeping over him. He tried to sit but ended up just collapsing to his knees, his mind worn and empty.

Medivh was at his side in a moment, passing a palm over the lad's forehead. Khadgar tried to move the hand away, but found that he lacked the energy.

"Rest," said Medivh. "Recover your strength. The worst is over."

Khadgar nodded, blinking. He looked at the bodies around the fire. Medivh could have slain him as easily, in the library. What stayed his hand, then? Some recognition of Khadgar? Some bit of memory or of humanity?

The young mage managed, "Those things." His voice sounded slurred, "What were . . ."

"Orcs," said the Magus. "Those were orcs. Now no more questions for the moment."

To the east, the sky was lightening. To the south, there was the sound of bright horns and powerful hooves.

"The cavalry at last," said Medivh with a sigh. "Too loud and too late, but don't tell them that. They can pick up the stragglers. Now rest."

The patrol swept through the camp, half of them dismounting, the remainder pressing up along the road. The horsemen began checking the bodies. A detail was assigned to bury the members of the caravan.

The few dead orcs that Medivh had not set on fire were gathered and put on the main fire, their bodies charring as their flesh turned to ash.

Khadgar didn't remember Medivh leaving him, but he did return with the patrol's commander. The commander was a stocky, older man, his face weathered by combat and campaign. His beard was already more salt than pepper, and his hairline had receded to the back of his head. He was a huge man, made all the more imposing by his plate armor and greatcape. Over one shoulder Khadgar could see the hilt of a huge sword, the crosspiece huge and jeweled.

"Khadgar, this is Lord Anduin Lothar," said Medivh, "Lothar, this is my apprentice, Khadgar of the Kirin Tor."

Khadgar's mind spun and caught first on the name. Lord Lothar. The King's Champion, boyhood companion of both King Llane and Medivh. The blade on his back had to be the Great Royal Sword, pledged to defend Azeroth, and . . .

Did Medivh just say Khadgar was his *apprentice*?

Lothar dropped to one knee to bring himself level with the young man, and looked at him, smiling. "So you finally got an apprentice. Had to go to the Violet Citadel to find one, eh, Med?"

"Find one of suitable merit, yes," said Medivh.

"And if it ties the local hedge wizards' undies in a bundle, so much the better, eh? Oh, don't look at me like that, Medivh. What has this one done to impress you?"

"Oh, the usual," said Medivh, showing his teeth in a

feral grin in response. "Organized my library. Tamed a gryphon on the first try. Took on these orcs single-handed, including a warlock."

Lothar let out a low whistle, "He organized *your* library? I *am* impressed." A smile flashed beneath his graying moustache.

"Lord Lothar," managed Khadgar finally. "Your skill is known even in Dalaran."

"You rest, lad," said Lothar, putting a heavy gauntlet on the young mage's shoulder. "We'll get the rest of those creatures."

Khadgar shook his head. "You won't. Not if you stay on the road."

The King's Champion blinked in surprise, and Khadgar was not sure if it was because of his presumption or his words.

"The lad's right, I'm afraid," said Medivh. "The orcs have taken to the swamp. They seem to know the Black Morass better than we do, and that's what makes them so effective here. We stay on the roads, and they can run circles around us."

Lothar rubbed the back of his head with his gauntlet. "Maybe we could borrow some of those gryphons of yours to scout."

"The dwarves that trained them may have their opinions about loaning out their gryphons," said Medivh. "But you might want to talk to them, and to the gnomes as well. They have a few whirligigs and sky-engines that might be more suitable for scouting."

Lothar nodded, and rubbed his chin. "How did you know they were here?"

"I encountered one of their advance scouts near my domain," said Medivh, as calmly as if he was discussing the weather. "I managed to squeeze out of him that there was a large party looking to raid along the Morass Road. I had hoped to arrive in time to warn them." He looked at the devastation around them.

The sunlight did little to help the appearance of the area. The smaller fires had burned out, and the air smelled of burning orcflesh. A pallid cloud hung over the site of the ambush.

A young soldier, little more than Khadgar's age, ran up to them. They had found a survivor, one that was pretty badly chewed up, but alive. Could the Magus come at once?

"Stay with the lad," said Medivh, "He's still a little woozy from everything." And with that the master mage strode across the scorched and bloody ground, his long robes trailing him like a banner.

Khadgar tried to rise and follow him, but the King's Champion put his heavy gauntlet on his shoulder and held him down. Khadgar struggled only for a moment, then returned to a seated position.

Lothar regarded Khadgar with a smile. "So the old coot finally took on an assistant."

"Apprentice," said Khadgar weakly, though he felt the pride rising in his chest. The feeling brought a new strength to his mind and limbs. "He's had many assistants. They didn't last. Or so I heard."

"Uh-huh," said Lothar. "I recommended a few of those assistants, and they came back with tales of a haunted tower and a crazy, demanding mage. What do you think of him?"

Khadgar blinked for moment. In the past twelve hours, Medivh had attacked him, shoved knowledge into his head, dragged him across the country on gryphon-back, and let him face off a handful of orcs before swooping in for the rescue. On the other hand, he had made Khadgar his apprentice. His student.

Khadgar coughed and said, "He is more than I expected."

Lothar smiled again and there was genuine warmth in the smile. "He is more than anyone expected. That's one of his good points." Lothar thought for a moment and said, "That is a very politic and polite response."

Khadgar managed a weak smile. "Lordaeron is a very politic and polite land."

"So I've noticed in the King's Council. 'Dalaran ambassadors can say both yes and no at the same time, and say nothing as well.' No insult intended."

"None taken, my lord," said Khadgar.

Lothar looked at the lad. "How old are you, lad?"

Khadgar looked at the older man. "Seventeen. Why?"

Lothar shook his head and grunted, "That might make sense."

"Make sense how?"

"Med, I mean Lord Magus Medivh, was a young man, several years younger than yourself, when he fell ill. As a result, he never dealt much with someone of your age."

"Ill?" said Khadgar. "The Magus was ill?"

"Seriously," said Lothar. "He fell into a deep sleep, a coma they called it. Llane and I kept him at Northshire Abbey, and the holy brothers there fed him broth to keep him from wasting away. For years he was like that, then, snap, he woke up, right as rain. Or almost."

"Almost?" asked Khadgar.

"Well, he missed a large piece of his teenage years, and a few additional decades as well. He fell asleep a teenager and woke up a grown man. I always worry that it affected him."

Khadgar thought about the master mage's mercurial temperament, his sudden mood swings, and the child-like delight with which he approached battling the orcs. Were Medivh a younger man, would his actions make more sense?

"His coma," said Lothar, and shook his head at the memory. "It was unnatural. Med calls it a 'nap,' like it was perfectly reasonable. But we never found out why it happened. The Magus might have puzzled it out, but he's shown no interest in the matter, even when I've asked."

"I am Medivh's apprentice," said Khadgar simply. "Why are you telling me this?"

Lothar sighed deeply and looked out over the battle-scarred ridge. Khadgar realized that the King's Champion was a basically honest individual, who would not last a day and a half in Dalaran. His emotions were plain on his weathered, open face.

Lothar sucked on his teeth, and said, "To be honest, I worry about him. He's all alone in his tower. . . ."

"He has a castellan. And there's Cook," put in Khadgar.

". . . with all of his magic," continued Lothar. "He just seems alone. Tucked up there in the mountains. I worry about him."

Khadgar nodded, and added to himself, *and that is why you tried to get apprentices from Azeroth in there. To spy on your friend. You worry about him, but you worry about his power as well.* Aloud, Khadgar said, "You worry if he's all right."

Lothar gave a shrug, revealing both how much he did worry and how much he was willing to pretend otherwise.

"What can I do to help?" asked Khadgar. "Help him. Help you."

"Keep an eye on him," said Lothar. "If you're an apprentice, he should spend more time with you. I don't want him to . . ."

"Fall into another coma?" suggested Khadgar. *At a time when these orcs are suddenly everywhere.* For his part, Lothar rewarded him with another shrug.

Khadgar gave the best smile he could manage, "I would be honored to help you both, Lord Lothar. Know that my loyalty must be to the master mage first, but if there is anything a *friend* would need to know, I will pass it along."

Another heavy pat of the gauntlet. Khadgar marveled at how badly Lothar concealed his concerns. Were all the natives of Azeroth this open and guileless? Even now, Khadgar could see there was something else Lothar wanted to speak of.

"There's something else," said Lothar. Khadgar just nodded politely.

"Has the Lord Magus spoken of the Guardian to you?" he asked.

Khadgar thought of pretending to know more than he did, to draw out more from this older, honest man. But as the thought passed through his head, he discarded it. Best to hold to the truth.

"I have heard the name from Medivh's lips," said Khadgar. "But I know nothing of the details."

"Ah," said Lothar. "Then let it be as if I said nothing to you."

"I'm sure we will talk of it in due course," added Khadgar.

"Undoubtedly," said Lothar. "You seem like a trustworthy sort."

"After all, I've only been his apprentice for a few days," said Khadgar lazily.

Lothar's eyebrows raised, "A few days? Exactly how long have you been Medivh's apprentice?"

"Counting until dawn tomorrow?" said Khadgar, and allowed himself a smile. "That would be one."

Medivh chose that moment to return, looking more haggard than before. Lothar raised his eyebrows in a hopeful question, but the Magus merely shook his head. Lothar frowned deeply, and after exchanging a few pleasantries, left to oversee the rest of salvage and clean-up. The half of the patrol that had moved ahead along the road had returned, but had found nothing.

"Are you up for travel?" asked Medivh.

Khadgar pulled himself to his feet, and the sandy ridge in the middle of the Black Morass seemed like a ship pitching on a rough sea.

"Well enough," he said. "I don't know if I can handle a gryphon, though, even with . . ." he let his voice trail off, but touched his forehead.

"It's just as well," said Medivh. "Your mount got spooked by the arrows, and headed for the high country. We'll have to double up." He raised the rune-carved whistle to his lips and let out a series of short, sharp blasts. Far above, there was the shriek of a gryphon on the wing, circling high above them.

Khadgar looked up and said, "So, I'm your apprentice."

"Yes," said Medivh, his face a calm mask.

"I passed your tests," said the youth.

"Yes," said Medivh.

"I'm honored, sir," said Khadgar.

"I'm glad you are," said Medivh, and a ghost of a smile crossed his face. "Because now starts the hard part."

FIVE
Sands in an Hourglass

"I've seen them before," said Khadgar.

It was seven days after the battle in the swamp. With their return to the tower (and a day of recovery on Khadgar's part), the young mage's apprenticeship had begun in earnest. The first hour of the day, before breakfast, Khadgar practiced his spells under Medivh's tutelage. From breakfast until lunch and through lunch until supper, Khadgar would assist the master mage with various tasks. These consisted of making notes as Medivh read off numbers, running down to the library to recover this book or that, or merely holding a collection of tools as the Magus worked.

Which was what he was doing at this particular moment, when he finally felt comfortable enough with the older mage to tell him what he knew about the ambush.

"Seen who before?" replied his mentor, peering through a great lens at his current experiment. On his fingers the master mage wore small pointed thimbles ending in infinitely-thin needles. He was tuning something that looked like a mechanical bumblebee, which flexed its heavy wings as his needles probed it.

"The orcs," said Khadgar. "I've seen the orcs we fought before."

"You didn't mention them when you first arrived," said Medivh absentmindedly, his fingers dancing in odd precision, lancing the needles into and out of the device. "I remember asking you about other races. There was no mention. Where have you seen them?"

"In a vision. Soon after I arrived here," Khadgar said.

"Ah. You had a vision. Well, many get them here, you know. Moroes probably told you. He's a bit of a blabbermouth, you know."

"I've had one, maybe two. The one I am sure about was on a battlefield, and these creature, these orcs, were there. Attacking us. I mean, attacking the humans I was with."

"Hmmm," said Medivh, the tip of his tongue appearing beneath his moustache as he moved the needles delicately along the bumblebee's copper thorax.

"And I wasn't here," continued Khadgar. "Not in Azeroth, or Lordaeron. Wherever I was, the sky was red as blood."

Medivh bristled as if struck by an electric shock. The intricate device beneath his tools flashed brightly as the wrong parts were touched, then screamed, and then died.

"Red skies?" he said, turning away form the workbench and looking sharply at Khadgar. Energy, intense and uncaring, seemed to dance along the older man's dark brows, and the Magus's eyes were the green of a storm-tossed sea.

"Red. Like blood," said Khadgar. The young man had thought he was becoming used to Medivh's sudden and mercurial moods, but this struck him with the force of a blow.

The older mage let out a hiss. "Tell me about it. The world, the orcs, the skies," commanded Medivh, his voice like stone. "Tell me *everything.*"

Khadgar recounted the vision of his first night there, mentioning everything he could remember. Medivh interrupted constantly—what were the orcs wearing, what was the world like. What was in the sky, on the horizon. Were there any banners among the orcs. Khadgar felt his thoughts were being dissected and examined. Medivh pulled the information from Khadgar effortlessly. Khadgar told him everything.

Everything except the strange, familiar eyes of the warrior-mage commander. He did not feel right mentioning that, and Medivh's questions seemed to concentrate more on the red-skied world and the orcs than the human defenders. As he described the vision, the older mage seemed to calm down, but the choppy sea still remained beneath his bushy brows. Khadgar saw no need to upset the Magus further.

"Curious," said Medivh, slowly and thoughtfully, after Khadgar had finished. The master mage leaned back in his chair and tapped a needle-tipped finger to his lips. There was a silence that hung over the room like a shroud. At last he said, "That is a new one. A very new one indeed."

"Sir," began Khadgar.

"Medivh," reminded the master mage.

"Medivh, sir," began Khadgar again. "Where do these visions come from? Are they hauntings of some past or portents of the future?"

"Both," said Medivh, leaning back in his chair. "And neither. Go fetch an ewer of wine from the kitchen. My work is done for the day, I'm afraid, its nearly time for supper, and this may take some explaining."

When Khadgar returned, Medivh had started a fire in the hearth and was already settling into one of the larger chairs. He held out a pair of mugs. Khadgar poured, the sweet smell of the red wine mixing with the cedar smoke.

"You do drink?" asked Medivh as an afterthought.

"A bit," said Khadgar. "It is customary to serve wine with dinner in the Violet Citadel."

"Yes," said Medivh. "You wouldn't need to if you just got rid of the lead lining for your aqueduct. Now, you were asking about visions."

"Yes, I saw what I described to you, and Moroes . . ."

Khadgar hesitated for a moment, hoping not to further blacken the castellan's reputation for gossip, then decided to press on. "Moroes said that I was not alone. That people saw things like that all the time."

"Moroes is right," said Medivh, taking a long pull from the wine and smacking his lips. "A late harvest vintage, not bad at all. That this tower is a place of power should not surprise you. Mages gravitate toward such places. Such places are often where the universe wears thin, allowing it to double back on itself, or perhaps even allowing entry to the Twisting Nether and to other worlds entirely."

"Was that what I saw, then," interrupted Khadgar, "another world?"

Medivh held up a hand to hush the younger man. "I am just saying that there are places of power, which for one reason or another, become the seats of great power. One such location is here, in the Redridge Mountains. Once long ago something powerful exploded here, carving out the valley and weakening the reality around it."

"And that's why you sought it out," prompted Khadgar.

Medivh shook his head, but instead said, "That's one theory."

"You said there was an explosion long ago that created this place, and it made it a place of magical power. You then came. . . ."

"Yes," said Medivh. "That's all true, if you look at it

in a linear fashion. But what happens if the explosion occurred because I would eventually come here and the place needed to be ready for me?"

Khadgar's face knitted. "But things don't happen like that."

"In the normal world, no, they do not," said Medivh. "But magic is the art of circumventing the normal. That's why the philosophical debates in the halls of the Kirin Tor are so much buffle and blow. They seek to place rationality upon the world, and regulate its motions. The stars march in order across the sky, the seasons fall one after the other with lockstepped regularity, and men and women live and die. If that does not happen, it's magic, the first warping of the universe, a few floorboards that are bent out of shape, waiting for industrious hands to pry them up."

"But for that to happen to the area to be prepared for you . . ." started Khadgar.

"The world would have to be very different than it seems," answered Medivh, "which it truly is, after all. How does time work?"

Khadgar was not thrown as much by Medivh's apparent change of topic. "Time?"

"We use it, trust it, measure by it, but what *is* it?" Medivh was smiling over the top of his cup.

"Time is a regular progression of instants. Like sands through an hourglass," said Khadgar.

"Excellent analogy," said Medivh. "One I was going to use myself, and then compare the hourglass with the mechanical clock. You see the difference between the two?"

Khadgar shook his head slowly as Medivh sipped on his wine.

Eventually, the mage spoke, "No, you're not daft, boy. It's a hard concept to wrap your brain around. The clock is a mechanical simulation of time, each beat controlled by a turning of the gears. You can look at a clock and know that everything advances by one tic of the wheel, one slip of the gears. You know what is coming next, because the original clockmaker built it that way."

"All right," said Khadgar. "Time is a clock."

"Ah, but time is also an hourglass," said the older Mage, reaching for one planted on the mantel and flipping it over. Khadgar looked at the timepiece, and tried to remember if it was there before he had brought up the wine, or even before Medivh reached for it.

"The hourglass also measures time, true?" said Medivh. "Yet here you never know which particle of sand will move from the upper half to the lower half at any instant. Were you to number the sands, the order would be slightly different each time. But the end result is always the same—all the sand has moved from the top to the bottom. What order it happens in does not matter." The old man's eyes brightened for a moment. "So?" he asked.

"So," said Khadgar. "You're saying that it may not matter if you set up your tower here because an explosion created this valley and warped the nature of reality around it, or that the explosion occurred *because* you would eventually be come here, and the nature of the universe needed to give you the tools you wanted to stay."

"Close enough," said Medivh.

"So what these visions are, then, are bits of sand?" said Khadgar. Medivh frowned slightly but the youth pressed on. "If the tower is an hourglass, and not a clock, then there are bits of sand, of time itself, that are moving though it at any time. These are unstuck, or overlap each other, so that we can see them, but not clearly. Some of it is parts of the past. Some of it is parts of the future. Could some of it be of other worlds as well?"

Medivh now was thinking deeply himself. "It is possible. Full marks. Well thought out. The big thing to remember is that these visions are just that. Visions. They waft in and out. Were the tower a clock, they would move regularly and be easily explained. But since the tower is an hourglass, then they don't. They move at their own speed, and defy us to explain their chaotic nature." Medivh leaned back in his chair. "Which I, for one, am quite comfortable with. I could never really favor an orderly, well-planned universe."

Khadgar added, "But have you ever sought out a particular vision? Wouldn't there be a way to discover a certain future, and then make sure it happened?"

Medivh's mood darkened. "Or make sure it never comes to pass," he said. "No, there are some things that even a master mage respects and stays clear of. This is one of them."

"But . . ."

"No buts," said Medivh, rising and setting his empty mug on the mantelpiece. "Now that you've had a bit of wine—let's see how that affects your magical control. Levitate my mug."

Khadgar furrowed his brow, and realized that his voice had been slightly slurred. "But we've been drinking."

"Exactly," said the master mage. "You will never know what sands the universe will throw in your face. You can either plan to be eternally vigilant and ready, eschewing life as we know it, or be willing to enjoy life and pay the price. Now try to levitate the mug."

Khadgar didn't realize until this moment how much he had drunk, and tried to clear the mushiness from his mind and lift the heavy ceramic mug from the mantel.

A few moments later, he was heading for the kitchen, looking for a broom and a pan.

In the evenings, Khadgar's time was his own, to practice and research, as Medivh dealt with other matters. Khadgar wondered what the other matters were, but assumed they included correspondence, for twice a week a dwarf on gryphon-back arrived at the topmost tower with a satchel, and left with a larger satchel.

Medivh gave the young man free license in the library to research as he saw fit, including the myriad questions that his former masters in the Violet Citadel had requested.

"My only demand," said Medivh with a smile, "is

that you show me what you write before you send it to them." Khadgar must have shown his embarrassment, because Medivh added, "Not because I fear you'll keep something from me, Young Trust, but because I'd hate for them to know something that I had forgotten about."

So Khadgar plunged into the books. For Guzbah he found an ancient, well-read scroll with an epic poem, its numbered stanzas precisely detailing a battle between Medivh's mother Aegwynn and an unnamed demon. For Lady Delth he made a listing of the moldering elven tomes in the library. And for Alonda he plunged through those bestiaries he could read, but could not push the number of troll species past four.

Khadgar also spent his free time with his lock picks and his personal opening spells. He still sought to master those books that foiled his earlier attempts to crack them open. These tomes had strong magics on them, and he could spend an evening among his divinations before getting even the first hint what style of spell protected its contents.

Lastly, there was the subject of the Guardian. Medivh had mentioned it, and Lord Lothar had assumed that the Magus had confided in it to the young man, and backed off quickly when the King's Champion had found it not to be the case.

The Guardian, it seemed, was a phantom, no more or no less real than the time-skewed visions that seemed to move through the tower. There was a mention in passing of a Guardian (always capitalized) in this elven tome, a reference in the Azeroth's royal histories of a Guardian attending this wedding or that funeral, or being in the vanguard of some attack. Always present, but never identified. Was this Guardian a position, or, like Medivh's supposed near-immortal mother, a single being?

There were other phantoms that orbited this Guardian as well. An order of some sort, an organization—was the Guardian a holy knight? And the word "Tirisfal" was written in the margins of one grimoire, and then erased, such that only Khadgar's skill at examination told him what was once written there by the carving the pen had done in the parchment. A name of a particular Guardian, or the organization, or something else entirely?

It was the evening that Khadgar found this word, four days after the incident with the mug, that the young man fell into a new vision. Or rather, a vision snuck up on him and surrounded him, swallowing him whole.

It was the smell that came to him first, a soft vegetable warmth among the moldering texts, a fragrance that slowly rose into the room. The heat rose in the room, not uncomfortably, but as a warm damp blanket. The walls darkened and turned green, and vines trellised up the sides of the bookcases, passing through and replacing the volumes that were there and spreading wide, flat leaves. Large pale moonflowers and crimson star orchids sprouted among the stacked scrolls.

Khadgar took a deep breath, but more from anticipation than fear. This was not the world of harsh land and orc armies that he had seen before. This was something different. This was a jungle, but it was a jungle on this world. The thought comforted him.

And the table disappeared, and the book, and Khadgar was left sitting at a campfire with three other young men. They seemed to be about his age, and were on some sort of expedition. Sleeping rolls had been laid out, and the stewpot, empty and already cleaned, was drying by the fire. All three were dressed for riding, but their clothes were well tailored and of good quality.

The three men were laughing and joking, though, as before, Khadgar could not make out the exact words. The blond one in the middle was in the midst of telling a story, and from his hand motions, one involving a nicely apportioned young woman.

The one on his right laughed and slapped a knee as the blond one continued his tale. This one ran his fingers through his hair, and Khadgar noticed that his dark hair was already receding. That was when he realized he was looking at Lord Lothar. The eyes and nose were his, and the smile just the same, but the flesh was not yet weathered and his beard was not graying. But it was him.

Khadgar looked at the third man, and knew at once it had to be Medivh. This one was dressed in a dark green hunter's garb, his hood pulled back to reveal a young, mirthful face. His eyes were burnished jade in the light of the campfire, and he favored the blond one's story with an embarrassed smile.

The blond one in the center made a point and motioned to the young Medivh, who shrugged, clearly embarrassed. The blond one's story apparently involved the future Magus as well.

The blond one had to be Llane, now King Llane of Azeroth. Yes, the early stories of the three of them had found their way even into the Violet Citadel's archives. The three of them often wandered through the borders of the kingdom, exploring and putting down all manner of raiders and monsters.

Llane concluded his story and Lothar nearly fell back over the log he was sitting upon, roaring with laughter. Medivh suppressed a laugh himself into his curled hand, looking like he was merely clearing his throat.

Lothar's laughter subsided, and Medivh said something, opening his palms upward to make a point. Lothar *did* pitch backward now, and Llane himself put his face in his hand, his body heaving in amusement. Apparently whatever Medivh said topped Llane's story entirely.

Then something moved in the surrounding jungle. The three stopped their revelry at once—they must have heard it. Khadgar, the ghost at this gathering, more felt it instead; something malevolent lurking at the borders of the campfire.

Lothar rose slowly and reached for a great, wide-bladed sword laying in its sheath at his feet. Llane stood up, reaching behind his log to pull out a double-headed ax, and motioned for Lothar to go one way, Medivh to go the other. Medivh had risen as well by this point, and though his hands were empty he, even at this age, was the most powerful of the three.

Llane with his broadax loped forward to one side of the campsite. He might have imagined himself as stealthy, but Khadgar saw him move with firm-footed deliberation. He wanted whatever was there at the edge to reveal itself.

The thing obliged, bursting from its place of concealment. It was half again as tall as any of the young men, and for one instant he thought it was some gigantic orc.

Then he recognized it from bestiaries that Alonda had him peruse. It was a troll, one of the jungle breed, its blue-hued skin pale in the moonlight, its long gray hair lacquered upright into a crest that ran from its forehead back to the nape of the neck. Like the orcs, it had fangs jutting from its lower jaw, but these were rounded, peglike tusks, thicker than the sharp teeth of the orcs. Its ears and nose were elongated, parodies of human flesh. It was dressed in skins, and chains made of human finger bones danced on its bare chest.

The troll let out a battle roar, baring its teeth and its chest in rage, and feinted with its spear. Llane swung at the outthrust weapon, but his blow went wide. Lothar charged from one side, and Medivh came up as well, eldritch energy dancing off his fingertips.

The troll sidestepped Lothar's greatsword, and danced back another step when Llane shredded the air with his huge ax. Each step covered more than a yard, and the two warriors pressed the troll each time it retreated. It used the spear more as a shield than a weapon, holding the haft two-handed and knocking aside the blow.

Khadgar realized the creature wasn't fighting to kill the humans, not yet. It was trying to pull them into position.

In the vision, the young Medivh must have realized the same thing, because he shouted something to the others.

But by this time it was too late, for two other trolls chose that moment to leap from their hiding places on either side of the combat.

Llane, for all his planning, was the one caught by surprise, and the spear skewered his right arm. The broadax's blade bit into the earth as the future king screamed a curse.

The other two concentrated on Lothar, and now the warrior was being forced back, using his broad blade with consummate dexterity, foiling first one thrust, then the other. Still, the jungle trolls showed their strategy—they were driving the two warriors apart, separating Llane from Lothar, forcing Medivh to choose.

Medivh chose Llane. From his phantom viewpoint Khadgar guessed it was because Llane was already wounded. Medivh charged, his hands flaming. . . .

And caught the butt end of the troll's spear in the face, as the troll slammed the heavy haft against

Medivh's jaw, then turned and with one elegant motion pummeled the wounded Llane. Medivh went down, and so did Llane, and the ax, spun out of the future sovereign's hand.

The troll hesitated a moment, trying to determine who to kill first. It chose Medivh, sprawled on the ground at its feet, the closer of the two. The troll raised the spear and the obsidian point glowed evil in the moonlight.

The young Medivh choked off a series of syllables. A small tornado of dust rose from the ground and flung itself into the troll's face, blinding it. The troll hesitated for a moment, and clawed at its dusty orbs with one hand.

The hesitation was all Medivh needed, for he lunged forward, not with a spell, but with a simple knife, plunging it into the back of the troll's thigh. The troll gave a scream in the night, stabbing blindly. The spear dug into where Medivh had been, for the young mage had rolled to one side and was now rising, his fingertips crackling.

He muttered a word and lightning gathered in a ball between his fingers and lanced forward. The troll jolted from the shock and hung for a moment, caught in a blue-limned seizure. The creature fell to its knees, and even then was not done, for it tried to rise, its rheumy red eyes burning with hatred for the wizard.

The troll never got its chance, for a shadow rose behind it, and Llane's recovered ax gleamed briefly in the moonlight before coming down on the troll's head, bisecting it at the neck. The creature sprawled forward, and the two young men, as well as Khadgar, turned to the trolls battling with Lothar.

The future champion was holding his own, but just barely, and had backed almost across the entire campsite. The trolls had heard the death scream of their brother, and one continued to press his attack as the other charged back to deal with the two humans. It let out an inarticulate bellow as it crossed the campsite, its spear before it like a knight on horseback.

Llane charged in return, but at the last moment veered to one side, dancing aside the spear's point. The troll took two more steps forward, which brought him up to the campfire itself, and where Medivh was waiting.

Now the mage seemed to be full of energy and, limned by the coals before him, looked demonic in his demeanor. He had his arms wide, and he was chanting something harsh and rhythmic.

And the fire itself leaped up, taking a brief animated form of a giant lion, and leaped on the attacking troll. The jungle troll screamed as the coals, logs, and ash wrapped itself around him like a cloak, and would not be shrugged off. The troll flung itself on the ground and rolled first one way and then the other, trying to dampen the flame, but it did no good. Finally the troll stopped moving entirely, and the hungry flames consumed it.

For his part, Llane continued his charge and buried

his ax in the side of the surviving troll. The beast let out a howl, but its moment's hesitation was all that Lothar needed. The champion batted away the out-thrust spear with a backhanded blow, then with a level, precise swing cut the troll's head cleanly from its shoulders. The head bounced into the brush, and was lost.

Llane, though bleeding from his own wound, slapped Lothar on the back, apparently taunting him for taking so long with his troll. Then Lothar put a hand to Llane's chest to quiet him, and pointed at Medivh.

The young mage was still standing over the fire, his hands held open, but fingers hooked like claws. His eyes were glassy in the surviving firelight, and his jaw was tightly clenched. As the two men (and the phantom Khadgar) ran over to him, the young man pitched backward.

By the time the pair reached Medivh, he was breathing heavily, and his pupils were wide in the moonlight. Warriors and vision visitor leaned over him, as the young mage strained to push the words out of his mouth.

"Watch out for me," he said, looking at neither Llane nor Lothar, but at Khadgar. Then the young Medivh's eyes rolled up in his head and he lay very still.

Lothar and Llane were trying to revive their friend, but Khadgar just stepped back. Had Medivh truly seen him, as the other mage, the one with his eyes on the war-swept plains, had? And he had heard him, clear words spoken almost to the depth of his soul.

Khadgar turned and the vision dropped away as quickly as a magician's curtain. He was back in the library again, and he almost stumbled into Medivh himself.

"Young Trust," said Medivh, the version much older than the one laying on the ground in the vanished vision. "Are you all right? I called out, but you did not answer."

"Sorry Med . . . sir," said Khadgar, taking a deep breath. "It was a vision. I was lost in it, I'm afraid."

Medivh's dark brows drew together. "Not more orcs and red skies?" he asked seriously, and Khadgar saw a touch of the storm in those green eyes.

Khadgar shook his head and chose his words carefully. "Trolls. Blue trolls, and it was a jungle. I think it was this world. The sky was the same."

Medivh's concern deflated and he just said, "Jungle trolls. I met some once, down south, in the Stranglethorn Vale. . . ." The mage's features softened as he himself seemed to become lost in a vision of his own. Then he shook his head, "But no orcs this time, right? You are sure."

"No, sir," said Khadgar. He did not want to mention that it was that battle he was witnessing. Was it a bad memory for Medivh? Was this the time when he slipped into the coma?

Looking at the older mage, Khadgar could see much of the young man from the vision. He was taller, but slightly stooped from his years and researches, yet there was the young man wrapped within the older form.

Medivh for his part said, "Do you have 'Song of Aegwynn'?"

Khadgar shook himself out of his thoughts. "The song?"

"Of my mother," said Medivh. "It would be an old scroll. I swear I can't find anything here since you've cleaned!"

"It is with the other epic poetry, sir," said Khadgar. *He should tell him about the vision,* he thought. Was this a random event, or was it brought on by his meeting of Lothar? Was finding out about things triggering visions?

Medivh crossed to the shelf, and running a finger along the scrolls, pulled the needed version, old, and well worn. He unwound it partway, checked it against a scrap of paper in his pocket, then rewound and replaced it.

"I have to go," he said suddenly. "Tonight, I'm afraid."

"Where are we going?" asked Khadgar.

"I go alone, this time," said the elder mage, already striding toward the door. "I will leave instructions for your studies with Moroes."

"When will you return?" shouted Khadgar after his retreating form.

"When I am back!" bellowed Medivh, taking the stairs up two at a time already. Khadgar imagined the castellan already at the top of the tower, with his runic whistle and tame gryphon at the ready.

"Fine," said Khadgar, looking at the books. "I'll just sit here and figure out how to tame an hourglass."

SIX

Aegwynn and Sargeras

Medivh was gone a week, all told, and it was a week well spent for Khadgar. He installed himself in the library, and had Moroes bring his meals there. On more than one occasion he did not even reach his quarters in the evening, rather spending the time sleeping on the great library tables themselves. Ultimately, he was searching for visions.

His own correspondence went unanswered as he plumbed the ancient tomes and grimoires on questions about time, light, and magic. His early reports had drawn quick responses from the mages of the Violet Citadel. Guzbah wanted a transcription of the epic poem of Aegwynn. Lady Delth declared that she recognized none of the titles he sent her—could he send them again, this time with the first paragraph of each, so she knew what they were? And Alonda was adamant that there had to be a fifth breed of troll, and that Khadgar had obviously not found the proper bestiaries. The young mage was delighted to leave their demands unanswered as he sought out a way of taming the visions.

The key to his incantation, it seemed, would be a simple spell of farseeing, a divination that granted sight of distant objects and far-off locations. A book of priestly magic had described it as an incantation of holy vision, yet it worked as well for Khadgar as it did for their clerics. While that priestly spell functioned over space, perhaps with modification it could function over time. Khadgar reasoned that this would normally be impossible given the flow of time in a determinant, clockwork universe.

But it seemed that within the walls of Karazhan, at least, time was an hourglass, and identifying bits of disjointed time was more likely. And once one hooked into one grain of time, it would be easier to move that grain to another.

If others had attempted this within the walls of Medivh's Tower, there was no clue within the library, unless it was within the most heavily guarded or unreadable of the tomes located on the iron balcony. Curiously, the notes in Medivh's own hand were uninterested in the visions, which seemed to dominate other notes from other visitors. Did Medivh keep that information in another location, or was he truly more interested in matters beyond the walls of the citadel than the activities within it?

Refitting a spell for a new activity was not as simple as changing an incantation here, altering a motion there. It required a deep and precise understanding of how divination worked, of what it revealed and how. When a hand-motion changes, or the type of incense used is deleted, the result is most likely complete failure, where the energies are dissipated harmlessly. Occasionally the energies may go wild and out of control, but usually the only result of a failed spell is a frustrated spellcaster.

In his studies, Khadgar discovered that if a spell fails in a spectacular fashion, it indicates that the failed spell is very close to the final intended spell. The magics are trying to close the gap, to make things happen, though not always with the results intended by the caster. Of course, sometimes these failed magic-users did not survive the experience.

During the process, Khadgar was afraid that Medivh would return at any time, wafting back into the library, looking for the well-read epic poem or some other bit of trivia. Would he tell his master what he was trying? And if he did, would Medivh encourage him, or forbid him from trying to find out?

After five days, Khadgar felt he had the spellmaking complete. The framework remained that of the farseeing, but it was now empowered with a random factor to allow it to reach through and search out the discontinuities that seemed to exist within the tower. These bits of misplaced time would be a little brighter, a little hotter, or simply a little odder than the immediate surroundings, and as such attract the full force of the spell itself.

The spell, if it functioned, should in addition tune in the vision better. This would collect the sounds at the other end and remove the distortion, concentrating them in the same fashion as an elderly person cupping a hand to the ear to hear better. It would not work for sounds beyond the central location as well, but should clarify what individuals were saying in addition to what the caster was seeing.

The evening of the fifth day, Khadgar had completed his calculations, the neat rows and orders of power and casting laid out in a simple script. Should something go horribly wrong, at least Medivh would figure out what had happened.

Medivh, of course, kept a fully equipped pantry of spell components, including a larder of aromatic and thaumaturgic herbs, and a lapidarium of crushed semiprecious stones. Of these Khadgar chose amethyst to lay out his magical circle, in the library itself, crisscrossing it with runes of powered rose quartz. He reviewed the words of power (most of them known to the young mage before he left Dalaran) and worked through the motions (almost all of them original). Dressed in conjuration robes (more for luck than effect), he stepped within the casting circle.

Khadgar let his mind settle and become calm. This was no quickly-cast battle spell, or some offhand cantrip. Rather this was a deep and powerful spell, one that, if within the Violet Citadel, would set off the warning abjurations of other mages and bring them flying to him.

He took a deep breath, and began to cast.

Within his mind, the spell began to form, a warm, hot ball of energy. He could feel it congeal within him, as rainbow ripples moved across the surface. This was the core of the spell, usually quickly dispatched to alter the real world as its caster saw fit.

Khadgar fitted the sphere with the attributes he desired, to seek out the bits of time that seemed to haunt the tower, sort through them, and bring together a single vision, one that he could witness spread before him. The ideas seemed to sink with the imaginary sphere in his mind, and in return the sphere seemed to hum at a higher pitch, awaiting only release and direction.

"Bring me a vision," said the young mage. "Bring me a vision of the young Medivh."

With the sound of an egg imploding the magic was gone from his mind, seeping into the real world to carry out his bidding. There was a rush of air, and as Khadgar looked around, the library began to transform, as it had before, the vision moving slowly into his space and time.

Only when it suddenly got colder did Khadgar realize he had called up the wrong vision.

It moved through the library suddenly, a cold draft as if someone had left a window open. The breeze went from a draft to a chill to an arctic blast, and despite his own knowledge that it was merely illusion, Khadgar shivered to his core.

The walls of the library fell away as the vision took hold with an expanse of white. The chill wind curled around the books and manuscripts and left a blanket of snow as it passed, thick and hard. Tables, shelves, and chairs were obscured and then eliminated with the swirls of thick heavy flakes.

And Khadgar was on a hillside, his feet disappearing at his knees into a bank of snow, but leaving no mark. He was a ghost within this vision.

Still, his breath frosted and curled upward as he looked around him. To his right was a copse of trees, dark evergreens loaded down by the passing snowstorm. Far to his left was a great white cliff. Khadgar thought it some chalky substance, and then realized that it was ice, as if someone had taken a frozen river and uprooted it. The ice river was as tall as some of the mountains on Dalaran, and small dark shapes moved above it. Hawks or eagles, though they would have to be of immense size if they were truly near the icy cliffs.

Ahead of him was a vale, and moving up the vale was an army.

The army melted the snow as it passed, leaving a smudged mark of black behind it like a slug's trail. The members of the army were dressed in red, wearing great horned helms and long, high-backed black cloaks. They were hunters, for they wore all manner of weapons.

At the head of the army, its leader bore a standard, and atop the standard rode a dripping, decapitated head. Khadgar thought it some great green-scaled beast, but stopped himself when he realized it was a dragon's head.

He had seen a skull of such a creature in the Violet Citadel, but never thought that he would see one that had recently been alive. How far back had his vision truly thrown him?

The army of giant-things were bellowing what could have been a marching song, though it could just as easily have been a string of curses or a challenging cry. The voices were muddled, as if they were at the bottom of a great well, but at least Khadgar could hear them.

As they grew closer, Khadgar realized what they were. Their ornate helmets were not helms, but rather horns that jutted from their own flesh. Their cloaks were not garments but great batlike wings that jutted from their backs. Their red-tinged armor was their own thick flesh, glowing from within and melting the snow.

They were demons, creatures from Guzbah's lectures and Korrigan's hidden pamphlets. Monstrous beings that exceeded even the orcs in their bloodthirst and sadism. The great, broad-bladed swords were clearly bathed in crimson, and now Khadgar could see that their bodies were spattered with gore as well.

They were here, wherever and whenever here was, and they were hunting dragons.

There was a soft, distorted sound behind him, no more than a footfall on a soft carpet. Khadgar turned, and he realized that he was not alone on the hillock overlooking the demon hunting party.

She had come up from behind him unawares, and if she saw him, she paid him no mind. Just as the demons seemed a blight incarnate on the land, so, too, did she radiate her own sense of power. This was a brilliant power that seemed to fold and intensify as she glided along atop the surface of the snow itself. She was real, but her white leather boots left only the faintest marks in the snow.

She was tall and powerful and unafraid of the abomination in the valley below. Her garb was as white and unspoiled as the snow around them, and she wore a vest made of small silver scales. A great white hooded fur cape with a lining of green silk billowed behind her, held at her throat by a large green stone which matched her eyes. She wore her blond hair simply, held in place by a silver diadem, and seemed less affected by the cold than the ghostly Khadgar.

Yet it was her eyes that held his attention—green as summer forest, green as polished jade, green as the ocean after a storm. Khadgar recognized those eyes, for he had felt the penetrating gaze of similar eyes, but from her son.

This was Aegwynn. Medivh's mother, the powerful near-immortal mage that was so old as to become a legend.

Khadgar also realized where he must be, and this was Aegwynn's battle against the demon hordes, a legend saved only in fragments, in the cantos of an epic poem on the library shelf.

With a pang Khadgar realized where his spell had gone wrong. Medivh had asked for that scroll before leaving, the last time Khadgar had seen him. Had the spell misfired, passing through a vision of Medivh himself most recently into the very legend that he was checking?

Aegwynn frowned as she looked down on the demonic hunting party, the single line dividing her eyebrows showing her displeasure. Her jade eyes flashed, and Khadgar could guess that a storm of power was brewing within her.

It did not take long for that anger to be released. She raised an arm, chanted a short, clipped phrase, and lightning danced from her fingertips.

This was no mere conjurer's bolt, nor even the harshest strike of a summer thunderstorm. This was a shard of elemental lightning, arcing through the cold air and finding its ground in the surprised demonic armor. The air split down to its most basic elements as the bolt cleaved through it, and the air smelled sharp and bitter in its passing, the air thundering in to replace the space the bolt had briefly filled. Despite himself, despite knowing that he was phantom, despite knowing that this was a vision, despite all this and the fact that the noise was muted by his ghostly state, Khadgar grimaced and recoiled at the flash and metallic tolling of the mystic bolt.

The bolt struck the standard bearer, the one bearing the severed head of the great green dragon. It immolated the demon where he stood, and those around it were blasted from their feet, falling like hot coals in the snow. Some did not rise again.

But the majority of the hunting party were outside the spell's effect, whether by accident or design. The demons, each one larger than ten men, recoiled in shock, but that lasted only a moment. The largest of them bellowed something in a language that sounded like broken metal bells, and half of the demons took wing, charging Aegwynn's (and Khadgar's) position. The other half pulled out heavy bows of black oak and iron arrows. As they fired the arrows, they ignited, and a rain of fire descended upon them.

Aegwynn did not flinch, but merely raised a hand in a sweeping motion. The entire sky between her and the fiery rain erupted in a wall of bluish flame, which swallowed the orange-red bolts as if they had simply fallen into a river.

Yet the bolts were merely to provide cover for the attackers, who burst through the blue wall of fire as it dissipated and dropped on Aegwynn from above. There had to be at least twenty of them, each a giant, darkening the skies with their huge wings.

Khadgar looked at Aegwynn and saw that she was smiling. It was a knowing, self-confident smile, and one that the young mage had seen on Medivh's face, when they had fought the orcs. She was more than confident.

Khadgar looked down the valley to where the archers had been. They had abandoned their useless missiles but now were gathered together, chanting in a low, buzzing tone. The air warped around them, and a hole appeared in reality, a dark malignancy against the pristine white. And from that hole dropped more demons—creatures of every description, with the heads of animals, with flaming eyes, with wings of bats and insects and great scavenging birds. These demons joined the choir and the rift opened farther, sucking more and more of the spawn of the Twisting Nether into the cold northern air.

Aegwynn paid the chanters and reinforcements no mind, but rather coolly concentrated on those dropping on her from above.

She passed her hand, palm up. Half of those that flew were turned to glass, and all of them were knocked from the sky. Those that had been turned to crystal shattered where they struck with discordant chords. Those that were still living landed with a heavy thump, and rose again, their ichor-splattered weapons drawn. There were ten left.

Aegwynn placed her left fist against her upright right palm, and four of the survivors melted, their ruddy flesh melting off the bones as they slumped into the snow banks. They screamed until their decaying throats filled with their own desiccated flesh. There were six left.

Aegwynn clutched at the air and three more demons exploded as their interiors turned into insects and ripped them from the inside out. They didn't even have time to scream as their forms were replaced by swarms of gnats, bees, and wasps, which boiled out toward the forests. There were three left.

Aegwynn pulled her hands apart and a demon had its arms and legs ripped from its torso by invisible hands. Two left. Aegwynn raised two fingers and a demon turned to sand, its dying curse lost on the chill breeze.

One left. It was the largest, the leader, the bellower of orders. At close range Khadgar could see that its bare chest was a pattern of scars, and one eye socket was empty. The other burned with hate.

It did not attack. Neither did Aegwynn. Instead they stopped, frozen for a moment, while the valley beneath them filled with demons.

Finally the great behemoth of a demon snarled. His voice was clear but distant to Khadgar's ears.

"You are a fool, Guardian of Tirisfal," it said, wrapping its lips around the uncomfortable human language.

Aegwynn let out a laugh, as sharp and as thin as a

glass dagger. "Am I, foulspawn? I came here to spoil your dragon hunt. It seems that I have succeeded."

"You are an overconfident fool," slurred the demon. "While you have been fighting only a few, my brothers in sorcery have brought in others. A legion of others. Every incubus and petty demon, every nightmare and shadow-hound, every dark lord and captain of the Burning Legion. All have come here while you have fought these few."

"I know," said Aegwynn, calmly.

"You *know*?" bellowed the demon with a throaty laugh. "You know that you are alone in the wilderness, with every demon raised against you. You *know*?"

"I know," said Aegwynn, and there was smile in the voice. "I know you would bring as many of your allies as possible. A Guardian would be too great a target for you to resist."

"*You know*?" shouted the demon again. "And you came anyway, alone, to this forsaken place?"

"I know," said Aegwynn. "But I never said I was alone."

Aegwynn snapped her fingers and the sky suddenly darkened, as if a great flock of birds had been disturbed, and blocked the sun.

Except they were not birds. They were dragons. More dragons than Khadgar even imagined existing. They hovered in place on their great wings, waiting for the Guardian's signal.

"Foulspawn of the Burning Legion," said Aegwynn. "It is you that are the fool."

The demonic leader let out a cry and raised its blood-spattered sword. Aegwynn was too quick for it, and raised a hand, three fingers outstretched. The foulspawn's scar-ridden chest evaporated, leaving only a cloud of bloody motes. His brawny arms fell away to each side, its abandoned legs folded and it collapsed, and its head, registering nothing so much as a look of shocked surprise, fell into the melting snow and was lost.

That was the signal for the dragons, for as one they turned on the collected horde of summoned demons. The great flying creatures swooped down from all sides, and flame sprung from their open maws. The front rows of demons were immolated, reduced to no more than ash in an instant, while others struggled to pull out their weapons, to ready their own spells, to flee the field.

In the center of the army, a chant went up, this one an intense pleading, and a passionate cry. These were the most powerful of the demonic spellcasters, who concentrated their energies as those at the borders fought off the dragons at deadly cost.

The demons regrouped and retaliated, and dragons now began to fall from the sky, their bodies riddled by iron arrows and flaming bolt, by sorcerous poisons and by maddening visions. Still, the circle around the center of the demons shrank as more and more of the dragons took their revenge against the demons for the hunt, and the cries in the center became more desperate and indistinct.

Khadgar looked at Aegwynn, and she was standing stock-still in the snow, her fists clenched, her green eyes blazing with power, her teeth locked in a hideous grin. She was chanting, too, something dark and inhuman and beyond even Khadgar's ability to recognize. She was fighting the spell the demons had constructed, but she was pulling energy from it as well, bending mystic force contained within back on itself, like layers of steel in a sword's blade are folded back on themselves to make the blade stronger and more potent.

The cries of the demons in the center reached a fever pitch, and now Aegwynn was shouting herself, a nimbus of energy coalesced around her. Her hair was loose and flying now, and she raised both arms and unleashed the last words of her conjuration.

And there was a flash at the center of the demonic horde, at the center where the casters chanted and screamed and prayed. It was a rip in the universe, this time a bright rip, as if a doorway into the sun itself had been opened. The energy spiraled outward, and the demons did not even have time to scream as it overtook them, burning them out and leaving the shadows of their afterimage as their only testament.

All of the demons were caught, and a few of the dragons as well who strayed too close to the center of the demonic horde. They were caught like moths in a flame and snuffed out just as surely.

Aegwynn let out a ragged breath and smiled. It was the smile of the wolf, of the predator, of the victor.

Where the demonic horde had been there was now a pillar of smoke, rising to the heavens in a great cloud.

But as Khadgar watched, the cloud flattened and gathered in on itself, growing darker and more intense, like the anvil of a thunderhead. Yet in redoubling itself, it grew stronger, and its heart grew blacker, verging on shades of purple and ebony.

And from out of the darkened cloud Khadgar saw a god emerge.

It was a titanic figure, larger than any giant of myth, greater than any dragon. Its skin looked like it was cast in bronze, and it wore black armor made of molten obsidian. Its great beard and wild hair were made of living flames, and huge horns jutted from above its dark brow. Its eyes were the color of the Infinite Abyss. It strode out of the dark cloud, and the earth shook where its feet fell. It carried a huge spear engraved with runes that dripped burning blood, and it had a long tail ending in a fireball.

What dragons were left fled the field, heading for the dark forest and the distant cliffs. Khadgar could not blame them. As much power as Medivh held within him, as much great power that his mother now showed, it was like two small candles compared to the raw power of this lord of the demons.

"Sargeras," hissed Aegwynn.

"Guardian," thundered the great demon, in a voice as deep as the ocean itself. In the distance, the ice cliffs collapsed rather than echo this hellish voice.

The Guardian pulled herself up to her full height,

brushed back a stray blond hair, and said, "I have broken your toys. You are finished here. Flee while you still have your life."

Khadgar looked at the Guardian as if she had lost her mind. Even to his eyes she was exhausted from her experience, almost as empty as Khadgar had been against the orcs. Surely this titanic demon could see through the ruse. The epic poem spoke of Aegwynn's victory. Was he about to witness her death, instead?

Sargeras did not laugh, but his voice rolled across the land, pressing down on Khadgar nonetheless. "The time of Tirisfal is about to end," said the demon. "This world will soon bow before the onslaught of the Legion."

"Not as long as there is a Guardian," said Aegwynn. "Not as long as I live, or those who come after me." Her fingers curled slightly, and Khadgar could see that she was summoning power within herself, gathering her wits, her will, and her energy into one great assault. Despite himself, Khadgar took a step back, then another, then a third. If his elder self could see him in the vision, if young Medivh could see him, could not these two great powers, mage and monster, see him as well?

Or was he too small to notice, perhaps?

"Surrender now," said Sargeras. "I have use of your power."

"No," said Aegwynn, her hands in tight balls.

"Then die, Guardian, and let your world die with you," said the titanic demon, and raised his bleeding rune-spear.

Aegwynn raised both hands, and unleashed a shout, half-curse and half-prayer. A flaming rainbow of colors unseen on this world erupted from her palms, snaking upward like a sentient strike of lightning. It struck like a dagger thrust in the center of Sargeras's chest.

It seemed to Khadgar like a bow-shot fired against a boat, as small and as ineffective. Yet Sargeras staggered under the blow, taking a half-step backward and dropping his huge spear. It struck the ground like a meteorite hitting the earth, and the snow rippled beneath Khadgar's feet. He fell to one knee, but looked up at the demon lord.

When Aegwynn's spell had struck, there was a darkness spreading. No, not a darkness, but rather a coolness, the heated bronze flesh of the titan-demon dying and being replaced with a cold, inert mass. It radiated from the center of its chest like a wildfire, leaving consumed flesh behind it.

Sargeras regarded the growing devastation with surprise, then alarm, then fear. He raised a hand to touch it, and it spread to that limb as well, leaving an inert mass of rough, black metal behind. Now Sargeras starting chanting himself, pulling together what energies he possessed to reverse the process, to staunch the flow, to put out the consuming fire. His words grew hotter and more passionate, and his unaffected skin flicked with renewed intensity. He was glowing like a sun, shouting curses as the dark coolness reached where his heart should have been.

And then there was another flash, this one as intense as the one that consumed the demon horde, centered on Sargeras himself. Khadgar looked away, looked at Aegwynn, who watched as the fire and darkness consumed her foe. The brightness of the light dimmed the day itself, and long shadows stretched out behind the mage.

And then it was over. Khadgar blinked as his eyes regained their sight. He turned back to the vale and there was the titanic Sargeras, inert as a thing made of wrought iron, the power burned out of him. Beneath his weight, the heated arctic ground started to give way, and slowly his dead form fell forward, remaining whole as it mashed into the ground. The air around them was still.

Aegwynn laughed. Khadgar looked at her, and she looked drained, both by exhaustion and by madness. She rubbed her hands and chuckled and started to walk down toward the toppled titan. Khadgar noticed that she no longer rested delicately atop the drifts, but now had to slog her way down the hill.

As she left him, the library began to return. The snow began to sublimate in thick clouds of steam, and the shadowy forms of the shelves, the upper gallery, and the chairs slowly made themselves visible.

Khadgar turned slightly, back toward where the table should have been, and everything was back to normal. The library reasserted its reality with a firm suddenness.

Khadgar let out a chill breath and rubbed his skin. Cool, but not cold. The spell had worked well enough, in generalities if not particulars. It had called the vision, but not the desired one. The question was what went wrong, and what was the best way to fix it.

The young mage reached for his scribe's pouch, pulling from it a blank sheet of parchment and tools. He fitted a metal nub to the end of his stylus, melted some of the octopus ink in a bowl, and quickly began to note everything that happened, how he cast the initial spell, to Aegwynn sinking deeper in the snow as she walked away.

He was still working an hour later when there was a cadaverous cough at the doorway. Khadgar was so wrapped up in thought that he did not notice until Moroes coughed a second time.

Khadgar looked up, mildly irritated. There was something important he was about to write, but it was eluding him. Something that was just at the corner of his mind's eye.

"The Magus is back," said Moroes. "Wants you up at the observatory level."

Khadgar looked at Moroes blankly for a moment, before the words gained purchase in his mind. "Medivh's back?" he managed at last.

"That's what I said," groaned Moroes, each word given grudgingly. "You're to fly to Stormwind with him."

"Stormwind? Me? Why?" managed the younger mage.

"You're the apprentice, that's why," scowled Moroes. "Observatory, top level. I've summoned the gryphons."

Khadgar looked at his work—line upon line of neat handwriting, delving into every detail. There was something else that he was thinking about. Instead he said, "Yes. Yes. Let me gather my things up. Finish this."

"Take your time," said the castellan. "It's only the Magus that wants you to fly with him to Stormwind Castle. Nothing important." And Moroes faded back into the hallway. "Top level," came his disembodied voice, almost as an afterthought.

Stormwind! thought Khadgar, *King Llane's castle.* What would be important enough for him to have to go there? Perhaps a report of the orcs?

Khadgar looked at his writing. With the news that Medivh was back, and that they would leave soon, his thoughts were disrupted, and now his mind was on the new task. He looked at the last words he wrote on the parchment.

Aegwynn has two shadows, it said.

Khadgar shook his head. Whatever course his mind was following was gone now. He carefully blotted the excess ink to make sure it did not smear, and set the pages aside. Then he gathered his tools, and quickly headed for his quarters. He would have to change into traveling clothes if he was going gryphon-back, and would need to pack his good conjuring cloak if he was going to meet royalty.

SEVEN
Stormwind

Up until then, the greatest buildings that Khadgar had ever seen had been the Violet Citadel itself, on Cross Island outside the city of Dalaran. The majestic spires and great halls of the Kirin Tor, roofed by thick slate the color of lapis lazuli, which gave the citadel its name, had been a point of pride for Khadgar. In all his travels through Lordaeron and into Azeroth, nothing, not even Medivh's Tower, came close to the ancient grandeur of the citadel of the Kirin Tor.

Until he came to Stormwind.

They had flown through the night, as before, and this time the young mage was convinced he had slept while guiding the gryphon through the chill night air. Whatever knowledge Medivh had placed in his mind was still operating, for he was sure with his ability to guide the winged predator with his knees, and felt quite at home. The part of his brain where the knowledge resided felt no pain this time, but rather a slight thrumming, like the mental tissue had healed over, leaving scar tissue, taking the knowledge within but still recognizing it as a separate part of him.

He woke as the sun crested the horizon behind him, and panicked momentarily, causing the great flier to bank slightly, dragging it away from following in Medivh's wake. Ahead of him, sudden and brilliant in the morning sun, was Stormwind.

It was a citadel of gold and silver. The walls in the morning light seemed to glow with their own radiance, burnished like a chalice under a castellan's cleaning. The roofs glittered as if crafted from silver, and for a moment Khadgar thought they were set with innumerable small gems.

The young mage blinked and shook his head. The golden walls became mere stone, though polished to a fine luster in some places, intricately carved in others. The roofs of silver were merely dark slate, and what he thought were gemstones merely collected dew rainbowing back the dawn.

And yet Khadgar was still astounded by the city's size. As great if not greater than anything in Lordaeron, and seen from this great height, it spread out before him. He counted three full sets of walls ribboned around the central keep, and lesser barriers separating different wards. Everywhere he looked, there was more city beneath him.

Even now, in the dawn hours, there was activity. Smoke rose from morning fires, and already people were clotting in the open marketplaces and commons. Great wains were lumbered out of the main gates, loaded with farmers heading for the neat, ordered fields that spread out from the city's walls like skirts, stretching almost to the horizon.

Khadgar could not identify half the buildings. Great towers could have been universities or granaries, as far as he could tell. A surging river cascade had been harnessed by massive waterwheels, but to what purpose he could not guess. There was a sudden flame far to his right, though whether from a foundry, a captive dragon, or some great accident was a mystery.

It was the greatest city he had ever seen, and at its heart was Llane's castle.

It could be no other. Here the walls seemed to be truly made of gold, set with silver around the windows. The royal roof was shod with blue slate, as deep and luxurious as a sapphire's, and from its myriad towers Khadgar could see pennants with the lion's head of Azeroth, the sigil of King Llane's household and symbol of the land.

The castle complex seemed to be a small city in itself, with innumerable side buildings, towers, and halls. Arching galleries spanned between buildings, at lengths that Khadgar thought impossible without magical aide.

Perhaps such a structure could only be crafted with magic, thought Khadgar, and realized that perhaps this was one reason Medivh was so valued here.

The older mage raised a hand and circled over one particular tower, its topmost floor a level parapet. Medivh pointed down—once, twice, a third time. He wanted Khadgar to land first.

Pulling from the scabbed-over memories, Khadgar brought the great gryphon down neatly. The great eagle-headed beast churned its wings backward like a great sail, slowing to a delicate landing.

There was a delegation already waiting for him. A group of retainers in blue livery surged forward to take the reins and fit the gryphon's head with a heavy hood. The alien memories told Khadgar that this was similar to a falconer's snood, restricting the raptor's vision. Another had a bucket of warm cow guts, which were carefully presented before the gryphon's snapping beak.

Khadgar slid from the gryphon's back and was greeted warmly by Lord Lothar himself. The huge man seemed even larger in an ornate robe and cape, topped with a inscribed breastplate and filigreed mantle hanging on his shoulder.

"Apprentice!" said Lothar, swallowing Khadgar's hand in his huge meaty paw. "Good to see you're still employed!"

"My lord," said Khadgar, trying not to wince from the pressure of the larger man's grip. "We flew through the night to get here. I don't . . ."

The rest of Khadgar's statement was swept away in a flurry of wings and the panicked squawk of a gryphon. Medivh's mount tumbled out of the sky, and the Magus was less graceful in his landing. The huge flier slid across the width of the turret and almost fell off the other side, and Medivh pulled hard on the reins. As it was, the gryphon's great foreclaws clutched at the crenellated wall, and almost tipped the older mage over the side.

Khadgar did not wait for comment from Lord Lothar, but bolted forward, followed by the host of blue-clad retainers, and Lothar lumbering up behind them.

Medivh had already dismounted by the time they had reached him, and handed the reigns to the first of the retainers. "Blasted crosswind!" said the older mage irritably. "I told you this was the precisely wrong spot for an aviary, but no one listens to the mage around here. Good landing, lad," he added as an afterthought, as the servants swarmed over his gryphon, trying to calm it down.

"Med," said Lothar, holding out a hand in greeting. "It is good you could come."

Medivh just scowled. "I came as soon as I could," the wizard snapped, responding to some affront that passed Khadgar by entirely. "You have to get along without me sometimes, you know."

If Lothar was surprised by Medivh's attitude, he said nothing of it. "Good to see you anyway. His Majesty . . ."

"Will have to wait," finished Medivh. "Take me to the chamber in question, now. No, I know the way myself. You said it was Huglar and Hugarin. This way, then." And with that the Magus was off, toward the side stairs that spiraled into the tower proper. "Five levels down, then a cross bridge, then three levels up! Horrible place for an aviary!"

Khadgar looked at Lothar. The larger man rubbed his beefy hand up over his balding pate, and shook his head. Then he started after the man, Khadgar in tow.

Medivh was gone by the time they reached the bottom of the spiral, though a litany of complaints and the occasional curse could be heard up ahead, diminishing fast.

"He's in a fine mood," said Lothar, "Let me walk you to the mage-chambers. We'll find him there."

"He was very agitated last night," said Khadgar, by way of apology. "He had been gone, and apparently your summons reached Karazhan shortly after he had returned."

"Has he told you what all this is about, Apprentice?" asked Lothar. Khadgar had to shake his head.

Champion Anduin Lothar frowned deeply. "Two of the great sorcerers of Azeroth are dead, their bodies burned almost beyond recognition, their heart pulled from their very chests. Dead in their chambers. And there is evidence—" Lord Lothar hesitated for a moment, as if trying to choose the right words. "There is evidence of demonic activity. Which is why I sent the fastest messenger to fetch the Magus. Perhaps he can tell us what happened."

"Where are the bodies?" shouted Medivh, as Lothar and Khadgar finally caught up with him. They were near the top of another of the spires of the castle, the city spread out before them in a great open bay window opposite the door.

The room was a shambles, and looked like it had been searched by orcs, and sloppy orcs at that. Every book had been pulled from the shelves, and every scroll unrolled, and in many cases shredded. Alchemic devices were smashed, powders and poultices scattered about in a fine dusting, and even the furniture broken.

In the center of the room was a ring of power, an inscription carved into the floor itself. The ring was two concentric circles, incised with words of power between them. The incisions in the floor were deep and filled with a sticky dark liquid. There were two scorch marks on the floor, each man-sized, situated between the circle and the window.

Such incised rings had only one purpose to them, as far as Khadgar knew. The librarian in the Violet Citadel was always warning about them.

"Where *are* the bodies?" repeated Medivh, and Khadgar was glad that he was not expected to provide the answers. "Where are the remains of Huglar and Hugarin?"

"They were removed soon after they were found," said Lothar calmly. "It was unseemly to leave them here. We didn't know when you would arrive."

"You didn't know *if* I would arrive, you mean," snapped Medivh. "All right. All right. We can still salvage something. Who has come into this room?"

"The Conjurer-Lords Huglar and Hugarin," began Lothar.

"Well, of *course,*" said Medivh sharply. "They had to be here if they died here. Who else?"

"One of their servants found them," continued Lothar. "And I was called. And I brought several guardsmen to move the bodies. They have not been interred yet, if you wish to examine them."

Medivh was already deeply in thought. "Hmmm? The bodies, or the guardsmen? No matter, we can take care of that later. So that's a servant, yourself, and about four guards, would you say? And now myself and my apprentice. No one else?"

"No one I can think of," said Lothar.

The Magus closed his eyes and muttered a few words under his breath. It might have been either a curse or a spell. His eyes flew open. "Interesting. Young Trust!"

Khadgar took a deep breath. "Lord Magus."

"I need your youth and inexperience. My jaded eyes may see what I'm expecting to see. I need fresh eyes. Don't be afraid to ask questions, now. Come here and stand in the center of the room. No, don't cross the circle itself. We don't know if it has any lingering enchantments on it. Stand here. Now. What do you sense?"

"I see the wrecked room," started Khadgar.

"I didn't say see," said Medivh sharply. "I said sense."

Khadgar took a deep breath and cast a minor spell, one that sharpened the senses and helped find lost articles. It was a simple divination, one he had used hundreds of times in the Violet Citadel. It was particularly good for finding things that others wanted to keep hidden.

But even upon the first intoned words, Khadgar could feel it was different. There was a sluggishness to the magic in this room. Often magic had a feel of lightness and energy, but this felt more viscous, almost liquid in nature. Khadgar had never felt it before, and wondered if it was because of the circles of power, or powers and cantrips of the late mages themselves.

It was a thick feeling, like stale air in a room that had been shuttered for years. Khadgar tried to pull the energies together, but they seemed to resist, to follow his desires with only the greatest reluctance.

Khadgar's face grew stern as he tried to pull more of the power of the room, of the magical energies, into himself. This was a simple spell. If anything, it should be easier in a place where such castings would be commonplace.

And suddenly the young mage was inundated with the thick fetid feel of the magic. It was suddenly upon him and surrounding him, as if he had pulled the bottommost stone out and brought down a wall upon himself. The force of the dark, heavy magic fell upon him in a thick blanket, crushing the spell beneath him and driving him physically to his knees. Despite himself, he cried out.

Medivh was at his side at once, helping the young mage to his feet. "There, there," said the Magus, "I didn't expect you to succeed even that well. Good try. Excellent work."

"What is it?" managed Khadgar, suddenly able to breath again. "It was like nothing I've felt before. Heavy. Resistant. Smothering."

"That's good news for you, then," said Medivh. "Good that you sensed it. Good that you carried through. The magic has been particularly twisted here, a remnant of what occurred earlier."

"You mean like a haunting?" said Khadgar. "Even in Karazhan, I never . . ."

"No, not like that," said Medivh. "Something much worse. The two dead mages here were summoning demons. It's that taint that you feel here, that heaviness of magic. A demon was here. That is what killed Huglar and Hugarin, the poor, powerful idiots."

There was a silence of a moment, then Lothar said, "Demons? In the king's towers? I cannot believe . . ."

"Oh, believe," said Medivh. "No matter how learned and knowledgeable, how wise and wonderful, how powerful and puissant, there is always one more sliver of power, one more bit of knowledge, one more secret to be learned by any mage. I think these two fell into that trap, and called upon forces from beyond the Great Dark Beyond, and paid the price for it. Idiots. They were friends and colleagues, and they were idiots."

"But how?" said Lothar. "Surely there were to be protections. Wards. This is a mystic circle of power."

"Easily breached, easy broken," said Medivh, leaning over the ring the glimmered with the dried blood of the two mages. He reached down and produced a thin straw that had laid over the cooling stones. "A-hah! A simple broom straw. If this was here when they began their summonings, all the adjurations and phylacteries in the world would not protect them. The demon would consider the circle to be no more than an arch, a gateway into this world. He would come out, hellfire blazing, and attack the poor fools who brought him into this world. I've seen it before."

Khadgar shook his head. The thick darkness that seemed to press in on all sides of him seemed to lift somewhat, and he gathered his wits about him. He looked around the room. It was already a disaster area—the demon had torn everything apart in its assault. If there was a broom straw breaking the circle, then it surely should have been moved elsewhere during the battle.

"How were the bodies found?" asked Khadgar.

"What?" said Medivh, with a sharpness that almost made Khadgar jump.

"I'm sorry," Khadgar responded quickly. "You said I should ask questions."

"Yes, yes, of course," said Medivh, cooling his harsh tone only a notch. To the King's Champion he said, "Well, Anduin Lothar, how were the bodies found?"

"When I came in, they were on the ground. The servant had not moved them," said Lothar.

"Faceup or facedown, sir?" said Khadgar, as calmly as he could. He could feel the icy stare of the elder mage. "Heads toward the circle or toward the window?"

Lothar's face clouded in memory. "Toward the circle. And facedown. Yes, definitely. They were badly scorched all over, and we had to turn them over to make sure it was Huglar and Hugarin."

"What are you driving at, Young Trust?" said the Magus, now seated by the open window, stroking his beard.

Khadgar looked at the two scorch marks between the malfunctioned protective circle and the window, and tried to think of them both as bodies and not think of them as once-living mages. "If you hit someone from the front, they fall backward. If you hit someone from the back, they fall forward. Was the window open when you arrived?"

Lothar looked at the open bay window, the great city beyond forgotten for the moment. "Yes. No. Yes, I think it was. But it could have been opened by the servant. There was a horrible stench—that's what brought attention to it in the first place. I can ask."

"No need," said Medivh. "The window was likely open when your servant entered." The Magus rose and walked to where the scorch marks were. "So you think, Young Trust," he said, "that Huglar and Hugarin were standing here, watching the magic circle, and something came in the window and hit them from the back." For effect he smacked himself against the back of the head with an open palm. "They fell forward, and were burned in that position."

"Yes, sir," said Khadgar. "I mean, it's a theory."

"A good one," said Medivh. "But wrong, I'm afraid. In the first place, the two mages would be standing there, facing nothing at all, *unless* they were looking at the magic circle. Therefore they were summoning a demon. Such a circle would not be used otherwise."

"But . . ." started Khadgar, and the Magus froze his words in his throat with a harsh glance.

"*And,*" continued Medivh, "while that would work with a single attacker with a sap or a club, it does not function as well for the dark energies of demons. Had the beast breathed fire, it could have caught both men standing, killed them, and only after being set alight, the bodies fell forward. You said the bodies were burned front and back?" He put that question to Lothar.

"Yes," said the King's Champion.

Medivh held a palm up in front of him. "Demon breathes fire. Burns the front. Huglar (or Hugarin) falls forward, flames spread to the back. Unless the demon hit Hugarin (or Huglar) in the back, then turned them over to make sure the front was burned, then turned them over again. Hardly likely—demons are not that methodical."

Khadgar felt his face warm from embarrassment. "I'm sorry. It was just a theory."

"And a good one," said Medivh quickly. "Just in error, that's all. You're right, the window would be open, because that was how the demon left the tower. It is at large in the city right now."

Lothar cut short a curse, and said, "Are you sure?"

Medivh nodded. "Completely. But it will probably be laying low for the moment. Even killing two fools like Huglar and Hugarin by surprise would tax any but the most powerful creature's abilities."

"I can organize search parties within the hour," said Lothar.

"No," said Medivh. "I want to do this myself. No use throwing away good lives after bad. I'll want to see the remains, of course. That will tell me what we're dealing with here."

"We moved them to a cool room in the wine cellar," said Lothar. "I can take you there."

"In a moment," said Medivh. "I want to look about here for a moment. Will you grant me and my apprentice a moment or ten alone?"

Lothar hesitated for a moment, then said, "Of course. I will be right outside." As he said the last he looked at Khadgar sharply, then left.

The door's latch clicked shut and there was silence in the room. Medivh moved from table to table, pawing through the shredded tomes and torn papers. He held up a piece of correspondence with a purple seal, and shook his head. Slowly, he crumbled the piece of paper in his hand.

"In *civilized* countries," he said, his voice slightly strained, "apprentices don't disagree with their masters. At least in public." He turned toward Khadgar and the youth saw the older man's face was a mass of storm clouds.

"I am sorry," said Khadgar. "You said I should ask questions, and the position of the bodies did not seem right at the time, but now that you mention how the bodies were burned . . ."

Medivh held up a hand and Khadgar silenced himself. He paused a moment, then let out a slow exhalation. "Enough. You did the right thing, no more or less than asked by me. And if you hadn't spoken up, I wouldn't have realized the demon probably skittered down the tower itself, and wasted more time searching the castle complex. But, you asked questions because you don't know much about demons, and that is ignorance. And ignorance I will *not* tolerate."

The elder Magus looked at Khadgar, but there was a smile at the corner of his lips. Khadgar, sure that the storm had passed, lowered himself onto a stool. Despite himself, he still said, "Lothar . . ."

"Will wait," said Medivh, nodding. "He waits well, that Anduin Lothar. Now, what did you learn of demons in your time at the Violet Citadel?"

"I've heard the legends," said Khadgar. "In the First Days, there were demons in the land, and great heroes arose to drive them out." He thought of the image of Medivh's mother blasting the demons to bits, and facing down their Lord, but said nothing. No need to make Medivh angry again now that he'd calmed down.

"That's the basics," said Medivh. "What we tell the hoi polloi. What do you know in addition?"

Khadgar took a deep breath. "The official teachings in the Violet Citadel, in Kirin Tor, is that demonology is to be eschewed, avoided, and abjured. Any attempt to summon demons are to be found out and stopped at once, and those involved are to be expelled. Or worse. There were stories, among the young students, when I was growing up."

"Stories grounded in fact," said Medivh. "But you're a curious lad, you know more, I assume?"

Khadgar tilted his head in thought, choosing words carefully. "Korrigan, our academic librarian, had an extensive collection of . . . material at his disposal."

"And needed someone to help organize it," said Medivh dryly. Khadgar must have jumped, because Medivh added, "That was a guess, only, Young Trust."

"The material is mostly folk legends and the reports of the local authorities involving demon worshipers. Most of it was along the lines of individuals committing foul acts in the name of some old demon from the legends or another. Nothing about the actions of truly summoning a demon. No spells, no arcane writings." Khadgar motioned toward the protective circle. "No ceremonies."

"Of course," said Medivh. "Even Korrigan would not inflict that on a student. If he has such things, he would keep them separate."

"From that, the general belief is that when the demons were defeated, they were driven out of this world entirely. They were pushed out of the world of light and living, and into their own domain."

"The Great Dark Beyond," said Medivh, intoning the phrase like a prayer.

"They are still out there, or so the legend goes," said Khadgar, "and they want to come back in. Some say they come to the weak-willed in their sleep and urge them to find old spells and make sacrifices. Sometimes it is to open the way for them to come back fully. Others say they want worshipers and sacrifices to make this world like it once was, bloody and violent, and only then would they return."

Medivh was quiet for a moment, stroking his beard, then said, "Anything else?"

"There's more. Details and individual stories. I've seen carvings of demons, pictures, diagrams." Again Khadgar felt a rising need to tell Medivh about the vision, about the demon army. Instead he said, "And there is that old epic poem, the one about Aegwynn, fighting a horde of demons in a far-off land."

The mention of that brought a gentle, knowing smile to Medivh's face, "Ah yes, "The Song of Aegwynn." You'll find that poem in a lot of powerful mages' quarters, you know."

"My teacher, Lord Guzbah was interested in it," said Khadgar.

"Is he, now?" said Medivh, smiling. "With all due

respect, I don't know if Guzbah is quite ready for that poem. At least not in its true form." He peaked his eyebrows. "What you have is basically true. A lot of people couch it in the form of legends and fairy stories, but I think you know as well as I do that demons are real, and are out there, and yes, form a threat to those of us who walk this sunlit world, as well as other worlds. I think, now, I definitely *think*, that your red-sunned world was another place, a different world, on the far side of the Great Dark Beyond. The Beyond is a prison for these demons, a place without light or succor, and they are very, very jealous and very, very anxious to get back in."

Khadgar nodded, and Medivh continued, "But your assumption that their victims are weak-willed is in error, though again an error that is well-intended. There are more than enough venal farmhands who invoke a demonic force for revenge against a former lover, or stupid merchants who burn an invoice from a debtor with a black candle, badly mangling the ancient name of some once-great demonic power. But just as often there are those who walk willingly to the abyss, who feel themselves safe and sure and knowledgeable that they are beyond any blandishment or threat, that they are powerful enough to harness the demonic energies that surge beyond the walls of the world. They are in many ways even more dangerous than the common rabble, for as you know, a near-failure in spellcasting is more deadly than a complete failure."

Khadgar could only nod, and wondered if Medivh

had the power of the mind, "But these were powerful mages—Huglar and Hugarin, I mean."

"The most powerful in Azeroth," said Medivh. "The wisest and finest wizards, magical advisors to King Llane himself. Safe, sage, and sinecured!"

"Surely they would know better?" asked Khadgar.

"You would think so," said Medivh. "Yet, here we stand in the wreckage of their chambers, and their demon-burned bodies lay in the wine cellar."

"Why would they do it, then?" Khadgar knitted his brows, trying not to offend. "If they knew so much, why did they try to summon a demon?"

"Many reasons," said Medivh with a sigh. "Hubris, that false pride that goes before the fall. Overconfidence, both in each individually and doubled it for working in tandem. And fear, I suppose, most of all."

"Fear?" Khadgar looked at Medivh quizzically.

"Fear of the unknown," said Medivh. "Fear of the known. Fear of things more powerful than they."

Khadgar shook his head. "What could be more powerful than two of the most advanced and learned wizards in Azeroth?"

"Ah," said Medivh, and a small smile blossomed beneath his beard. "That would be me. They killed themselves summoning a demon, playing with forces best left alone, because they feared *me.*"

"You?" said Khadgar, the surprise in his voice greater than he had intended. For a moment he feared offending the older mage once more.

But Medivh just took a deep breath and blew the air out slowly. Then he said, "Me. They were fools, but I blame myself as well. Come, lad, Lothar can wait. It's time I told you the story of the Guardians and of the Order of Tirisfal, which is all that stands between us and the Darkness."

EIGHT
Lessons

"To understand the Order," said Medivh, "you must understand demons. You must also understand magic." He lowered himself comfortably on one of the still-undamaged chairs. The chair also had one of the few unripped pillows upon it.

"Lord Medivh . . . Magus," said Khadgar. "If there is a demon abroad in Stormwind, we should concentrate on that, and not on history lessons that could wait until later."

Medivh looked down at his chest, and Khadgar feared that he risked another outburst from the elder mage. But the master mage merely shook his head, and smiled as he said, "Your concerns would be valid if the demon in question was a threat to those around it. Take my word for it, it is not. The demon, even were it one of the more powerful officers within the Burning

Legion, would have expended almost all its personal power in dealing with the two powerful mages that summoned it. It is of little matter, at least for the moment. What is important, is that you understand what the Order is, what I am, and why others are so deeply interested in it."

"But Magus. . ." started Khadgar.

"And the sooner I finish the sooner I will know that I can trust you with the information, and the sooner I will go out to deal with this petty demon, so if you truly want me to go you should let me finish, eh?" Medivh gave the younger mage a hard, knowing smile.

Khadgar opened his mouth to protest, but thought better of it. He slouched down against the wide ledge by the open window. Despite the efforts of the servants to remove the bodies from the tower, the stench of their death, a corrosive pallor, was still heavy in the air.

"So. What is magic?" asked Medivh, in the manner of a schoolmage.

"An ambient field of energy that pervades the world," said Khadgar, almost without thinking. It was catechism, a simple answer for a simple question. "It is stronger in some locations than others, but it is ever-present."

"Yes it is," said the older mage, "at least *now*. But imagine a time when it was not."

"Magic is universal," said Khadgar, knowing as soon as he said it that it was soon to prove not to be. "Like air or water."

"Yes, like water," said Medivh. "Now imagine a time

at the very start of things, when all the water in the world was in one location. All the rain and rivers and seas and streams, all the showers and creeks and tears, all in one location, in one well."

Khadgar nodded, slowly.

"Now, instead of water, it is magic we're talking about," said Khadgar. "A well of magic, the source, an opening into other dimensions, a shimmering doorway into the lands beyond the Great Dark, beyond the walls of the world. The first peoples to cast spells encamped around the well and distilled its raw power into magic. They were called the Kaldorei then. What they are called now, I cannot say." Medivh looked at Khadgar, but the younger mage kept his silence now.

Medivh resumed. "The Kaldorei grew powerful from their use of magic, but they did not understand its nature. They did not understand that there were other, powerful forces in the Great Dark Beyond, moving in the space between worlds, that hungered after magic and were very interested in any who tamed it and refined it to their own ends. These malign forces were abomination and juggernauts and nightmares from hundreds of worlds, but we call them simply demons. They sought to invade any world where magic was mastered and grown, and destroy it, keeping the energies for themselves alone. And the greatest of them, the master of the Burning Legion, was a demon named Sargeras."

Khadgar thought of the vision with Aegwynn and suppressed a shudder.

If Medivh noticed the young mage's reaction he did not say anything. "The Lord of the Burning Legion was both powerful and subtle, and worked to corrupt the early magic-users, the Kaldorei. He succeeded, for a dark shadow fell upon their hearts, and they enslaved other races, the nascent humans as well as others, in order to build their empire."

Medivh sighed, "Now in this time of the enslaving Kaldorei, there were those with greater vision than their brethren, who were willing both to speak out against the Kaldorei and to pay the price for their vision. These brave individuals, both Kaldorei and other races as well, saw the hearts of the ruling Kaldorei grow cold and dark, and the demonic power grow."

"So it came to pass that the Kaldorei were corrupted by Sargeras such that they nearly damned this world at its birth. The Kaldorei ignored those who spoke out against them, and opened the way for the most powerful of demons, Sargeras and his lot, to invade. Only by the heroic actions of a few was the shimmering doorway through the Great Dark shut, exiling Sargeras and his followers. But the victory was at great cost. The Well of Eternity exploded when the doorway was shut down, and the resulting explosion ripped the heart out of this world, destroying the Kaldorei lands and the very continent it rested upon. Those that shut the door were never seen again by living eyes."

"Kalimdor!" said Khadgar, interrupting despite himself.

Medivh looked at him, and Khadgar continued, "Its an old legend in Lordaeron! Once there was an evil race who meddled foolishly with great power. As punishment for their sins, their lands were broken and set beneath the waves. It was called the Sundering of the World. Their lands were called Kalimdor."

"Kalimdor," repeated Medivh. "Though you have the child's version of the tale, the bit we tell would-be mages to stress the dangers of what they are playing with. The Kaldorei were foolish, and destroyed themselves and nearly our world. And when the Well of Eternity exploded, the magical energies within scattered to the four corners of the earth, in an eternal rain of magic. And *that's* why magic is universal—it's the power of the well's death."

"But Magus," said Khadgar, "that was thousands of years ago."

"Ten thousand years," said Medivh, "give or take a score."

"How is it that the legend comes down to us? Dalaran itself has histories only going back twenty centuries, and the earliest of those are wrapped in legends."

Medivh nodded and took up the story again. "Many were lost in the sinking of Kalimdor, but some survived, and took their knowledge with them. Some of these surviving Kaldorei would found the Order of Tirisfal. Whether Tirisfal was a person, or a place, or a thing, or a concept, even I cannot say. They took the knowledge, of what had happened, and swore to keep it from ever happening again, and that is the bedrock of the Order.

"Now, the race of humans survived those dark days as well, and thrived, and soon, with magical energy worked into the fabric of the world itself, they too were scratching at the doors of reality, beginning to summon creatures from the Great Dark, prying at the shut gates of Sargaras's prison. That was when those Kaldorei who had survived and changed themselves came forward with the story of how their ancestors had almost destroyed the world.

"The first human mages considered what the surviving Kaldorei had said, and realized that even were they to lay down their wands and grimoires and ciphers, that others would seek, innocently or less so, ways to allow the demons access once more to our green lands. And so they continued the Order, now as a secret society among the most powerful of their mages. This Order of Tirisfal would choose one of its number, who would serve as the *Guardian* of the *Tirisfalen.* This guardian would be given the greatest of powers, and would be the gatekeeper of reality. But now the gate was not a single great well of power, but rather an infinite rain that continues to fall even today. It is nothing less than the heaviest responsibility in the world."

Medivh fell silent, and his eyes lost their focus briefly, as if he were suddenly swept into the past himself. Then he shook his head, returning to himself, but still did not speak.

"You are the Guardian," said Khadgar, simply.

"Aye," said Medivh, "I am the child of the greatest Guardian of all time, and was given her power soon after my birth. It was . . . too much for me, and I paid for it with a good piece of my youth."

"But you said the mages chose among themselves," said Khadgar. "Couldn't Magna Aegwynn have chosen an older candidate? Why chose a child, especially her own child?"

Medivh took a deep breath. "The first Guardians, for the first millennium, were chosen among the select group. The very existence of the Order was kept hidden, as was the wishes of the original founders. However, over time, politics and personal interests came into play, such that the Guardian soon became little more than a servant, a magical dogsbody. Some of the more powerful mages felt it was the Guardian's job to keep *everyone else* from enjoying the power that they themselves commanded. Like the Kaldorei before us, a shadow of corrupting power was moving through the members of the Order. More demons were getting through, and even Sargeras himself had manifested the smallest bits of himself. A mere fraction of his power, but enough to slay armies and destroy nations."

Khadgar thought of the image of Sargeras that fought Aegwynn in the vision. Could this have been a mere fraction of the great demon's power?

"Magna Aegwynn," Medivh said the words, then stopped. It was as if he was not used to speaking those words. "She who bore me was herself born nearly a thousand years ago. She was greatly gifted, and chosen by other members of the Order to become the Guardian. I believe the grayest of the graybeards of that time thought they could control her, and in doing so continue to use the Guardian as a pawn of their own political games.

"She surprised them."—and at this Medivh smiled. "She refused to be manipulated, and indeed fought against some of the greatest mages of her age when they themselves fell into demonic lore. Some thought that her independence was a passing thing, that when her time came, she would have to pass the mantle on to a more malleable candidate. Again, she surprised them, using the magics within her to live for a thousand years, unchanging, and to wield her power with wisdom and grace. So the Order and the Guardian split. The former can advise the latter, but the latter must be free to challenge the former, to avoid what happened to the Kaldorei.

"For a thousand years she fought the Great Dark, even challenging the physical aspect of Sargeras himself, who had instilled himself into this plane and sought to destroy the mythical dragons, adding their power to his own. Magna Aegwynn met him and defeated him, locking his body away in a place where none knows, keeping him forever from the Great Dark that is his power. That's in that epic poem, 'The Song of Aegwynn,' the one Guzbah wants. But she could not do it forever, and there must always be a Guardian.

"And then . . ." And again Medivh's voice faltered. "She had one more trick up her sleeve. Powerful she was, but she was still of mortal flesh. She was expected to pass on her power. Instead she fathered an heir on a conjurer from the Court of Azeroth itself, and she chose that child as her successor. She threatened the Order, saying that if her choice was not honored, she would not step down, and would rather take the power of the Guardian into death than allow another to have it. They felt they *might* be able to manipulate the child . . . me . . . better, and so they allowed it.

"The power was too much," said Medivh. "When I was a young man, younger than you, it awoke within me, and I slept for over twenty years. Magna Aegwynn had so much of a life, and I seem to have lost most of it." His voice faltered again. "Magna Aegwynn . . . my mother . . ." he began, but found he had nothing more to say.

Khadgar just sat there for a moment. Then Medivh rose, shook back his mane and said, "And while I slept, evil crept back into the world. There are more demons, and more of these orcs as well. And now members of my own Order are once more playing the dark road. Yes, Huglar and Hugarin were members of the Order, as have been others, like ancient Arrexis among the Kirin Tor. Yes, something similar happened to him, and while they covered it up neatly, you probably heard *something* about it. They feared my mother's power, and they fear me, and I have to keep their fear from destroying them. Such is the charge laid upon the Guardian of Tirisfal."

The older man launched himself to his feet. "I must be off!" he said.

"Off?" said Khadgar, suddenly surprised by the energy within the lanky frame.

"As you have so rightly noted, there is a demon abroad," said Medivh with a renewed smile. "Sound the hunter's horn, I must find it before it regains its wits and strength and kills others!"

Khadgar pulled himself upright. "Where do we start?"

Medivh pulled himself up short, and turned, looking slightly sheepishly at the younger man. "Ah. *We* are not starting anywhere. I am going to go. You're talented, but you're not up to demons quite yet. This battle is my own, Young Apprentice Trust."

"Magus, I am sure I can . . ."

But Medivh raised a hand to silence him.

"I also need you here to keep your own ears open," said Medivh, in a quieter voice. "I have no doubt that Old Lothar has spent the past ten minutes with his ear to the door, such that there will be a keyhole-shaped impression on the side of his face." Medivh grinned. "He knows a lot, but not all. That's why I had to tell you, so he doesn't pry too much out of you. I need someone to guard the Guardian, as it were."

Khadgar looked at Medivh and the older mage

winked. Then the Magus strode to the door and pulled it open with a quick motion.

Lothar did not stumble into the room, but he was there, right on the other side. He could have been listening, or just standing watch.

"Med," said Lothar with a game smile. "His Majesty . . ."

"His Majesty will understand perfectly," said Medivh, breezing right past the larger man. "That I would rather meet with a rampaging demon than the leader of a nation. Priorities and all that. In the mean time will you look after my apprentice?"

He said it all in a single breath, and then he was gone, out into the hall and down the stairs, leaving Lothar in mid-sentence.

The old warrior rubbed a great hand up over his balding pate, letting out an exaggerated sigh. Then he looked at Khadgar and let out another, deeper sigh.

"He's always been like this, you know," said Lothar, as if Khadgar truly did know. "I suppose you're hungry, at least. Let's see if we can find some lunch."

Lunch consisted of a cold game fowl looted from the cold room and tucked under Lothar's arm, and two mugs of ale the size of ewers, one in each meaty hand. The King's Champion was surprisingly at ease, despite the situation, and guided Khadgar out to a high balcony overlooking the city.

"My lord," said Khadgar. "Despite the Magus's request, I realize you have other work."

"Aye," said Lothar, "and most of it was taken care of while you were talking to Medivh. His majesty King Llane is in his quarters, as are most of the courtiers, under guard, in case that demon decided to hide in the castle. Also I have agents already spreading through the city, with orders to both report anything suspicious but not to make themselves suspicious. The last thing we need is a demon-panic. I've cast all my lines, and now there is nothing to do but wait." He looked at the younger man. "And my lieutenants know that I'll be on this balcony, as I always have a late lunch anyway."

Khadgar considered Lothar's words, and thought that the King's Champion was very much like Medivh—not only planning ahead a few moves, but delighting in telling others how he's planned things out. The apprentice picked at the sliced breast meat while Lothar tore into a drumstick.

The pair ate in silence for a long time. The fowl was anything but foul, for it was treated with a concoction of rosemary, bacon, and sheep's butter placed beneath the skin before roasting. Even cold it fell apart in the mouth. The ale for its part was pungent, rich with bottomland hops.

Beneath them the city unfolded. The citadel itself was atop a rocky outcropping that already separated the King from his subjects, and from the tower's additional height, the citizens of Stormwind looked like naught but small dolls busying themselves along crowded streets. Some sort of market day was playing out beneath them, brightly-tarped storefronts occupied with vendors bellowing (very quietly, it seemed to Khadgar at this altitude) the virtues of their wares.

For a moment Khadgar forgot where he was, and what he had seen, and why he was there in the first place. It was a beautiful city. Only Lothar's deep grumble brought him back to this world.

"So," said the King's Champion in his way of introspection. "How is he?"

Khadgar thought for a moment, and replied, "He is in good health. You have seen that yourself, milord."

"Bah," spat Lothar, and for a moment Khadgar thought the knight was choking on a large piece of meat. "I can see, and I know Med can dance and bluff his way past just about anyone. What I mean to say is, How *is* he?"

Khadgar looked out at the city again, wondering if he had Medivh's talent to bluster his way past the older man, to deny answers without causing affront.

No, he decided, Medivh played on loyalties and friendships older than he was. He had to find another way to respond. He let out a sigh and said, "Demanding. He's very demanding. And intelligent. And surprising. I feel I have apprenticed myself to a whirlwind, sometimes." He looked at Lothar, his eyebrows raised, hoping that this would be sufficient.

Lothar nodded, "A whirlwind, aye. And a thunderstorm, too, I suspect."

Khadgar shrugged awkwardly. "He has his moods, like anyone."

"Hmmpph," said the King's Champion. "An ostler has a mood and he kicks the dog. A mage has his moods and a town disappears. No offense meant."

"None taken, milord," said Khadgar, thinking of the dead mages in the tower room. "You ask how he is. He's all these things."

"Hmmmph," said Lothar again. "He's a very powerful person."

Khadgar thought *and you worry about him like the other wizards do.* Instead he said, "He speaks well of you."

"What did he say?" said Lothar, more quickly than perhaps he meant to.

"Only," Khadgar chose his words carefully, "that you served him well when he was ill."

"True enough," grunted the Champion, starting into the other drumstick.

"And that you are extremely observant," added Khadgar, feeling that this was a sufficient distillation of Medivh's opinion of the warrior.

"Glad to know he notices," said Lothar, with a full mouth. There was a pause between the two of them, as Lothar chewed and swallowed. "Has he mentioned the Guardian?"

"We have spoken," said Khadgar, feeling that he was on a very narrow verbal cliff. Medivh did not tell him how much Lothar knew. He settled for silence as the best answer, and let the statement hang in the air for a moment.

"And it is not the Apprentice's place to discuss the doings of the Master, eh?" said Lothar, with a smile that seemed just a jot too forced. "Come now, you're from Dalaran. That nest of mage-vipers has more secrets per square foot than any other place on the continent. No offense, again."

Khadgar shrugged off the comment. Diplomatically, he stated, "I notice that there is less obvious rivalry between mages here than in Lordaeron."

"And you mean to tell me that your teachers didn't send you out with a laundry list of things to pry out of the high Magus?" Lothar's grin deepened, and looked almost sympathetic.

Khadgar felt some heat in his face. The older warrior was firing bow shots increasingly close to the gold. "Any requests from the Violet Citadel are under Medivh's consideration. He has been *very* accommodating."

"Hmmph," snorted Lothar. "Must mean they aren't asking for the right stuff. I know the mages around here, including Huglar and Hugarin, the saints rest their souls, were always pestering him for this and that, and complaining to His Majesty or myself when they didn't get it. Like we had any control over him!"

"I don't think anyone does," said Khadgar, drowning any additional comment he might have made in his ale.

"Not even his mother, I understand," said Lothar. It

was a small comment, but it slipped in like a dagger thrust. Khadgar found himself wanting to ask Lothar more about her, but contained himself.

"I fear I am too young to know," he said. "I've read some on her. She seems like a powerful mage."

"And that power is in *him,* now," said Lothar. She whelped him from a conjurer of this very court, and weaned him on pure magestuff, and poured her power into him. Yes, I know all about it, pieced it together after he went into that coma. Too much, too young. Even now I'm concerned."

"You think he's too powerful," said Khadgar, and Lothar froze him with a sudden, penetrating stare. The young mage kicked himself for speaking his mind, practically accusing his host.

Lothar let out a smile and shook his head. "On the contrary, lad, I worry that he's not powerful *enough.* There are horrible things afoot in the kingdoms. Those orc-things you saw a month ago, they're multiplying like rabbits after a rain. And trolls, nearly extinct, have been seen more often. And Medivh is out hunting a demon even as we speak. Bad times are coming, and I hope, no, I *pray,* that he's up to it. We went for twenty-some years without a Guardian, when he was in a coma. I don't want to go another twenty, particularly at a time like this."

Khadgar felt embarrassed now. "So when you ask, How is he? You mean . . ."

"How *is* he?" finished Lothar. "I don't want him weakening at a time like this. Orcs, trolls, demons, and then there is . . ." Lothar let his voice trail off and looked at Khadgar, then said, "You know of the Guardian, by now, I can assume?"

"You can assume," said Khadgar.

"And the Order, too?" said Lothar, then he smiled. "No need to say anything, young man, your eyes gave yourself away. Never play cards with me, eh?"

Khadgar felt on the very precipice itself. Medivh warned him not to let too much loose to the Champion, but Lothar seemed to know as much as Khadgar knew. More, even.

Lothar spoke in a calm voice. "We would not send for Med for a simple matter of a magical misfire. Nor even two common conjurers being caught in their own spells. Huglar and Hugarin were two of our best, two of our most powerful. There was another, even more powerful, but she met an accident two months back. All three, I believe, were members of your Order."

Khadgar felt a chill creep up his back. He managed to say, "I don't think I'm comfortable speaking of this."

"Then don't," said Lothar, his brows furrowed like the foothills of some ancient mountain chain. "Three powerful mages, the most powerful in Azeroth. Not a patch on Med or his mother, mind you, but great and powerful wizards nonetheless. All dead. I can buy one mage being unlucky, or being caught unawares, but three of them? A warrior doesn't believe in that much coincidence.

"There's more," continued the King's Champion. "I

have my own ways of finding out things. Caravan traders, mercenaries, and adventurers that come into the city often find a receptive ear with old Lothar. Word comes from Ironforge and Alterac, and even from Lordaeron itself. There has been a plague of such mishaps, one after another. I think someone, or worse yet, some*thing* is hunting the great mages of this secret Order. Both here, and in Dalaran itself, I don't doubt."

Khadgar realized that the older man was studying his face as he spoke, and with a start he realized that this fit into the rumors he heard before leaving the Violet Citadel. Ancient mages, suddenly gone, and the upper echelons quietly hushing it up. The great secret among the Kirin Tor, part of a greater problem.

Despite himself, Khadgar looked away, out over the city. "Yes, Dalaran too, it seems," said Lothar. "Not much news comes from there, but I'm willing to bet that the news is similar, eh?"

"You think that the Lord Magus is in danger?" asked Khadgar. The desire to not tell Lothar anything was eroding by the obvious concern of the older warrior.

"I think Medivh is danger incarnate," said Lothar. "And I admire anyone willing to be under the same roof with him." It sounded like a joke, but the King's Champion did not smile. "But yes, something is out there, and it may be tied with the demons or the orcs or something much worse. And I would hate to lose our most powerful weapon at a time like this."

Khadgar looked at Lothar, trying to read the furrows of the older man's face. Was this old warrior worried about his friend, or worried about the loss of a magical protection? Was his concern about Medivh's safety, out in the middle of the wilderness, or that something was stalking them all? The older man's face seemed like a mask, and his deep sea-blue eyes gave no clue as to what Lothar was truly thinking.

Khadgar had expected a simple swordsman, a knight devoted to duty, but the King's Champion was more than this. He was pushing Khadgar, looking for weakness, looking for information, but to what end?

I need someone to guard the Guardian, Medivh had said.

"He is fine," said Khadgar. "You are worried about him, and I share your concerns. But he is doing well, and I doubt anything or anyone can truly hurt him."

Lothar's unfathomable eyes seemed to deflate for a moment, but only a flickering moment. He was going to say something else, to renew the prying, friendly inquisition, but a commotion within the tower drew both their attention away from the discussion, away from the now-empty mugs and the bare bones of the fowl.

Medivh swaggered into view, followed by a crew of servants and guardsmen. All complained about his presence, but none would (wisely) place a hand on him, and as a result followed him like a living, mewling comet's tale. The older mage strode out onto the parapet.

"I thought you a creature of habit, Lothar," said Medivh. "I knew you'd be out here taking afternoon tea!" The Magus beamed a warm smile, but Khadgar saw there was a slight, almost drunken sway to his walk. Medivh kept one arm behind him, concealing something.

Lothar rose, concern in his voice. "Medivh are you all right? The demon . . ."

"Ah, yes, the demon," said Medivh brightly and pulled his bloodied prize out from behind his back. He lobbed it at Lothar and Khadgar in a lazy, underhanded swing.

The red orb spun as it flew, spilling the last bits of blood and brains out before landing at Lothar's feet. It was a demon's skull, the flesh still adhered to it, with a mighty divot, like that of a great ax, driven into the center, right between the ramlike horns. The demon's expression, Khadgar thought, was one of both awe and indignation.

"You might want to have that stuffed," said Medivh, pulling himself seriously to his full height. "Had to burn the rest of it, of course. No telling what the inexperienced might do with a draught of demon's blood."

Khadgar saw that Medivh's face was more pinched than it had been earlier, and that the lines around his eyes were more prominent. Lothar may have caught it as well, and remarked, "You caught it quite quickly."

"Child's play!" said Medivh. "Once Young Trust here pointed out how the demon fled the castle, it was a simple matter to track it from the tower's base to a small escarpment. It was over before I knew it. Before it knew it either." The Magus swayed slightly.

"Come then," said Lothar, with a warm smile. "We

should tell the King. There should be reveling in your honor for this, Med!"

Medivh held up a hand. "You may revel without us, I am afraid. We should get back. Miles to go before we rest. Isn't that right, Apprentice?"

Lothar looked at Khadgar, again with a questioning, imploring look. Medivh looked calm but worn. He also looked expectant for Khadgar to support him this time.

The young mage coughed, "Of course. We left an experiment on the boil."

"Indeed!" said Medivh, picking up the lie immediately. "In our rush to get here, I had quite forgotten. We should make haste." The Magus wheeled and bellowed at the collected courtiers. "Make ready our mounts! We leave at once." The servants dissolved like a covey of quail. Medivh turned back to Lothar. "You will make our apologies to His Majesty, of course."

Lothar looked at Medivh, then at Khadgar, then at Medivh again. At last he sighed and said, "Of course. Let me lead you to the tower, at least."

"Lead on," said Medivh. "Don't forget to take your skull. I'd keep it myself, but I have one like it already."

Lothar hefted the ram-headed skull in one hand and brushed past Medivh, leading into the tower itself. As he passed, the Magus seemed to deflate, the air going out of him. He looked more tired than before, grayer than he had been moments earlier. He let out a heavy sigh and headed for the door himself.

Khadgar chased after him and caught him by the

elbow. It was light touch, but the elder mage suddenly pulled himself upright, flinching as if reacting to a blow. He turned to Khadgar, and his eyes seemed to mist over for a moment as he looked at the younger mage.

"Magus," said Khadgar.

"What is it now?" said Medivh in a hissing whisper.

Khadgar thought about what to say, how to risk the Magus's censure. "You're not well," he said, simply.

It was the right thing to say. Medivh gave an aged nod, and said, "I've been better. Lothar probably knows as well, but he won't challenge me on it. But I'd rather be home than here." He paused for a moment, and his lips formed a stiff line beneath his beard. "I was sick for a long time, here. Don't want to repeat the experience."

Khadgar didn't say anything, but only nodded. Lothar now stood at the door, waiting.

"You're going to have to lead the way back to Karazhan," said Medivh to Khadgar, loud enough for all nearby to hear. "This city life takes too much out of a man, and I could use a nap about now!"

NINE

The Slumber of the Magus

"This is very important," said Medivh, staggering slightly as he slid from the back of the gryphon. He looked haggard, and Khadgar assumed the battle with the demon had been worse than even he let on.

"I will be . . . unavailable for a few days," continued the older Mage. "If any messengers arrive during this time, I want you to keep track of my correspondence."

"I can do that," said Khadgar, "easily."

"No you can't," said Medivh, starting roughly down the stairs. "That is why I need to tell you how to read the ones with the purple seal. The purple seal is always Order business."

Khadgar said nothing this time, but just nodded.

Medivh slid on the edge of the stairs and stumbled, pitching forward headlong. Khadgar lunged to grab the older man, but the Magus had already caught himself against the wall and pulled himself upright. He didn't miss a beat, "In the library, there is a scroll. 'The Song of Aegwynn.' Tells of my mother's battle with Sargeras."

"The scroll that Guzbah wanted a copy of," said Khadgar, now watching the mage carefully as he lurched down the stairs ahead of him.

"The very one," said Medivh. "This is why he can't have it—we use it as cipher for Order communications. It is the master key. An identical scroll is with each of the members of the Order. If you take the standard alphabet, and move everything down, so the first letter is represented by the fourth, or the tenth, or the twentieth. It is a simple code. You understand?"

Khadgar started to say he did, but Medivh was already hurrying on, almost urgent in his need to explain.

"The scroll is the key," he repeated. At the top of the message, you'll see what looks like a date. It's not. It's a reference to the stanza, line, and word you start at. The first letter of that word becomes the first letter of the alphabet in the code. From there it proceeds normally, the next letter in alphabetic progression would be the second letter of the alphabet, and so on."

"I understand."

"No, you don't," said Medivh, rushed now and tired. "That's the cipher for the first sentence only. When you hit a punctuation mark, you go to the second letter in the word. That becomes the equivalent for the first letter of the alphabet for the cipher of that sentence. Punctuation is normal. Numbers are as well, but they are supposed to write things out, not use numerals. There's something else, but I'm missing it."

They were outside Medivh's personal quarters now. Moroes was already present, with a robe slung over his arm and a covered bowl resting on an ornate table. From the doorway Khadgar could smell the rich broth rising from the bowl.

"What should I do once I decipher the message?" asked Khadgar.

"Right!" said Medivh, as if some vital connection had snapped closed in his mind. "Delay. Delay first. Day or two, I may be up to it after that. Then equivocate. I am out on business, may return any time. Use the same cipher as you got, but make sure you mark it as the date. If all else fails, delegate. Tell whoever it is to use their own judgment, and I will lend what aid I can at the soonest moment. They always love that. Do *not* tell them I am indisposed—the last time I mentioned that, a horde of would-be clerics arrived to minister to my needs. I'm still missing silverware from that little visit."

The old mage took a deep breath, and seemed to deflate, supporting himself against the door frame. Moroes did not move, but Khadgar took a step forward.

"The fight with the demon," said Khadgar. "It was bad, wasn't it?"

"I've fought worse. Demons! Slope-shouldered, ram-headed brutes. Equal parts shadow and fire. More beast than human, more raw bile than both. Nasty claws. That's what you watch out for, the claws."

Khadgar nodded. "How did you defeat it?"

"Massive trauma usually will force out the life essence," said Medivh, "In this case, I took its head off."

Khadgar blinked. "You didn't have a sword."

Medivh smiled wearily. "Did I say I needed a sword? Enough. More questions when I am up to it." And with that he stepped into the room, and the ever-faithful Moroes closed the door on Khadgar. The last sound the youth heard was the exhausted groan of an old man who had finally found a resting place.

A week passed, and Medivh had not emerged from his quarters. Moroes would shuffle upstairs with a daily bowl of broth. Finally, Khadgar summoned sufficient nerve to look in. The castellan made no move to protest, other than a monosyllabic recognition of his presence there.

In repose Medivh looked ghastly, the light gone out of his shuttered eyes, the tension of life gone from his visage. He was dressed in a long nightshirt, propped up against the headboard, supported by pillows, his mouth open, his face pale, his usually animate form thin and haggard. Moroes would carefully spoon the broth into Medivh's mouth, and he would swallow, but otherwise not awaken. The castellan would change the bedding as well, then retire for the day.

Khadgar got a frisson of recognition, and wondered

if this was the same scene that played out in Medivh's youth, when his powers first surfaced, and when Lothar tended to him. He wondered how long the Magus would truly be out. How much energy had the battle with the demon taken out of him?

Normal communications came in, written in common hand and clear language. Some were delivered by gryphon-rider, others by horseback, and more than a few came with the regular supply wagons of traders seeking to fill Moroes's larders. They were for the most part mundane—ship movements and troop drills. Readiness reports. An occasional discovery of an ancient tomb or a forgotten artifact, or the recovery of a time-worn legend. The sighting of a waterspout, or a great sea turtle, or a crimson tide. Sketches of fauna that may have been new to the observer, but were better duplicated in the bestiaries already in the library.

And mention of the orcs, in ever-increasing numbers, particularly from the east. Rising sightings of them in the vicinity of the Black Morass. Increased guards on the caravans, locations of temporary camps, reports of raids, robberies, and mysterious disappearances. An increase in refugees heading for the protection of the larger walled towns and cities. And sketches from the survivors and the slant-browed, heavy-jawed creatures, including a detailed description of the powerful muscular systems that, Khadgar realized with a start, could only come from vivisecting the subject.

Khadgar began to read the mail to the wizard as he

slept, reading aloud the more interesting or humorous bits. The Magus made no response to encourage the younger mage, but neither did he forbid it.

The first purple-sealed letter arrived and Khadgar was immediately lost. Some of the letters made sense, but others quickly descended into gibberish. At first the younger mage panicked, sure that he had misunderstood some basic instruction. After a day of littering the quarters with notes and failed attempts, Khadgar realized what he had been missing—that the space between the words was considered a letter in the Order's cipher, shifting everything one more letter in the process. Once that realization dawned, the missive deciphered easily.

It was less impressive than it had seemed earlier when it was gibberish. A note from the far south, the peninsula of Ulmat Thondr, noting that all was quiet, there were no signs of orcs (though there was a rise in the number of jungle trolls of late) and that a new comet was visible along the southern horizon, with detailed notes (written out in words, not numbers). No response was requested, and Khadgar set it, and its translation, aside.

Khadgar wondered why the Order did not use a magical encoding or spell-based script. Perhaps not all members of the Order of Tirisfal were mages. Or that they were trying to hide it from other wizards, like Guzbah, and putting it in a magical script would draw their curiosity like bees to nectar. Most likely, Khadgar decided, it was out of Medivh's sheer cussedness to the point of making the other members of the Order use a poem praising his mother as the key.

A large package arrived from Lothar, distilling the previously-reported orc sightings and attacks and translating them onto a large map. Indeed, it seemed like armies of orcs were pouring out of the swampy territory of the Black Morass itself. Again, no response was asked. Khadgar considered sending Lothar a note regarding Medivh's state, but thought better of it. What could the Champion do, in any event, other than to worry? He did send a note, over his own signature, thanking him for the information and asking to be kept apprised.

A second week passed and they moved into a third, the master comatose, the student searching. Now armed with proper key, Khadgar started going through the older mail, some of it still held shut by violet dabs of sealing wax. Going through the old documents, Khadgar began to understand Medivh's often ambivalent feelings toward the Order. Oftimes the letters were little more than demands—this enchantment, that bit of information, a summons to come at once because the cows are off their feed or their milk has gone sour. The more complementary of the missives usually held some sort of sting—a request for a desired spell or a lost tome, wrapped up within its florid praise. Many held nothing but pedantic advice, pointing out in detail how this candidate or that would be a perfect apprentice (these were mostly unopened, he noticed). And there were continual reports of no news, no changes, nothing out of the ordinary.

The latter changed within the more recent messages (they were not dated, but Khadgar began to determine where they fell within a timeline, both by the yellowing of the parchment and the increasing fever-pitch of demands and advice). The tone became more consolatory with the sudden appearance of the orcs, particularly as they started raiding caravans. But the undercurrent of demands on Medivh's time remained, and even increased.

Khadgar looked at the old man lying on the bed and wondered what would possess him to help these people and help them on a regular basis.

And then there were the mystery letters—the occasional thanks, the references to some arcane text, a response to an unknown question—"Yes," "No," and "The emu, of course." During his vigil at Medivh's bedside one mystery letter arrived, without signature. It read "Prepare quarters. The Emissary will arrive shortly."

At the end of the third week two letters arrived one evening with a traveling merchant, one with the purple seal, the other red-sealed and addressed to Khadgar himself. Both were from the Violet Citadel of the Kirin Tor.

The letter to Khadgar began, in a spidery hand, "We regret to inform you of the sudden and unexpected death of the instructor mage Guzbah. We understand you have been in correspondence with the late mage and we share your emotion and sympathy at this time. If you have any correspondence, moneys, or information currently due to Guzbah, or are in possession of any of his property (in particular any of his books on loan), the return of that correspondence, money, information, or property would be appreciated, sent to the below address." A set of numbers and a lazy, illegible scrawl marked the bottom of the letter.

Khadgar felt as if he had been struck in the gut. Guzbah, dead? He turned the letter over, but no further information fell out. Stunned, he reached for the purple-sealed letter. This was in the same spider-hand, but once it was decoded held more information.

Guzbah was found slain in the library on the eve of the Feast of Scribes, in the midst of a reviewing *Denbrawn's Treatise on the "Song of Aegwynn."* (Khadgar felt a pang of remorse for not sending his former instructor the scroll.) He was apparently taken by surprise from a beast (presumably summoned) which ripped him apart. The death was quick but painful, and the explanation of how the body was found detailed to the point of excess. From the description of the body and the shambles of the library, Khadgar could only conclude that the "summoned beast" was a demon of the type Medivh had fought in Stormwind.

The letter continued, the words maintaining a cold, analytical tone that Khadgar found excessive. The writer noted that this was the seventh death within the year of a mage of the Violet Citadel, including that of the archmage Arrexis. It went on further to note that this was the first death of this type where the victim was not a member of the Order itself. The writer wanted to know if Medivh had been in contact with Guzbah, either directly or through his apprentice (Khadgar had a moment of déjà vu looking at his own name in print). The unknown author went forward to speculate that since he was not a member of the Order, Guzbah might be responsible for the summoning of the beast for some other matter, and if this was the case, then Medivh should be aware that Khadgar had been Guzbah's student at one point.

Khadgar felt a sharp pain of anger. How dare this mysterious writer (it had to be someone high within the Kirin Tor hierarchy, but Khadgar had no idea who) impinge both Guzbah and himself! Khadgar wasn't even present when Guzbah was killed! Perhaps this writer was the one responsible, or someone like Korrigan—the librarian was always researching demon-worshipers. Casting accusations about like that!

Khadgar shook his head and took a deep breath. No, such speculation was futile and fueled only by personal indignation, like so much of the politics of the Kirin Tor. The anger faded to sadness and realization that the mighty mages of the Violet Citadel were unable to stop this, that seven wizards (six of them members of this supposedly secret and powerful Order) had died, and all this writer could do was cast about aspersions in the desperate hope that there would be no additional deaths. Khadgar thought of Medivh's quick and decisive actions at Stormwind Keep, and marveled that there was no one of equal wit, drive, and intelligence within his own community.

The young mage picked up the encoded letter and examined it again in the wan candlelight. The Feast of Scribes was over a month and a half ago. It took this long for the message to cross the sea and reach them overland. A month and a half. Before Huglar and Hugarin were killed in Stormwind. If the same demon was involved, or even the same summoner, it would have to move between the two points very, very swiftly. Some of the demons in the vision had wings—was it possible for such a beast to move between the locations without anyone spotting it?

An errant and unexpected breeze wafted through. The hairs on the back of Khadgar's neck began to bristle, and he looked up in time to see the figure manifest within the room.

First there was smoke, red as blood, bubbling out from some pinprick hole in the universe. It coiled and curdled upon itself like milk rising through water, quickly forming a swirling mass, through which stepped the looming form of a great demon.

Its form was reduced from when Khadgar had seen it before, on the field of snow in the timelost vision. It had shrunk itself to allow it to fit within the confines of the room. Still its flesh was of bronze, its armor of jet-black iron, and its beard and hair of animated fire, huge horns erupting from a massive brow. It was weaponless, but seemed to need no weapons, for it moved with the comfortable grace of a predator that fears nothing.

Sargeras.

Khadgar was stunned into silence and immobility. Surely the wards Medivh had maintained would keep such a beast at bay? Yet here it was, entering the tower, entering the Magus's very room with the ease of a noble entering a commoner's shack.

The Lord of the Burning Legion did not look around, instead glided to the foot of the bed. He stood there for a long moment, the flames of his beard and hair flickering without sound, as he regarded the unconscious form before him. The demon stood watching the sleeping mage.

Khadgar held his breath and looked around the worktable. A few tomes, the candle backlit by a mirror for greater illumination. A letter opener used to break the purple seals. The young mage slowly reached for the opener, trying to move without attracting the great demon's attention. His fingers wrapped around it tightly, his knuckles white.

Still Sargeras stood at the foot of the bed. A long moment passed, and Khadgar tried to will himself to move. Either to flee or to attack. His muscles felt locked in position.

Medivh shifted in his bedding, mumbling something unheard. The demon lord raised a hand slowly, as if to pronounce a benediction on the Magus's inert form.

Khadgar gave a strangled cry and thrust himself up from his chair, letter opener clutched in his hand. Only at this moment did he realize that he held the opener in his wrong hand.

The demon looked up, and it was a lazy, smooth motion, as if the demon himself was sleeping, or far underwater. It regarded the charging youth, hand raised in a clumsy attack with a short, sharp dagger.

The demon smiled. Medivh shifted and muttered in his sleep. Khadgar drove the letter opener into the demon's chest.

And through the creature's body entirely. The thrust of his blow carried him forward, through the form of Sargeras, and sent him spinning toward the opposite wall. Unable to stop, he slammed into the wall, and the letter opener jangled to the stone floor.

Medivh's eyes popped open, and the Guardian sat up. "Moroes? Khadgar? Are you here?"

Khadgar pulled himself to his feet, looking around. The demon had vanished, popped like a soap bubble at the first touch of steel. He was alone in the room with Medivh.

"What are you doing on the floor, lad?" said Medivh. "Moroes could have gotten you a cot."

"Master, your wards!" said Khadgar. "They have failed. There was . . ." he stumbled for a moment, unsure that he should reveal he knew Sargeras by appearance. Medivh would catch something like that, and pester him until he revealed how he knew it.

"A demon," he managed. "There was a demon here."

Medivh smiled, looking well rested, the color returning to his face. "A demon? I think not. Hold." The Magus closed his eyes and nodded. "No, the wards are still in place. It would take more than a catnap for them to run out of energy. What did you see?"

Quickly Khadgar recounted the appearance of the demon from the cloud of boiling red milk, of it standing there, of it raising its hand. The Magus shook his head.

"I think that was another one of your visions," he said at last. "Some bit of time unstuck and displaced that fell into the tower, quickly banished."

"But the demon . . ." started Khadgar.

"The demon you described is no more, at least no more in this life," said Medivh. "He was slain before I was born, buried far beneath the sea. Your vision was of Sargeras, from 'The Song of Aegwynn.' You have the scrolls there. Deciphering messages? Yes. Perhaps that's what called that timelost wraith into my quarters. You should not be doing work here while I slept." He frowned slightly, as if he was thinking if he should be more upset or not.

"I'm sorry, I thought . . . I thought it would be best to not leave you alone?" Khadgar twisted it into a question, and it sounded a bit foolish.

Medivh chuckled and let a smile creep across his weathered features. "Well, I didn't say you couldn't, and I don't suppose Moroes would have stopped you, since that would reduce his need to be here." He rubbed a finger and thumb over his lips and through his beard. "I think I've had enough broth for one lifetime. And just to reassure you, I *will* check the tower's mystic wards. And show you how to do it as well. Now, aside from demon visions, did anything happen while I was gone?"

Khadgar summarized the messages he had received. The rising tide of orc incidents. Lothar's map. The mystery message about the Emissary. And the news of Guzbah's death.

Medivh grunted at the description of Guzbah's passing, and said, "So they're going to blame Guzbah until the next poor sod gets sliced open." He shook his head, then added, "Feast of the Scribes. That would be before Huglar and Hugarin died."

"By about a week and a half," said Khadgar. "Time enough for a demon to fly from Dalaran to Stormwind Keep."

"Or a man on gryphon-back," mused Medivh. "It's not all demons and magic in this world. Sometimes a simpler answer suffices. Anything else?"

"It sounds like these orcs are becoming much more numerous and dangerous," said Khadgar. "Lothar says they are moving from caravan raids to attacks on settlements. Small ones, but there are more people coming into Stormwind and the other cities all the time as a result.

"Lothar worries too much," said Medivh with a grimace.

"He's concerned," said Khadgar flatly. "He doesn't know what to expect next."

"On the contrary," said Medivh, letting out a long, mournful sigh. "If everything you tell me is true, then I'm afraid things are going *just* the way I expected!"

TEN
The Emissary

With Medivh's recovery things returned to normal, or as normal as anything was in the presence of the Magus. When the Magus was absent, Khadgar was left with instructions as to honing his magical skill, and when Medivh was in residence in the tower, the younger mage was expected to demonstrate those skills at the drop of hat.

Khadgar adapted well, and felt as if his power was a set of clothes, two sizes too big, that only now was he growing into. He could control fire at will now, summon lightning without a cloud in the sky, and cause small items to dance upon the table at the will of his own mind. He learned other spells as well—those that allowed one to know when and how a man died from a single bone of his remains, how to cause a ground-fog to rise, and how to leave magical messages for others to find. He learned how to restore the age lost to an inanimate object, strengthening an old chair, and its reverse, to pull all the youth from a newly-crafted club, leaving it dusty and brittle. He learned the nature of the protective wards, and was entrusted with keeping them intact. He learned the library of demons, though Medivh would not permit any to be summoned in his tower. This last order Khadgar had no desire to break.

Medivh was gone for brief periods of a day here, a few days there. Always instructions were left behind, but never explanations. Upon his return the Guardian looked more haggard and worn, and would push Khadgar testily to determine the youth's mastery over his craft, and to detail any news that had arrived in his absence. But there was no further repeat of his comatose rest, and Khadgar assumed that whatever the master was doing, it did not involve demons.

One evening in the library, Khadgar heard noises from the common area and stables below. Shouts, challenges, and responses, in low, illegible tones. By the time he reached a window overlooking that part of the castle, a group of riders were leaving the tower's walls.

Khadgar frowned. Were these some supplicants turned away by Moroes, or messengers with some other dark tidings for his master? Khadgar descended the tower to find out.

He caught sight of the new arrival only briefly—a flash of a black cloak stepping into a guest room along the lower levels of the tower. Moroes was there, candle in hand, blinders in place, and as Khadgar slipped down the last few steps he could hear the castellan say "... Other visitors, they were less careful. They're gone now."

Whatever response the new arrival made was lost, and Moroes pulled the door shut as Khadgar came up.

"A guest?" asked the young man, trying to see if there was any clue of the new arrival behind him. Only a closed door greeted his view.

"Ayep," replied the castellan.

"Mage or merchant?" asked the young mage.

"Couldn't say," said the castellan, already moving down the hall. "Didn't ask, and the Emissary didn't say."

"The Emissary," repeated Khadgar, thinking of one of the mystery letters from Medivh's great sleep. "So it's political, then. For the Magus."

"Assume so," said Moroes. "Didn't ask. Not my place."

"So it is for the Magus," said Khadgar.

"Assume so," said Moroes, with the same sleepy inflection. "We'll be told when we need to know." And with that he was gone, leaving Khadgar to stare at the shut door.

For the next day, there was the odd feeling of another presence in the tower, a new planetary body whose very gravity changed the orbits of all the others. This new planet caused Cook to shift to a larger set of pans, and Moroes to move through the halls at more random times than normal. And even Medivh himself would send Khadgar on some errand within the tower, and as the young mage left he would hear the whisper of a heavy cloak on the stonework behind him.

Medivh volunteered nothing, and Khadgar waited to be told. He dropped hints. He waited patiently. Instead he was sent to the library to continue his studies and practice his spells. Khadgar descended the curved stairs for half a rotation, stopped, then slowly climbed back up, only to see the back of a black cloak glide into the Guardian's laboratory.

Khadgar stomped down the stairs, considering options of who the Emissary was. A spy for Lothar? Some secretive member of the Order? Perhaps one of the members from the Kirin Tor, the one with the spidery handwriting and the venomous theories? Or maybe some other matter entirely? Not knowing was frustrating, and not being trusted by the Magus seemed to make matters worse.

"We'll be told when we need to know," Khadgar muttered, stomping into the library. His notes and histories were scattered on the tables, where he left them last. He looked at them, and the schematics of his vision-summoning spell. He had made a few amendments since his last attempt, hoping to temporally refine its results.

Khadgar looked at the notes and smiled. Then he picked up his vials of crushed gemstones, and headed downward—putting additional floors between himself and Medivh's audience chamber—to one of the abandoned dining halls.

Two levels lower was perfect. An ellipsoid of a room with stone fireplaces at each end, the great table put into service elsewhere, the ancient chairs lined across the wall from the single entrance. The floor was white marble, old and cracked but kept clean by Moroes's relentless industry and drive.

Khadgar laid out a magic circle of amethyst and rose quartz, still grinning as he laid out the lines. He was confident in his castings now, and did not need his ceremonial conjuration robes for luck. As he laid out the pattern of protection and abjuration, he smiled again. He was already shaping the energy within his mind, calling the required shades and types of magic, conforming them to their requisite shape, holding that fertile energy in abeyance until it was needed.

He stepped within the circle, spoke the words that needed to be spoken, made the motions with his hands in perfect harmony, and unleashed the energy within his mind. He felt the release as something connected within his mind and soul, and he called the magic forth.

"Show me what is happening in Medivh's quarters," he said, his mind giving off a nervous tic, hoping that the Guardian's wards did not apply to his apprentice.

Immediately, he knew the spell had gone wrong. Not in a major fashion, with the magical matrices collapsing upon themselves, but in a slight misfire. Perhaps the wards did work against him, redirecting his vision elsewhere, to another scene.

He knew he was off by several clues. First off, it was

now daylight, Second, it was warm. And last, the location was familiar.

He had not been here before, exactly, at least not in this particular spire, but it was clear he was at Stormwind Keep, overlooking the city below. This was one of the taller spires, and the room was similar in general design to that where the two members of the Order had met their end months earlier. Yet here the windows were large and opened onto great white parapets, and a warm scented breeze stirred diaphanous draperies. Multicolored birds perched within golden hoops around the perimeter of the room.

Before Khadgar a small table was set with white porcelain plates edged with gold, the knifes and forks made of the precious metal as well. Crystal bowls held fruits—fresh and unblemished, the morning dew still clinging to the dimples of the strawberries. Khadgar felt his stomach rumble slightly at the sight.

Around the table hovered a thin man unknown to Khadgar, narrow-faced and wide-foreheaded, with a slender moustache and goatee. He was draped in an ornate red quilt that Khadgar realized must be a dressing gown, cinched at the waist with a golden belt. He touched one of the forks, moving it a molecule's length sideways, then nodded in satisfaction. He looked up at Khadgar and smiled.

"Ah, you are awake," he said in a voice that almost sounded familiar to Khadgar as well.

For an instant, Khadgar thought that this vision

could see him, but no, the man was addressing someone behind him. He turned to see Aegwynn, as youthful and beautiful as she had been on the snowfield. (Was it earlier than that date? Later? He could not tell from her appearance.) She wore a white cape with green lining, but this was made of silk now, not fur, and her feet were shod not in boots but in simple white sandals. Her blond hair was held in place with a silver diadem.

"You seem to have gone to a great deal of trouble," she said, and her face was unreadable to Khadgar.

"With sufficient magic and desire, nothing is impossible," said the man, and turned over his hand, palm upward. Floating above his palm, a white orchid bloomed.

Aegwynn took the flower, raised it perfunctorily to her nose, then set it down on the table. "Nielas . . ." she began.

"Breakfast first," said the mage Nielas. "See what a court conjurer may whip up first thing in the morning. These berries were picked from the royal gardens not more than a hour ago. . . ."

"Nielas," Aegwynn said again.

"Followed by slices of butter-fed ham and syrup," continued the mage.

"Nielas," Aegwynn repeated.

"Then perhaps some eggs of the *vrocka,* poached at the table in the shells by a simple spell I learned out on the isles . . ." said the mage.

"I am leaving," said Aegwynn, simply.

A cloud passed over the mage's face. "Leaving? So

soon? Before breakfast? I mean, I thought we would have a chance to talk further."

"I am leaving," said Aegwynn. "I have my own tasks to complete, and little time for the pleasantries of the morning afterward."

The court conjurer still looked confused. "I thought that after last night you would want to remain in the castle, at Stormwind, for a while." He blinked at the woman, "Wouldn't you?"

"No," said Aegwynn. "Indeed, after last night, there is no need for me to remain at all. I have attained what I have come here for. There is no need for me to stay any longer."

In the present, Khadgar winced as the pieces fell into place. Of course the mage's voice sounded familiar.

"But I thought . . ." stammered the mage Nielas, but the Guardian shook her head.

"You, Nielas Aran, are an idiot," said Aegwynn simply. "You are one of the mightiest sorcerers in the Order of Tirisfal, and yet, you remain an idiot. That says something about the rest of the Order."

Nielas Aran bridled. He meant to look irritated, but only looked petulant. "Now, wait a moment. . . ."

"Surely you did not think that your natural charms alone brought me to your chamber, nor that your wit and sense of whimsy distracted me from our discussion of conjuration rites? Surely you realize that I cannot be impressed by your position as court conjurer like some village cowherd would? And surely you must realize that seduction works both ways? You are not *that* big an idiot, are you, Nielas Aran?"

"Of course not," said the court conjurer, clearly stung by her words but refusing to admit it. "I just thought that, like civilized people, we might share a moment of breakfast."

Aegwynn smiled, and Khadgar saw that it was a cruel smile. "I am as old as many dynasties, and got over my girlish indulgences early in my first century. I knew fully what I was doing coming to your chambers last night."

"I thought . . ." said Nielas. "I just thought . . ." He struggled for the right words.

"That you, of all the Order, would be the one to charm and tame the great, wild Guardian?" said Aegwynn, the smile growing wider. "That you could break her to your will, where all the others had failed, through your charm and wit and parlor tricks? Harness the power of the *Tirisfalen* to your own chariot? Come now, Nielas Aran. You have wasted much of your potential as it is, do not tell me that life in the royal court has corrupted you utterly. Leave me some respect for you."

"But if you weren't impressed," said Nielas, his mind wrapping around what Aegwynn was saying, "if you didn't want me, then why did we . . ."

Aegwynn provided the answer. "I came to Stormwind for one thing I could not provide for myself, a suitable father to my heir. Yes, Nielas Aran, you can tell your fellow mages in the Order that you managed to bed the great and mighty Guardian. But you will also have to tell them that you provided me with a way of passing on my power without the Order having any further say in it."

"I did?" The results of his actions began to sink in. "I suppose I did. But the Order would not like . . ."

"To be manipulated? To be countered? To be fooled?" said Aegwynn. "No, they will not. But they will not act against you, for fear that I truly do have some romantic interest in you. And take this solace—of all the mages, wizards, conjurers, and sorcerers, you were the one with the most potential. Your seed will protect and strengthen my child and make him the vessel for my power. And when he is born and weaned, you will even raise him, here, for I know he will follow my path, and even the Order would not want to miss that opportunity to influence him."

Nielas Aran shook his head. "But I . . ." He stopped for moment. "But did you . . ." He stopped again. At last when he spoke, there was finally some fire in his eyes, and steel in his voice. "Good-bye, Magna Aegwynn."

"Good-bye, Nielas Aran," said Aegwynn. "It has been . . . pleasant." And with that she turned on her heel and was gone from the room.

Nielas Aran, chief conjurer to the throne of Azeroth, conspirator in the Order of Tirisfal, and now father to the future Guardian Medivh, sat by the perfectly set table. He picked up a golden fork, turned it over and over in his fingers. Then he sighed, and dropped it on the floor.

The vision faded before the fork struck the marble floor, but Khadgar was aware of another noise, this one behind him. The sound of a boot scraping against cold stone. The soft scraping of a cloak. He was not alone.

Khadgar wheeled, but all he caught was a tantalizing glimpse of a black cloak's back. The Emissary was spying on him. Bad enough he was sent away each time Medivh met with the stranger—now the Emissary had run of the castle and was spying on him!

At once, Khadgar was on his feet and rushing for the entrance. By the time he reached the doorway, his prey was gone, but there was the sound of fabric brushing along stone down the stairs. Down toward the guest quarters.

Khadgar barreled forward down the stairs as well. The curve of the stairs would keep her to the outside rim, where the footing was broader and more sure. The younger mage had raced up and down these steps so many times he deftly danced down along the inner wall, skipping the stairs in twos and threes.

Halfway to the guest level Khadgar could see his prey's shadow against the outer wall. As he reached the guest level itself he could see the cloaked figure, moving swiftly out through the archway and toward its door. Once the Emissary reached the guest quarters, he would lose his chance. Khadgar vaulted the last four steps in a single bound, and leapt forward to grasp the cloaked figure by the arm.

His hand closed on fabric and firm muscle, and he spun his prey toward the wall. "The Magus will want to know you're spying. . . ." he began, but the words died in his mouth as the cloak fell open to reveal the Emissary.

She was dressed in traveling leathers, with high laced boots and black trousers and black silk blouse. She was well-muscled, and Khadgar had no doubt that she had ridden the entire way here. But her skin was green, and as the hood fell back it revealed a jut-jawed, fanged orcish face. Tall greenish ears poked up from the mass of ebony hair.

"Orc!" shouted Khadgar, and reacted with an automatic response. He raised a hand, muttering a word of power, summoning the forces to drive a bolt of mystic power through her.

He never had the chance to finish. At the first opening of his mouth, the orc woman lashed out with a roundhouse kick, bringing her leg up to chest level. Her knee brushed aside Khadgar's pointing hand, forcing his aim off. Her booted foot slammed into the side of Khadgar's cheek, staggering him.

Khadgar staggered back and tasted blood—he must have bitten his cheek as a result of the blow. He raised his hand again to fire a bolt, but the orc was still too fast, faster than the armor-bound warriors he had fought earlier. Already she had closed the distance between them, driving a hard fist into his stomach, driving the wind from his lungs and the concentration from his mind.

The young mage snarled, abandoning magic for the moment in favor of a more direct approach. Still smarting from the blow, he spun to one side, grasping the woman's arm and pulling her off-balance. A surprised look crossed the woman's jade-shaded face, but only for a moment. She planted her feet firmly on the ground, pulled Khadgar toward her, and neatly broke and reversed the hold.

Khadgar caught a whiff of spices as he was drawn close to the orc, and then she threw him, bodily, down the hallway. He slid along the stone floor, bumping into the wall and at last coming to rest at someone else's feet.

Looking up, Khadgar saw the castellan looking down on him, a look of vague concern on his face.

"Moroes!" shouted Khadgar. "Get back! Fetch the Magus! We have an orc in the tower!"

Moroes did not move, but instead looked up at the orcish woman with his bland, blinkered eyes. "You all right, Emissary?"

The woman smirked, her greenish lips tucked back, and wrapped her cloak around herself. "Never better. Needed a little exercise. The whelp was kind enough to oblige."

"Moroes!" spat the younger mage. "This woman is . . ."

"The Emissary. A guest of the Magus," said Moroes, adding blandly, "Came to get you. Magus wants to see you."

Khadgar pulled himself to his feet and looked sharply at the Emissary. "When you see the Magus, you're going to tell him you're snooping around?"

"Doesn't want to see her," corrected Moroes. "Wants to see you, Apprentice."

"She's an orc!" said Khadgar, louder and harsher than he meant to.

"Half-orc, really," said Medivh. He was bent over his workbench, fiddling with a golden device, an astrolabe. "I surmise her homeland has humans, or near-humans, or at least had them within living memory. Hand me the calipers, Apprentice."

"They tried to kill you!" shouted Khadgar.

"Orcs, you mean? Some did, true," said Medivh calmly. "*Some* orcs tried to kill me. And kill you as well. Garona wasn't in that group. I don't think she was, at any rate. She's here as a representative for her people. Or at least some of her people."

Garona. So the witch has a name, thought Khadgar. Instead he said, "We were attacked by orcs. I had a vision of attacks of orcs. I have been reading the communications from all over Azeroth, speaking of raids and attacks by orcs. Every mention of orcs speaks of their cruelty and violence. There seem to be more of them every day. This is a dangerous and savage race."

"And she dispatched you easily, I assume," said Medivh, looking up from his work.

Despite himself, Khadgar touched the corner of his mouth, where the blood had already dried. "That is completely beside the point."

"Completely," said Medivh. "And your point would be?"

"She is an orc. She is dangerous. And you have given her free rein in the tower."

Medivh grumbled, and there was steel in his voice. "She is a half-orc. She is about as dangerous as you are, given the situation and inclination. And she is my guest and should be accorded all the respect of a guest. I expect this from you regarding my guests, Young Trust."

Khadgar was silent for a moment, then tried a new approach. "She is the Emissary."

"Yes."

"Who is she the emissary *for*?"

"One or more of the clans that are currently inhabiting the Black Morass," said Medivh. "I'm not quite sure which ones, yet. We haven't gotten that far."

Khadgar blinked in surprise. "You let her into our tower, and she has no official standing?"

Medivh laid down the calibers and gave out a weary sigh. "She has presented herself to me as a representative of some of the orc clans that are presently raiding Azeroth. If this matter is going to be solved by any manner other than by fire and the sword, then someone has to start talking. Here is as good a place as any. *And*, by the way, this is considered *my* tower, not ours. You are my student here, my apprentice, and are here at my whim. And as my student, as my apprentice, I expect you to keep an open mind."

There was a silence as Khadgar tried to let this sink

in. "So she represents whom? Some, none, or all of the orcs?"

"She represents, for the moment, herself," said Medivh, letting out an irritated sigh. "Not all humans believe the same thing. There is no reason to believe that all orcs do, either. My question for you is, given your natural curiosity, why aren't you already trying to pull as much information out of her as possible, instead of telling me I should not do the same? Unless you doubt me and my abilities to handle a single half-orc?"

Khadgar was silent, doubly embarrassed both for his actions and for failing to see another way. Was he doubting Medivh? Was there even a chance that the Magus would act in a fashion not to uphold his Order? The thoughts churned within him, fueled by Lothar's words, the vision of the demon, and the politics of the Order. He wanted to warn the older man, but every word seemed to be turned back against him.

"I worry about you, at times," he said at last.

"And I worry about you as well," said the older mage, distractedly. "I seem to worry about a lot of things these days."

Khadgar had to make one last attempt. "Sir, I think this Garona is a spy," he said, simply. "I think she is here to learn as much as she can, to be used against you later."

Medivh leaned back and gave the young man a wicked smile. "That is very much the pot calling the kettle black, young mageling. Or have you forgotten the list of things your own masters of the Kirin Tor wanted you to wheedle out of me when you first got to Karazhan?"

Khadgar's ears were burning crimson as he left the room.

ELEVEN
Garona

He returned to his (well, Medivh's) library to find her going over his notes. An immediate rage blossomed in his chest, but the sting of her blows, and Medivh's chastisement, kept his anger in check.

"What are you doing?" he still said sharply.

Emissary Garona's fingers danced up from the papers. "Snooping, I believe you called it? Spying?" She looked up, a frown on her face. "Actually, I'm just trying to understand what you're doing here. It was left out in the open. Hope that is all right with you."

It is NOT all right with me, thought Khadgar, but instead he said, "Lord Medivh has instructed me to extend to you every courtesy. However, he may take umbrage if, in doing so, I allow you to blow yourself up in casting some ill-thought magical spell."

Garona's face was impassive, but Khadgar noted that she did lift her fingers from the pages. "I have no interest in magic."

"Famous last words," said Khadgar. "Is there something here I can help you with, or are you just snooping in general, seeing what you can come up with?"

"I was told you had a tome on Azeroth's kings," she said, "I would like to consult it."

"You can read?" asked Khadgar. It sounded harsher than he meant it. "Sorry. I meant to say . . ."

"Yes, surprisingly, I can read," said Garona, quickly and officiously. "I have picked up many talents over the years."

Khadgar scowled. "Second row, fourth shelf up. It's a red-bound book with gold trim." Garona disappeared into the stacks, and Khadgar took the opportunity to gather up his notes from the table. He would have to keep them elsewhere if the half-orc had free run of the place. At least it wasn't Order correspondence—even Mcdivh would have a fit if he turned over 'The Song of Aegwynn' to her.

His eyes went to the section where the scroll used as the key was kept. From where he was standing it looked undisturbed. No need to cause a scene here, but he would probably have to move it as well.

Garona returned with a massive tome in her hand, and raised a heavy eyebrow at Khadgar, forming a question. "Yes, that's the one," said the apprentice.

"Human languages are a bit . . . wordy," she said,

setting the tome down in the empty space that previously held Khadgar's notes.

"Only because we always have something to say," said Khadgar, trying to manage a smile. He wondered, did orcs have books? Did they read at all? They had spellcasters, of course, but did that mean they had any real knowledge?

"I hope I wasn't too hard on you, earlier in the hall." Her tone was glib, and Khadgar was sure that she would rather have seen him spit out a tooth. Probably this was what passed for an apology among the orcs.

"Never better," said Khadgar. "I needed the exercise."

Garona sat down and started pouring through the text. Khadgar noticed that she moved her lips as she read, and she had immediately turned toward the back of the book, to the recent additions about King Llane's reign.

Now, not in the immediate fire of combat, he could see that Garona was not the standard orc he had fought earlier. She was lean and well-muscled, unlike the lumpy, rough brutes he had battled at the caravan site. Her skin was smoother, almost human, and a lighter shade of green than the jade flesh of the orcs themselves. Her fangs were a bit smaller, and her eyes were a bit larger, more expressive than the hard crimson orbs of the orc warriors. He wondered how much of this was from her human heritage and how much from being female. He wondered if any of the orcs he had fought earlier were female—it was not obvious, and he had no desire to check at the time.

Indeed, without the green flesh, the disfigured, tusked face, and the hostile, superior attitude she might almost be attractive. Still, she was in *his* library, and going through *his* books (well, Medivh's library, and Medivh's books, but the Magus had entrusted them to *him).*

"So you are an Emissary," he said at last. He tried to keep his words light and conversational. "I was told of your impending arrival."

The half-orc nodded, concentrating on the words before her.

"Who are you emissaring *for*, exactly?"

Garona looked up, and Khadgar saw a flicker of irritation beneath her heavy brows. Khadgar felt good about bothering her, but at the same time wondered where the woman drew the line. He did not want to push too hard or too fast, lest he earn another beating, or another curt dismissal by the Magus.

At least this time he would get some information out before the battle. He said, "I mean, if you're the Emissary, that means that someone is giving you orders, someone is pulling your strings, someone you have to report back to. Whom do you represent?"

"I'm sure your Master, the Old Man, would tell you, if you asked," said Garona smoothly, but her eyes remained hard.

"I'm sure he would," Khadgar lied. "If I had the effrontery to ask him. So I ask you instead. Whom do you represent? What powers have you been granted? Are you here to negotiate, or demand, or what?"

Garona closed the book (Khadgar felt a small victory in distracting her from her task) and said, "Do all humans think alike?"

"It would be boring if we did," said Khadgar.

"I mean, does everyone agree about everything? Are people always agreeing to what their masters or superiors want?" said Garona. The hardness in her eyes faded just a touch.

"Hardly," said Khadgar. "One reason that there are so many tomes is that everyone has an opinion. And that is just the literate ones."

"So understand that there are differences of opinions among the orcs as well," said Garona. "The Horde is made of up of a number of clans, all with their own chieftains and war leaders. All orcs belong to a clan. Most orcs are loyal to their clan and their chieftain."

"What are the clans?" asked Khadgar. "What are they called?"

"Stormreaver is one," said the half-orc. "Blackrock. Twilight's Hammer. Bleeding Hollow. Those are the major ones."

"Sounds like a warlike bunch," said Khadgar.

"The homeland of the orc peoples is a harsh place," said Garona, "and only the strongest and best organized survive. They are no more than what their land has made them."

Khadgar thought of the blasted, red-skied land he had seen in the vision. This was the orcs' homeland, then. Some wasteland in another dimension. Yet how did they get here? Instead he said, "So which is your clan?"

Garona gave a snort that sounded like a bulldog sneezing. "I have no clan."

"You said all of your people belonged to a clan," said Khadgar.

"I said all *orcs*," said Garona. When Khadgar looked at her blankly, she held up her hand. "Look at this. What do you see?"

"Your hand," said Khadgar.

"Human or orc?"

"Orc," said Khadgar. It was obvious to him. Green skin, sharp yellowing nails, knuckles just a shade too large to be human.

"An orc would say that it's a human hand—too slender to be really useful, not enough muscle to hold an ax or bash a skull in properly—too pale, too weak, and too ugly." Garona lowered her hand and looked at the young mage through lowered brows. "You see the parts of me that are orcish. My orcish superiors, and all other orcs, see the parts of me that are human. I am both, and neither, and considered an inferior being by both sides."

Khadgar opened his mouth to argue, but thought twice of the matter and kept silent. His first reaction was to strike out at the orc he had found in the halls, not to see the human that was Medivh's guest. He nodded and said, "It must be difficult, then. Without a clan allegiance."

"I have turned it to my advantage," said Garona. "I can move between the clans more easily. As a lesser creature, I am assumed to not be always looking for an advantage to my native clan. I am disliked by all, so therefore I am not biased. Some chieftains find that reassuring. It makes me a better negotiator, and before you say it, a better spy. But better to have no allegiance than conflicting ones."

Khadgar thought of Medivh's own castigation of his Kirin Tor ties, but said, "And which clan do you represent at the moment?"

Garona gave a wry, fanged smile. "If I said Gizblah the Mighty, what would you say? Or perhaps I am on a mission for Morgax the Gray or Hikapik the Bloodrender. Would that tell you enough?"

"It might," said Khadgar.

"It wouldn't," said Garona, "because I made up all those names, just now. And the name of the faction that has sent me here would mean nothing to you either, not at the moment. Similarly, the Old Man's stated friendship with King Llane means nothing to our chieftains, and the name Lothar is nothing more than a curse invoked by the human peasants we encounter. Before we can have peace, before we can even start negotiating, we have to learn more about you."

"Which is why you're here."

Garona let out a deep sigh. "Which is why I am praying that you will leave me alone long enough so I can figure out what the Old Man is talking about when we have our discussions."

Khadgar was silent for a moment. Garona opened

the volume again, leafing through the pages to where she had stopped. "Of course, that goes both ways," Khadgar said, and Garona closed the book with an exasperated breath. "I mean, we need to know more about the orcs if we're going to do more than just battle them. If you're serious about peace."

Garona glared at Khadgar, and for a moment the young mage wondered if the half-orc was going to leap across the table and throttle him. Instead, her ears perked up, and she said, "Hold on. What's that?"

Khadgar felt it before he heard it. A sudden change in the air, like a window had been opened elsewhere in the tower. A bit of wind stirring up the dust in the hall. A wave of warmth passing through the tower.

Khadgar said, "Something is . . ."

Garona said, "I heard . . ."

And then Khadgar heard it as well, the sound of iron claws scraping against stone, and the warmth of the air increased as the hairs on the back of his neck rose.

And the great beast slouched into the library.

It was made of fire and shadow, its skin dark and containing the flickers of the flame within. Its wolflike face was framed by a set of ram's horns, that glowed like polished ebony. It looked biped, but walked on all fours, its long front claws scraping along the stone floors.

"What is . . ." hissed Garona.

"Demon," said Khadgar in a strangled voice, rising and backing away from the table.

"Your manservant said there were visions here. Ghosts. Is this one?" Garona stood up as well.

Khadgar wanted to explain no, that visions tended to encompass the area entirely, shifting you to the new place, but he instead he just shook his head.

The beast itself was perched in the doorway, sniffing the air. The creature's eyes blazed with flame. Was the beast blind, and could only detect by scent? Or was it detecting a new thing in the air, a spice that it had not expected?

Khadgar tried to pull the energies into his mind, but at first his heart quailed and his mind went empty. The beast continued to sniff, turning in place until it faced the pair.

"Get to the high tower," said Khadgar quietly. "We have to warn Medivh." Out of the corner of his eye he saw Garona nod, but her eyes did not leave the beast. A trickle of sweat dropped down her long neck. She shifted slightly to one side.

The movement was enough, and everything happened at once. The beast crouched and leapt across the room. Khadgar's mind cleared, and with a quick efficiency he pulled the energies into himself, raised his hand, and buried a bolt of mystic energy into the creature's chest. The energy ripped through the beast's chest and splattered out its back, sending pieces of flaming flesh in all directions, but it did not deter it in the slightest.

It landed on the study table, its claws digging into

the hardwood, and bounded again, this time for Khadgar. The young mage's mind went blank for a second, but a second was all it took for the slope-shouldered demon to close the distance between them.

Something else grabbed him and yanked him out of the way. He smelled musky cinnamon and heard a deep-throated curse as he spun out of the path of the loping demon. The beast sailed through the space that until recently had been occupied by the apprentice, and let out a scream of its own. A long ragged tear had appeared along the creature's left side, and was oozing burning blood.

Garona released Khadgar from her grip (a weak, humanish grip, but still enough to drive the air from his lungs). In her other hand, the apprentice noticed that Garona held a long-bladed knife, crimson with its first strike, and Khadgar wondered where she had hid it while they were arguing.

The creature landed, wheeled, and tried to make an immediate, clumsy second assault, its iron-shod talons outstretched, its mouth and eyes blazing with flame. Khadgar ducked, then came up with the heavy red volume of *The Lineage of Azeroth's Kings*. He hefted the massive tome into the creature's face, then ducked again. The beast sailed past him, landing back near the door. It let out a retching, choking noise, and shook his ram-horned head to dislodge the weighty grimoire. Khadgar saw there was a line of burning blood etched along the creature's right side. Garona had struck a second time.

"Get Medivh," shouted Khadgar. "I'll get it away from the door."

"What if it wants me, instead?" responded Garona, and for the first time, Khadgar heard a ripple of fear in her voice.

"It doesn't," said Khadgar grimly. "It kills mages."

"But you . . ."

"Just go," said Khadgar.

Khadgar broke to the left, and, true to his fears, the demon followed him. Instead of heading toward the door. Garona broke for the right, and started climbing the far bookcase.

"Get Medivh!" shouted Khadgar, darting down one of the rows of books.

"No time," responded Garona, still climbing. "See if you can delay it in one of the rows."

Khadgar turned at the far end of the long bookshelves, and turned. The demon had already leapt over the study table and was now prowling down the row between the bookcases, between histories and geographies. In the shadow between the rows the creature's flaming eyes and mouth stood out in stark relief, and acrid smoke now roiled from its wounded sides.

Khadgar cleared his mind, stuffed down his fear, and fired off a mystic bolt. A globe of fire or a shard of lightning might be more effective, but the beast was surrounded by his books.

The bolt smashed into the creature's face, staggering it back a pace. It growled and crept forward again.

He repeated the process like a ritual—clear the mind, fight the fear, raise a hand, and invoke the word. Another bolt splanged off its ebony horns, ricocheting upward. The beast halted, but only for a moment. Now its maw seemed a twisted, flame-filled smile.

A third time he invoked the power of the mystic bolt, but now the creature was close, and it flashed in its face, but save for illuminating its amused features, did nothing. Khadgar smelled its sour, burning flesh, and heard a deep clicking within the beast's throat—laughter?

"Get ready to run!" shouted Garona, from somewhere to his right and above.

"What are you . . ." started Khadgar, already backing up.

"Run!" she shouted, and pushed off with her feet. The half-orc had climbed to the top of the bookcases, and now shoved them apart, toppling the cases like giant dominos. A deep crash of thunder resounded as each bookcase tipped over its neighbor, spilling volumes and crushing everything in its path.

The last bookcase smashed against the wall and splintered, the force of the impact driving it to the ground. Garona slid down from her now wobbling perch, long-bladed knife drawn. She tried to peer through the churning dust.

"Khadgar?" she said.

"Here," said the apprentice, plastered against the

back wall, where the iron pedestals rose to support the upper stacks on the balcony above. His face was pale even for a human.

"Did we get it?" she demanded, still in a half-crouch, expecting a new assault at any moment.

Khadgar pointed to the edge of what was until seconds before the end of the row of shelves. Now the entire lower floor was a ruins of shattered cases and ruined volumes. Reaching out of the tattered wreckage was a muscular, mangled arm made of dull flame and twisted shadow. Its iron claws were already red with rust, and warm blood was already pooling on the floor. Its outstretched hand was a mere foot from where Khadgar splayed himself.

"Got it," said Garona, sliding the knife back into sheath beneath her blouse.

"You should have listened," said Khadgar, choking on the dust. "Should have gotten Medivh."

"It would have sliced you open before I got up two flights of stairs," said the half-orc. "And then who would be left to explain things to the Old Man?"

Khadgar nodded, and then a thought furrowed his brow. "The Magus. Did he hear this?"

Garona nodded in agreement. "He should have come down. We made enough noise here to wake the dead."

"No," said Khadgar, heading for the entrance to the library. "What if there was more than one demon? Come on!"

Without thinking, Garona drew her knife and followed the human out of the room.

They found Medivh sitting in his laboratory, at the same workbench that Khadgar had left him no more than an hour previously. Now the golden instrument he was working on was in twisted pieces, and an iron hammer rested at one side of the bench.

Medivh started when Khadgar burst into the room, followed closely by Garona. The apprentice wondered, had he been dozing through all this?

"Master! There is a demon in the tower!" blurted Khadgar.

"A demon, again?" said Medivh wearily, rubbing one eye with the flat of his palm. "It was a demon the first time. The last time it was an orc."

"Your student is correct," said Garona. "I was in the library with him when it attacked. Large creature, bestial, but cunning. Made of fire and darkness, and its wounds burned and smoked."

"It was probably nothing more than another vision," said Medivh, turning back to his work. He picked up a mangled piece of the device and looked at it, as if seeing it for the first time. "They happen here, the visions. I think Moroes warned you about them."

"It was not a vision, Master," said Khadgar. "It was a demon, of the type you fought at Stormwind Keep. Something has gotten past the wards and attacked us."

Medivh's gray brows arched in suspicion. "Something get past my wards again? Ridiculous." He closed his eyes and traced a symbol in the air, "No. Nothing is amiss. None of the wards are tripped. You are here. Cook is in the kitchen, and Moroes is in the hall outside the library right now."

Khadgar and Garona exchanged a glance. Khadgar said, "Then you should come at once, Master."

"Must I?" said Medivh. "I have other things to worry about, of this I'm sure."

"Come and see," said Khadgar.

"We believe the beast to be dead," said Garona. "But we don't want to risk the lives of your servants on our beliefs."

Medivh looked at the smashed device, shook his head, and set it down. He seemed irritated by it. "As you wish. Apprentices are not supposed to be this much trouble."

By the time they reached the library, however, Moroes was standing there, dustpan and broom in hand, surveying the damage. He looked up, slightly lost, as the two mages and the half-orc entered.

"Congratulations," said Medivh, the lines of his frown cutting deeply across his face. "I think it's a bigger mess now than when you first arrived. At least then I had shelving. Where is this supposed demon?"

Khadgar walked over to where the demon's hand had jutted out, but now all that remained was one of the bookcases pressed flat on the floor. Even the blood was missing.

"It was here," said Garona, looking as surprised as

Khadgar. "It came in, and attacked us." She grasped the edge of the case, trying to pry it up, but the massive oak was too heavy for her. After she struggled a moment, she said, "We both saw it."

"You saw a vision," said Medivh sternly. "Didn't Moroes warn you about this?"

"Ayep," confirmed Moroes. "I did at that." He tapped the sides of his blinders for effect.

"Master, it did attack us," said Khadgar. "We damaged it with our own spells. The Emissary here wounded it, twice."

"Hmmph," grunted the Magus. "More likely you overreacted when you saw it, and did most of the damage yourselves. These are fresh scratches on the table. From the demon?"

"He had iron claws," said Khadgar.

"Or perhaps from your own mystic bolts, flung around like beads at a Stormwind streetfair?" Medivh shook his head.

"My knife bit into something hard and leathery," said Garona.

"No doubt some of the books themselves," said the Magus. "No, were there a demon, its body would still be here. Unless someone cleaned it up. Moroes, do you happen to have a demon in your dustbin?"

"Don't believe so," said the castellan. "I could check."

"Don't worry, but leave your tools for these two." To the younger mage and the half-orc he said, "I expect you to get along. In light of this, you two get to straighten up the library. Young Trust, you have betrayed your name, and so must make restitution now."

Garona would not relent, "But I saw—"

"You saw a phantom," interrupted Medivh in an authoritative tone, his brows knitted. "You saw a piece of somewhere else. It would not have harmed you. It never does. Your friend here," and he motioned at Khadgar, "tends to see demons where there are none. That worries me a bit. Perhaps you can try not to see any when you are cleaning up. Until you do, I am not to be disturbed!"

And with that, he was gone. Moroes laid the broom and dustpan on the floor and followed him.

Khadgar looked around at the debris of the room. More than just a broom would be needed here. Cases were toppled and in a couple places shattered entirely, and books were flung randomly about, some with their spines broken and their covers torn. Could it have been a time-lost vision?"

"This was no illusion that attacked us," said Garona moodily.

"I know," said Khadgar.

"So why doesn't he see it?" asked the half-orc.

"That I don't know," said the apprentice. "And I worry about finding out the answer."

TWELVE
Life in Wartime

It took only several days to put the library back in proper order. Most of the scattered books were at least near to where they needed to be, and the rarer, more magical, and trapped volumes were on the upper balcony and had been untouched by the fracas. Rebuilding some of the cases took time, however, and Garona and Khadgar turned the empty stables into a makeshift carpentry shop, and they tried to restore (and in some cases replace) the shattered cases.

Of the demon, there was no trace, save for the damage wrought. The claw marks remained in the table, and the pages of *The Lineage of Azeroth's Kings* were badly mangled and torn, as if by massive jaws. Yet there was no body, no blood, no remains to drop at Medivh's feet.

"Maybe it was rescued," suggested Garona.

"It was pretty dead when we left it," responded

Khadgar, at the time trying to remember if he had put epic poetry on the shelf above or below romantic epics.

"Something rescued the body," said Garona. "The same person who popped it in here would have popped him out."

"And the blood as well," reminded Khadgar.

"And blood as well," repeated the half-orc. "Perhaps it was a tidy demon."

"That's not the way magic works," said Khadgar.

"Perhaps not your magic, the magic you learned," said Garona. "Other peoples could have other magics. The old shamans among the orcs had one way of magic, the warlocks that cast spells have different ones. Maybe it's a spell you never heard of."

"No," said Khadgar simply. "It would have left some kind of a marker. A bit of the caster behind. Some residual energy that I could feel, even if I could not identify it. The only spellcasters active in the tower have been myself and the Magus. I know that through my own spells. And I checked the wards. Medivh was right—they were all operating. No one should have been able to break into the tower, magically or otherwise."

Garona shrugged. "But there are odd things about this tower as well, correct? Could the old rules not apply here?"

It was Khadgar's turn to shrug. "If that's the case, we're in a lot more trouble than I imagined."

Khadgar's relationship with the half-orc seemed to improve over the course of repairing the library, and when his back was to her, or she was in the stacks, her voice sounded almost human. Still, she remained guarded about whom she represented, and Khadgar for his part remained watchful. He kept track of what references she used and what questions she asked.

He also tried to keep track of any communications she made, to the point of wrapping the guest quarters with his own web of detection spells, to inform him if she had left the room or sent word out. If she had, her methods foiled even Khadgar's detection, which made him more nervous as opposed to assuring him. If she was doing anything with the knowledge she had gained, she was keeping it to herself.

And true to her word, Garona began sharing her own knowledge about the orcs. Khadgar began to assemble a picture of how the orcs were ruled (by strength and warrior prowess) as well as the different clans within. Once she got rolling, the Emissary made very clear her opinion of the various clans, whose leaders she tended to think of as lumpen oafs who are only thinking of where their next battle is coming from. As she described the multi-clan orcish nation, the Horde, Khadgar quickly understood that the dynamics were ever-changing and fluid at best.

A large chunk of the Horde was the conservative Bleeding Hollow clan. A powerful group with a long history of conquest, the clan was less powerful in that its aged leader, Kilrogg Deadeye, had become more unwilling to throw lives away in combat. Garona explained that in orcish politics, older orcs become more pragmatic, which is often mistaken for cowardice by the younger generation. Kilrogg had killed three of his sons and two grandsons already who thought they could rule the clan better.

The clan known as the Blackrock appeared to have another large chunk of the Horde, its leader was Blackhand, who had as his chief recommendation for leader the ability to thump anyone else who wanted the title. A chunk of Blackrock had already splintered off, knocked out a tooth, and called themselves the Black Tooth Grin. Charming names.

There were other clans: Twilight's Hammer, which reveled in destruction, and the Burning Blade, who seemed to have no leader, but rather served as an anarchic gathering within the chaos of the Horde. And smaller clans, like the Stormreavers, that were led by a warlock. Khadgar suspected that Garona was reporting to someone within the Stormreavers, if only because she had less to complain about with them than the others.

Khadgar took what notes he could, and assembled into reports for Lothar. A larger amount of communications was coming in from all points in Azeroth, and now it seemed that the Horde was spilling out of the Black Morass in all directions. The orcs that were considered mere rumors a year ago were now omnipresent, and Stormwind Keep was mobilizing to meet the threat. Khadgar kept the ever-worsening news from Garona, but fed to Lothar what details he could glean, down to clan rivalries and favorite colors

(The Blackrock clan, for example, favored red for some reason).

Khadgar also tried to communicate what he had learned to Medivh, but the Magus was surprisingly disinterested. Indeed, the Magus's conversations with Garona were not as common as they once were, and on several occasions Khadgar discovered that Medivh had left the tower without informing him. Even when he was present, Medivh seemed more distant. More than once Khadgar had come upon him, seated in one of his chairs in the observatory, staring out into the Azerothean night. He seemed moodier now, quicker to disagree, and less willing to listen than before.

His disaffected mood was clear to the others as well. Moroes would give Khadgar a painful, long-suffering look as he left the master's chambers. And Garona herself brought up the subject as they reviewed the maps of the known world (which were made in Stormwind, and as such woefully incomplete even when talking about Lordaeron).

"Is he always like this?" she asked.

Khadgar responded stoically, "He has many moods."

"Yes, but when I first encountered him, he seemed alive, engaged, and positive. Now he seems more . . ."

"Distracted?"

"Addled," said Garona, twisting her lips in disgust.

Khadgar could not disagree. Later that evening, Khadgar reported to the Magus a slew of new message translations, all with the purple seal, all begging for aid against the orcs.

"The orcs are not demons," said Medivh. "They are flesh and blood, and as such the worry of warriors, not wizards."

"The messages are quite dire," said Khadgar. "It sounds like the lands closest to the Black Morass are being abandoned, and refugees flooding into Stormwind and the other cities of Azeroth. They are pressed thin."

"And so they depend on the Guardian to ride to their rescue. Bad enough I must guard the watchtowers on the Twisting Nether to watch for demons, and to hunt down the mistakes of these amateurs. Now I must rescue them against other nations? Will I be asked to support Azeroth in a trade dispute with Lordaeron next? Such matters should not be our worry."

"There may not be an Azeroth without your help. Lothar is . . ."

"Lothar is a fool," muttered Medivh. "An old mother hen that sees threats everywhere. And Llane is little better, seeing nothing that could break his walls. And the Order, all the mighty mages, they have quarreled and argued and spat among themselves so now they don't have the power to repel a new invader. No, Young Trust, this is the little stuff. Even if the orcs succeeded in Azeroth, they would need a Guardian, and I would be here for them."

"Master, that's . . ."

"Sacrilege? Blasphemy? Betrayal?" The Magus

sighed and pinched the bridge of his nose. "Perhaps. But I am a man made old before my time, and I have paid a great price for my unwanted power. Permit me to rail against the clockworks that rule my life. Go now. I'll return to your tales of woe in the morning."

As he was closing the door, Khadgar heard Medivh add, "I am so tired of worrying about everything. When can I worry about myself?"

"The orcs have attacked Stormwind," said Khadgar. It was three weeks later. He laid the missive on the table between him and Garona.

The half orc stared at the red-sealed envelope like it was a venomous snake. "I am sorry," she said at last. "They will not as a rule take prisoners."

"The orc forces were repelled this time," said Khadgar. "Thrown back before they reached the gates by Llane's troops. From the descriptions, it sounds like Kilrogg's Bleeding Hollow and the Twilight's Hammer clans. There seemed to be a lack of coordination between the major forces."

Garona gave a bulldog-sneeze grunt and said, "The Twilight's Hammer should have never be put on an assault in a siege situation. Kilrogg likely was trying to decimate a rival, and use Stormwind as his anvil to do so."

"So even in the midst of an attack, they continue to brawl and betray each other," said Khadgar. He wondered if his own reports to Lothar had given them the information they needed to break the assault.

Garona shrugged, "Very much like humans." She motioned to the books piled high on the study table. "In your histories, there are continual justifications for all manner of hellish actions. Claims of nobility and heritage and honor to cover up every bit of genocide, assassination, and massacre. At least the Horde is honest in their naked lust for power." She was silent for a moment, then added, "I don't think I could have helped them."

"The orcs, or Stormwind?" asked Khadgar.

"Either," said Garona. "I did not know about any attack on Stormwind, if that's what you're hinting at, though anyone with half an ounce of sense would know that a Horde would strike against the biggest target as soon as possible. You know that from our discussions. You also know that they'll pull back, regroup, kill a few leaders, and then come back in greater numbers."

"I can guess, yes," said Khadgar.

Garona added, "And you already sent a letter to the Champion at Stormwind just to that affect."

Khadgar thought he kept his face passive, but the orc emissary gave a wide smile. "Yes, you did."

Khadgar now felt his face turn flush, but pressed his point. "Actually, the question I have is, Why haven't *you* been reporting to your masters?"

The green-fleshed woman leaned back in her seat. "Who's to say I haven't?"

"I do," said Khadgar. "Unless you're a better mage that I am."

A small tic at the corner of Garona's mouth betrayed her. "You haven't been reporting in at all, have you?" asked Khadgar.

Garona was silent for a moment, and Khadgar let the silence fill the library. At length she said, "Let's just say I've been having a problem with divided loyalties."

"I thought you had no allegiances," said Khadgar.

Garona ignored him. "I was sent here, ordered here, by a warlock named Gul'dan. Spellcaster. Leader of the Stormreavers. Very influential in the Horde. Very interested in the mages of your world."

"And the orcs have the tendency to strike the biggest target first. Medivh," said Khadgar.

"Gul'dan said Medivh was special. From which secret divination or spice-fueled meditation he used to come to that conclusion, I don't know." Garona avoided Khadgar's glance. "I met several times with Medivh in the field, then agreed to come to the tower here as an emissary. I was supposed to trade basic information and report back to Gul'dan as much as I could about Medivh's strengths. So you were right from the start—I was here as a spy."

Khadgar sat down across from her. "You wouldn't have been the first," he said. "So why didn't you report back?"

Garona was silent for a moment. "Medivh . . ." she started, then stopped. "The Old Man . . ." another pause. "He saw through it all at once, of course, and he still told me what I wanted to know. Most of it, at least."

"I know," said Khadgar. "He had the same affect on me."

Garona nodded. "At first I thought he was just being pompous, sure in his power, like some orc chieftains I've known. But there's something else. It's as if he feels that by giving me the knowledge, he knew I would be changed by it, and would not betray his trust."

"Trust," said Khadgar. "That's a big thing for Medivh. He seems to exude it. Standing next to him, you feel he knows what he's doing."

"Right," said Garona, "and orcs are drawn to power naturally. I figured I could tell Gul'dan that I was held prisoner, unable to respond, and so I learned more, and eventually . . ."

"You didn't want to see him hurt," finished Khadgar.

"As Moroes would say, 'ayep'," said Garona. "He put a lot of trust in me, and he puts it in you, too. After watching your vision-power thing, I told him about it. I figured that might have brought the demon down on us. He said he knew and it didn't bother him. That you were naturally curious, and it served you well. He stands by his people."

"And you can't hurt someone like that," said Khadgar.

"Ayep. He made me feel human. And I haven't felt human in a long, long time. The Old Man, Magus Medivh, seems to have a dream of more than one force battling another for domination. With his power, he could have destroyed us all, yet he does not. I think he believes in something better. I want to believe his dream as well."

The two sat there for a while in silence. Somewhere in the distance, Moroes or Cook moved along the hallway.

"And recently . . ." said Garona. "Has he ever been like this before?"

She sounded like Lothar—trying to ask without seeming too concerned. Khadgar shook his head. "He's always been erratic. Eccentric. But I've never seen him this . . . depressed."

"Brooding," added Garona. "Neutral. Up to now I've always assumed he would be on the side of the Kingdom of Azeroth. But if Stormwind itself is attacked and still he does nothing . . ."

"It may be his own training," said Khadgar, choosing his words carefully. He did not want to reveal the Order to Garona, regardless of her current feelings. "He has to take a very long view on things. It sometimes cuts him off from others."

"Which is why he takes in strays, I suppose," said Garona. Another silence, then she added, "I am not sorry that Stormwind repelled the invaders. You don't destroy something like that from without. You have to do something within to weaken the walls first."

"I'm glad you're not there as a general," said Khadgar.

"Chieftain," said Garona. "Like I'd get a chance."

"There is something," said Khadgar, then stopped. Garona tilted her heavily mawed head toward him.

"You sound like someone looking for a favor," she said.

"I have never asked you about troop strengths, and positions. . . ."

"About obvious spy stuff."

"But," said Khadgar, "they were amazed by the huge numbers of orc warriors on the field. They fought them back, but were surprised that the swamps of the Black Morass could hold that many soldiers. Even now they're worried about the forces that could be hiding within the marshlands."

"I know nothing of troop dispositions," said Garona. "I have been here, spying on you, remember?"

"True," said Khadgar. "But I also know you talked of your homeland. How did you get from there to here? Was it some spell?"

Garona sat quietly for a moment, as if trying to resolve something in her mind. Khadgar expected a flip comment, or a redirection of the subject, or even another question in response. Instead she said, "We call our world Draenor. It is a savage world, filled with badlands and bluffs and hardscrabble vegetation. Inhospitable and stormy . . ."

"And it has a red sky," added Khadgar.

Garona looked at the young mage. "You have spoken with other orcs? Prisoners, perhaps? I was unaware the humans took orc prisoners."

"No, a vision," said Khadgar. The memory seemed half a lifetime away. "Much like you saw the first time we met. It was the first time I had seen orcs. I remember there were huge numbers of them."

Garona let out a bulldog snort. "Your visions probably reveal more than you say, but you have a good picture. Orcs are fecund, and large litters are common, because so many die before they reach a warrior's age.

"It was a hard life, and only the strong, the powerful, and the smart survived. I was in the third group, but still I was a near-outcast, surviving as best I could at the fringes of the clan. That would be the Stormreavers, at the time, at least when the order went out."

"Order?"

"We were put on the march, every warrior and every capable hand. Grunt labor and swordsmen, all ordered to pack up their weapons, tools, and belongings, and head for the Hellfire Peninsula. There a great portal had been erected by Gul'dan and other powerful warlocks. A portal that broke through the space between the worlds."

Garona sucked on a fang, remembering. "It was a great set of standing stones, hauled there to frame a rip in space itself. Within the rip were the colors of darkness, a swirl like oil on the surface of a polluted pool. I got the feeling that rip had been forged by greater hands, and the warlocks had just contained it.

"Many of the most hardened warriors feared the space between the pillars, but the chieftains and underchiefs made passionate speeches about what was to be found on the other side. A world of riches. A world of plenty. A world of soft creatures who would be easily dominated. All this they promised.

"Some still resisted. Some were slain, and others were forced through with axes resting against their backs. I was caught with a large group of laborers and shoved into the space between the pillars."

Garona fell silent for a moment. "It's called the Twisting Nether, and it was both instantaneous and eternal. I fell forever, and when I emerged into the strange light, I was in a mad new world."

Khadgar added, "After promises of paradise, the Black Morass would be quite a letdown."

Garona shook her head. "It was a shock. I remember quailing at the first sight of the blue, hostile sky. And the land, covered with vegetation as far as the eye could see. Some could not take it and went mad. Many joined the Burning Blade, the chaos orcs thronging beneath their fire-orange pennant, that day."

Garona stroked her heavy chin. "I feared, but I survived. And I found my half-breed life gave me insight on these humans. I was part of an ambush party that attacked Medivh. He killed everyone else, but left me alive, and sent me with a message back to the Warlock Gul'dan. And after a while, Gul'dan sent me as his spy, but I found I had . . . difficulty . . . betraying the Old Man's secrets."

"Divided loyalties," commented Khadgar.

"But to answer your question," said Garona, "no, I don't know how many clans have poured through the

Dark Portal from Draenor. And I don't know how long it will take for them to recover. And I don't know where the portal came from. But you, Khadgar, can find out."

Khadgar blinked. "Me?"

"Your visions," said Garona. "You seem to be able to summon up the ghosts of the past, even of faraway. I watched you call up a vision of Medivh's mother when I first met you. That was Stormwind we were at?"

"Yes," said Khadgar. "And that's why I still think the demon in the library was real—there was no background to the vision."

Garona waved off his comment. "But you can call up these visions. You can summon up the moment when the rift was first created. You can find out who brought the orcs through to Azeroth."

"Aye," said Khadgar. "And I bet it's the same mage or warlock that has been unleashing demons. It makes sense, that the two be linked." He looked at Garona. "You know, that would not be a question I would have thought of."

"I will provide the questions," said Garona, looking very pleased with herself, "if you provide the answers."

The empty dining room again. The ever-diligent Moroes had swept up the earlier casting circle, and Khadgar had to recast it with streams of crushed rose quartz and amethyst. Garona fit lit torches into the wall sconces, then stood in the center of the pattern, next to him.

"I'll warn you," he said to the half-orc. "This may not work."

"You'll do well," replied Garona. "I've seen you do it before."

"I'll probably get something," said Khadgar. "I just don't know what." He made the motions with his hands, and intoned the words. With Garona watching, he wanted to get everything just right. At last he released the mystical energy from the cage within his mind and shouted, "Show me the origin of the rift between Draenor and Azeroth!"

There was a change in the pressure, in the very weight of the air around them. It was warm, and night, but the night sky outside their window (for there was a window now in these quarters) was a deep red, the color of old, dried blood, and only a few weak stars pierced the envelope.

It was someone's quarters, likely an orc leader. There were fur rugs on the floor and a large platform that would serve as a bed. A low fire pit burned in the center of the room. Weapons hung on the stone walls, and there were a plethora of cabinets as well. One was open, showing a line of preserved *things,* some of which might have once belonged to human or human-ish creatures.

The figure in the bed tossed, turned, and then sat up suddenly, as awakening from a bad dream. He stared into the darkness, and his savaged, war-torn face was clear. Even by orc standards, he was an ugly representative of his race.

Garona let out a sharp gasp, and said, "Gul'dan."

Khadgar nodded and said, "He should not see you." This, then, was the warlock that had sent Garona to spy. He looked about as trustworthy as a bent gold piece. For the moment, he wrapped himself in his furs, and spoke.

"I can still see you," he said. "Even though I think I am awake. Perhaps I dream I am awake. Come forth, dream creature."

Garona gripped Khadgar's shoulder, and he could feel her sharp fingernails dig into his flesh. But Gul'dan was not speaking to them. Instead a new specter wafted into view.

It was tall and broad-shouldered, taller than any of the other three. It was translucent, as if it did not belong here either. It was hooded, and its voice reedy and distant. Though the only light was from the fire pit, the figure cast two shadows—one directly back from the flames, the other to one side, as if lit by a different source.

"Gul'dan," said the figure. "I want your people. I want your armies. I want your power to aid me."

"I have called upon my spirit protectors, creature," said Gul'dan, and Khadgar could hear a tremor in the orc's voice. "I have called upon my warlocks and they have quailed before you. I have called upon my mystic master and he has failed to stop you. You haunt my dreams, and now you come, a dream-creature, into my world. Who and what are you, truly?"

"You fear me," said the tall figure, and at the sound of his voice, Khadgar felt a cold hand run down his spine, "for you do not understand me. See my world and understand your fear. Then fear no more."

And with that the tall hooded figure shaped a ball out of the air, as light and clear as a soap bubble. It floated, about a foot in diameter, and within it showed a tableau of a land with blue sky and green fields.

The cloaked figure was showing him Azeroth.

Another bubble followed, and then another, and then a fourth. The sun-dappled fields of summer grain. The swamps of the Black Morass. The ice fields of the north. The shining towers of Stormwind Keep.

And a bubble that contained a lonely tower cradled within a crater of hills, lit by clear moonlight. He was showing the orc spellcaster Karazhan.

And there was another bubble, a fleeting one, that showed some dark scene far beneath the waves. It seemed an errant thought, one that was quickly eradicated. Yet Khadgar got the feeling of power. There was a grave beneath the waves, a crypt, one that surged with power like a heartbeat. It was there for an instant, and then gone.

"Gather your forces," said the cloaked figure. "Gather your armies and warriors and laborers and allies, and prepare them for a journey through the

Twisting Nether. Prepare them well, for all this will be yours when you succeed."

Khadgar shook his head. The voice stung at him like an errant gnat. Then he realized who it was and his heart quailed.

Gul'dan was up on his knees, his hands clasped before him. "I shall do so, for yours in power most supreme. But who are you truly, and how will we reach this world?"

The figure raised his hands to his hood, and Khadgar shook his head. He didn't want to see it. He knew but he did not want to see it.

A deeply lined face. Graying brows. Green eyes that sparkled with hidden knowledge and something dangerous. Next to him, Garona let out a gasp.

"I am the Guardian," said Medivh to the orc warlock. "I will open the way for you. I will smash the cycle and be free."

THIRTEEN

The Second Shadow

"No!" shouted Khadgar, and the vision ebbed at once. They were alone in the dining hall once more, at the center of an ornate pattern made of crushed agates and rose quartz.

His ears tingled and the corners of his vision seemed to close in on him. He had sunk to one knee, but was unaware that he had even moved. Above him and to his right, Garona's voice sounded hushed, almost strangled.

"Medivh," she said quietly. "The Old Man. It couldn't be."

"It can be," said Khadgar. His stomach felt like knotted snakes were churning within his flesh. His mind was already racing, and though he fervently wished to deny it, he knew its destination.

"No," said Garona, grimly. "It must be a misfire. A

false vision. We went looking for one thing and found something else. You said that's happened before."

"Not like this," said Khadgar. "We may not be shown what we want, but we are always shown the truth."

"Perhaps its just a warning," said the half-orc.

"It makes sense," said Khadgar, and there was the sound of rust and regret in his voice. "Think about it. That's why the wards were still intact after we were attacked. He was already within the wards, and summoned the demon within."

"It didn't seem like him," said Garona. "Perhaps it was an illusion, some magical fakery. It didn't seem like him."

"It was him," said the apprentice, rising now. "I know the master's voice. I know the master's face. In all his moods and manners."

"But it was like someone else was wearing that face," said Garona. "Something false. Like he was a set of clothes, or a suit of armor, that someone else was wearing."

Khadgar looked at the half-orc. Her voice was tremulous, and tears pooled in the corners of her wide eyes. She wanted to believe. She truly wanted to believe.

Khadgar wanted to believe as well. He nodded slowly. "It could be a trick. It still could be him. He could be tricking that orc, convincing him to come here. Maybe a vision of the future?"

Now it was Garona's turn to shake her head. "No. That was Gul'dan. He's here already. He herded us through the portal. This was in the past, this was their first meeting. But why would Medivh want to bring the orcs to Azeroth?"

"It explains why he hasn't done much to oppose them," said Khadgar. He shook his head, trying to loosen the thoughts that were lodged there. So many things suddenly made more sense. Odd disappearances. Little interest in the increasing number of orcs. Even bringing a half-orc into the castle.

He regarded Garona and wondered how deeply she was involved in the plot. She seemed completely taken aback by the news, yet was she a conspirator, or another pawn in the shadowplay that Medivh seemed to be running?

"We need to find out," he said simply. "We need to know why he was there. What he was doing. He is the Guardian—we should not condemn him on a single vision."

Garona nodded slowly. "So we ask him. How?"

Khadgar opened his mouth to respond, but another voice sounded through the halls.

"What's all this brouhaha?" said Medivh, rounding the corner at the dining hall's entrance.

Khadgar's throat constricted and went dry.

The Magus stood in the doorway, and Khadgar looked at him, hunting for something in his walk, his appearance, his voice. Anything to betray his presence. There was nothing. This was Medivh.

"What are you children up to?" said the Magus, his gray brows furrowing.

Khadgar struggled for an answer, but Garona said, "The Apprentice was showing me a spell he was working on." Her voice fluttered.

Medivh grunted. "Another of your visions, Young Trust? They're bad enough around here, without you calling up the past. Come out of there at once—we have work to do. And you as well, Emissary."

His voice was measured and understanding, but firm. The stern voice of the wise mentor. Khadgar took a step forward, but Garona grabbed him by the arm.

"Shadows," she hissed.

Khadgar blinked, and looked at the Magus again. Impatience showed on his face now, and disapproval. His shoulders were still broad, he held himself upright despite the pressures on him. He was dressed in robes Khadgar had seen him wear often before.

And behind him trailed two shadows. One directly away from the torch, and the other, equally dark, at an odd angle.

Khadgar hesitated, and Medivh's disapproval deepened, a storm gathering on his face. "What is the matter, Young Trust?"

"We should clean up our mess," said Khadgar, trying to be light. "Don't want to make Moroes work too hard. We will catch up."

"Negotiation is not part of an apprentice's duties," said Medivh. "Now come here at once."

No one moved. Garona said, "Why doesn't he come into the room?"

Why indeed, thought Khadgar. Instead he said, "One question, Master?"

"What now?" grunted the master mage.

"Why did you visit the orc Gul'dan's dreams?" said Khadgar, feeling his throat tighten as he asked, "Why did you show the orcs how to come to this world?"

Medivh's glare shifted to Garona. "I was unaware Gul'dan told you of me. He didn't strike me as being unwise, or a chatterbox."

Garona took a step back, but this time Khadgar restrained her. She said, "I didn't know. Until now."

Medivh snorted. "It matters little. Now come here. Both of you."

"Why did you show the orcs the way here?" repeated Khadgar.

"You do not negotiate with your betters!" snapped the mage.

"Why did you bring the orcs to Azeroth?" asked Khadgar, pleading now.

"It is none of your business, child. You *will* come here! Now!" The Magus's face was livid and twisted.

"With respect, sir," said Khadgar, and his words felt like dagger-thrusts, "no, I will not."

Medivh thundered in rage. "Child, I will have you . . ."and as he spoke, he stepped into the room.

Sparks flew up at once, bathing the older mage in a shower of light. The Magus staggered back a step, then raised his hands, and muttered a curse.

"What?" began Garona.

"Circle of Warding," snapped Khadgar. "To keep summoned demons at bay. The Magus cannot cross it."

"But if it only affects demons, why not? Unless . . ." Garona, looked at Khadgar. "No," she said. "Can the circle hold him back?"

Khadgar thought of jackstraw laid across the wards in the tower at Stormwind, and at the energy blossoming by the doorway. He shook his head.

Instead he shouted at the Magus, "Is this what you did to Huglar and Hugarin? And Guzbah? And the others? Did they figure things out?"

"They were further from the truth than you were, child," said the illuminated Magus through gritted teeth, "But I had to be careful. I forgave your curiosity for your youth, and thought that loyalty—" He grunted now as the protective wards resisted him. "—I thought that loyalty still mattered in this world."

The protective wards blazed as Medivh moved into them, and Khadgar could see the fields distorting around the Magus's outstretched palms. The flickering of the sparks seemed to catch Medivh's beard on fire, and smoke curled up like horns from his forehead.

And then Khadgar's heart sank, for he realized that what he was seeing was another image, this one laid over the image of the beloved mage. The image that belonged to the second shadow.

"He's going to get through," said Garona.

Khadgar gritted his teeth, "Eventually. He's pouring huge amounts of power into breaking the circle."

"Can he do that?" asked the half-orc.

"He's the Guardian of Tirisfal," said Khadgar. "He can do whatever he wants. It just takes time."

"Well, can we get out of here?" Garona sounded panicked now.

"Only way out is past him," said Khadgar.

Garona looked around. "Blow out a wall, then. New exit."

Khadgar looked at the stonework of the tower, but shook his head.

"Well, try something!"

"I'll try this," said Khadgar. Before them, the figure of Medivh, taller now and wreathed in lightning, loomed up in the smoke.

Calming himself, he pulled the magical energies into himself. He made the motions he had made only minutes before, and intoned the words lost to mortal men, and when he had compressed the energies into a single ball of light, he released it.

"Bring me a vision," said Khadgar, "of one who has fought this beast before!"

There was a brief bit of disorientation, and for a moment Khadgar thought the spell had misfired and transported them to the observatory atop the tower. But no, it was now night around them, and an imperious, angry female voice split the air.

"You *dare* strike your own mother?" shouted Aegwynn, her own face livid with rage.

Aegwynn stood at one end of the observatory deck,

Medivh at the other. It was Medivh as he knew him—tall, proud, and apparently worried. Neither she nor the past-Medivh paid any attention to either Khadgar or Garona. With a start, Khadgar realized that the present incarnation of Medivh was present as well, sparkling along one wall. The pair from the past ignored him as well, but the present-Medivh was watching the spectacle played out before them.

"Mother, I thought you were being hysterical," said the past-Medivh.

"So a mystic bolt would bring me to my senses?" snapped the previous Guardian. Khadgar saw that she was much older now. Her blond hair was now white, and there were tight wrinkles around her eyes and mouth. Still, she held the presence of the earlier forms he had seen. "Now," she said, "answer my question."

"Mother, you're not seeing things right," said the past-Medivh.

"Answer," snapped Aegwynn sternly. "Why did you bring the orcs to Azeroth?"

"No wonder he was so testy when you asked him that," said Garona. Khadgar shushed her, and kept an eye on the present-Medivh. The present incarnation had ceased to press against the walls of the wards, and his face seemed to have lost its emotion.

"Mother?" said the present-Medivh. His face looked credulous.

"You don't *HAVE* an answer, do you?" said Aegwynn. "This is some little game you're playing. Some challenge for Llane and Lothar to amuse themselves with? The power of the *Tirisfalen* is no game, child. There are more orcs coming in all the time, and I am hearing of caravans being raided near the Black Morass. A novice could track back to your Portal, but only your mother would be able to taste the power that wrapped it. Again, child, how do you account for yourself?"

Khadgar wilted under the older woman's invective, and half-expected the past-Medivh to flee the room. Instead, Medivh surprised him. He laughed deeply.

"Does your mother's disproval amuse you, child?" said Aegwynn sternly.

"No," said Medivh, flashing a deep, predatory grin. "But my mother's stupidity does."

Khadgar looked across the room, and saw the present-Medivh flinch at the sound of his past incarnation's words.

"You dare," thundered Aegwynn, raising her hand. A sphere of blazing-white light erupted from her palm and lanced toward the past-Medivh. The Magus raised a hand and turned it aside with ease.

"I do, Mother," said the phantom of the past. "And I have the power for it. The power that you invested me with at my conception, a power that I did not want or request." The phantom-Medivh gestured, and the top-most floor was alight with a blazing bolt. Aegwynn caught the energy herself, but Khadgar noted that she had to raise both hands, and still was staggered back.

"But *why* did you let the orcs into Azeroth?" hissed

the older woman. "There is no need. You put entire populations at risk, and to what end?"

"To break the cycle, of course," said the past-Medivh. "To smash the clockwork universe that you have built for me. Everything in its place, including your child. If you could not continue on as Guardian, your hand-picked, born and groomed successor would, but would be locked into his script as tightly as any of your other pawns."

The present-Medivh had sunk to his knees, his eyes locked on the tableaux before him. He was mouthing the words that his past-self had spoken.

Garona tugged on Khadgar's sleeve, and he nodded. The pair left the heart of the wards, and began to edge around the room, trying to ease behind the present incarnation of the Magus.

"But, the risk, child . . ." said Aegwynn.

"Risk?" said Medivh. "Risk to whom? Not to me, not with the power of the *Tirisfalen* at my command. To the rest of the Order? They worry more about internal politics than demons. To the human nations? Fat and happy, protected from dangers that they do not even know about? Is anyone important really at risk?"

"You're playing with forces greater than yourself, Son," said Aegwynn. Khadgar and Garona were nearly to the door, but the present-Medivh was held rapt by the vision.

"Oh, of course," said the Magus's past with a snarl. "Thinking that I could handle powers like that would be the sin of Pride. Sort of like thinking you could match wits with a demon lord and come out on top."

They were behind Medivh now, and Garona reached for the knife inside her blouse. Khadgar stopped her hand and shook his head. They slipped behind Medivh. Tears were starting to form at the old man's eyes.

"What happens if these orcs succeed?" said Aegwynn. "They worship dark gods and shadows. Why would you give Azeroth to them?"

"*When* they succeed," said the past Medivh, "they will make me their leader. They respect strength, Mother, unlike you or the rest of this sorry world. And thanks to you, I am the strongest thing in this world. And I will have broken the shackles that you and others have placed on me, and I will rule."

There was a silence in the vision, and Khadgar and Garona froze, holding their breath. Would the present Medivh notice them in the silence?

Aegwynn, speaking from the years past, held his attention. "You are not my son," she said.

The present Medivh put his face in his hands. His past version said, "No. I have never been your son. Never truly yours, in any case."

And the past Magus laughed. It was a deep, thundering laugh that Khadgar had heard before, on the icy steppes, when last these two battled.

Aegwynn looked shocked, "Sargeras?" she spat, in final recognition. "I killed you."

"You killed a body, witch. You only killed my physical form!" snarled the Medivh of the past, and already Khadgar could see the overlay of the second being, the alternate shadow, that consumed him. A creature of shadow and flame, with a beard of fire and great ebon horns. "Killed it and hid it away in a tomb beneath the sea. But I was willing to sacrifice it to gain a greater prize."

Despite herself, Aegwynn put a hand over her stomach.

"Yes, Mother dear," said the past Medivh, the flames licking at his beard, the horns forming out of smoke before his brows. He was Medivh, but Sargeras as well. "I hid in your womb, and passed into the slumbering cells of your unformed child. A cancer, a blight, a birth defect that you would never surmise. Killing you was impossible, seducing you unlikely. So I made myself your heir."

Aegwynn shouted a curse and lurched her hands upward, her anger wrapped around words not made for human voices. A bolt of scintillating rainbow energy struck the Medivh/Sargeras creature full in the chest.

The phantom of the past staggered back one step, then two, then raised a single hand and caught the energy cast at him. The room smelled of cooking meat, and the Sargeras/Medivh snarled and spat. He invoked a spell of his own, and Aegwynn was flung across the room.

"I cannot kill you, Mother," snapped the demonic form. "Some part of me keeps me from doing that. But I *will* break you. Break you and banish you, and by the time you've healed, by the time you've walked back from where I will send you, this land will be mine. This land, and the power of the Order of Tirisfal!"

In the present day, Medivh let out the howl of a lost soul, screaming to the heavens for forgiveness that will never be forthcoming.

"That's our cue," said Garona, pulling on Khadgar's robe. "Let's get while the getting is good."

Khadgar hesitated for a moment, then followed her to the stairs.

They tumbled down the stone stairs three at a time, almost slamming into Moroes.

"Excited," he noted calmly. "Problem?"

Garona hurdled down past the castellan, but Khadgar grabbed the older man and said, "The master has gone mad."

"More than usual?" replied Moroes.

"It's not a joke," said Khadgar, then his eyes lit up. "Do you have the whistle to summon gryphons?"

The servant raised a rune-carved piece of metal. "Wish me to summon . . ."

"I'll do it," said Khadgar, grabbing the item from his hands, and hurtling after Garona. "He'll be after us, but you had better run as well. Take Cook and flee as far as you can."

And with that Khadgar was lost to view.

"Flee?" said Moroes to the apprentice's retreating form; then he snorted. "Wherever would I go?"

FOURTEEN
Flight

They had made it several miles when the gryphon began to misbehave. Only a single beast had answered Khadgar's summons, and bridled as Garona approached it. Only by sheer strength of will did the young mage get the gryphon to accept the half-orc's presence. They could hear Medivh screaming and cursing long after they have left the circle of hills. They tilted the gryphon toward Stormwind, and Khadgar dug his heels deeply into the gryphon's haunches.

They had made good speed, but now the gryphon bucked beneath him, trying to tear at the reins, trying to turn back toward the mountains. Khadgar tried to break the beast, to keep it to its course, but it became increasingly agitated.

"What's wrong with it?" asked Garona over his shoulder.

"Medivh is calling it back," said Khadgar. "It wants to go back to Karazhan."

Khadgar wrestled with the reins, even tried the whistle, but at last had to admit defeat. He brought the gryphon down on a low, bare tor, and slid from its back after Garona had climbed off. As soon as he touched ground, the gryphon was aloft again, beating its heavy wings against the darkening air, climbing to return the call of its master.

"Think he will follow?" asked Garona.

"I don't know," said Khadgar. "But I don't want to be here if he does. We'll make for Stormwind."

They stumbled about for most of the evening and night, finding a dirt track, then following it in the general direction of Stormwind. There was no immediate pursuit nor strange lights in the sky, and before dawn the pair rested briefly, huddling beneath a great cedar.

They saw no one alive during the next day. There were houses burned to the foundations, and clumps of newly hummocked earth that marked buried families. Overturned and smashed carts were common, as were great burned circles heaped with ash. Garona noted that this was how the orcs dealt with their dead, after the bodies had been looted.

The only animals they saw were dead—disemboweled pigs by a shattered farmhouse, the skeletal remains of a horse, consumed save for the frightened, twisted head. They moved in silence through one despoiled farmstead after another.

"Your people have been thorough," Khadgar said at last.

"They pride themselves on such matters," said Garona, grimly.

"Pride?" said Khadgar, looking around him. "Pride in destruction? In despoiling? No human army, no human nation would burn down everything in its path, or kill animals without purpose."

Garona nodded. "It is the orc way—do not leave enough standing that their foes could use against them. If they could not use it immediately—as fodder, as quarters, as plunder, then it should be put to the torch. The borders of orc clans are often desolate places, as each side seeks to deny the other resources."

Khadgar shook his head. "These are *not* resources," he said hotly. "These are lives. This land was once green and verdant, with fields and forests. Now it's a wasteland. Look at this! Can there be any peace between humans and orcs?"

Garona said nothing. They continued in on silence that day, and camped in the shambles of an inn. They slept in separate rooms, he in the wreckage of the common room, she moving farther back to the kitchen. He didn't suggest they stay together, and neither did she.

Khadgar was awakened by the growls of his stomach. They had fled the tower with little but what they had on their backs, and save for some foraged berries and ground nuts, they had not eaten in over a day.

The young mage extricated himself from the rain-damp straw tic that made his bed, his joints protesting. He had not camped in the open since his arrival at Karazhan, and he felt out of shape. The fear of the previous day had ebbed entirely, and he wondered about his next move.

Stormwind was their stated target, but how would he get someone like Garona into the city? Maybe find something to disguise her. Or did she even want to come? Now that she was free of the tower, maybe it would be better for her to rejoin Gul'dan and the Stormreaver clan.

Something moved along the wrecked side of the building. Probably Garona. She had to be as hungry as Khadgar. She hadn't complained, but he assumed from the wreckage left behind that orcs required a lot of food to keep them in top fighting form.

Khadgar stood up, shook the cobwebs from his mind, and leaned out the remains of a window to ask her if there was anything left in the kitchen.

And was faced with one edge of a huge double-bladed ax, leveled at his neck.

At the opposite end of the ax was the jade-green face of an orc. A real orc. Khadgar had not realized until now how accustomed to Garona's face he had become, such that the heavy jaw and sloped brow were a shock to him.

The orc growled, "Wuzzat?"

Khadgar slowly raised both hands, all the while calling up in his mind the magical energy. A simple spell, enough to knock the creature aside, to get Garona and get away.

Unless Garona had brought them here, he suddenly realized.

He hesitated, and that was enough. He heard something behind him, but did not get to turn as something large and heavy came down on the back of his neck.

He could not have been out long—long enough for a half-dozen orcs to spill into the room and start pushing through the rubble with their axes. They wore green armbands. Bleeding Hollow clan, his memory told him. He stirred, and the first orc, the one with the double-bladed ax, spun on him again.

"Wharsyurstuth?" said the orc. "Wharyuhidit?"

"What?" asked Khadgar, wondering if it was the orc's voice or his own ears that were mangling the language.

"Your stuff," said the orc, slower. "Your gear. You gots nothing. Where did you hide it?"

Khadgar spoke without thinking. "No stuff. Lost it earlier. No stuff."

The orc snorted. "Then you die," he snarled, and raised his blade.

"No!" shouted Garona from the ruined doorway. She looked like she had spent a bad night, but had a brace of hares on a leather thong hanging from her belt. She had been out hunting. Khadgar felt mildly embarrassed for his earlier thoughts.

"Git out, half-breed," snapped the orc. "None of your business."

"You're killing my property, that makes it my business," said Garona.

Property? thought Khadgar, but held his tongue.

"Prop'ty?" lisped the orc. "Who's you to have prop'ty?"

"I am Garona Halforcen," snarled the woman, twisting her face into a mask of rage. "I serve Gul'dan, warlock of the Stormreaver clan. Damage my property and you'll have to deal with him!"

The orc snorted again. "Stormreavers? Pah! I hear they are a weak clan, pushed around by their warlock!"

Garona gave him a steely glare. "What I *hear* was that Bleeding Hollow failed to support the Twilight Hollow clan in the recent attack on Stormwind, and that both clans were thrown back. I *hear* that humans beat you in a fair fight. Is that true?"

"Dat's beside the point," said the Bleeding Hollow orc. "Dey had horses."

"Maybe I can . . ." said Khadgar, trying to rise to his feet.

"Down, slave!" shouted Garona, cuffing him hard and sending him backward. "You speak when spoken to, and not before!"

The lead orc took the opportunity to take a step forward, but as soon as Garona had finished she wheeled again, and a long-bladed dagger was pointed at the orc's midsection. The other orcs backed away from the brewing fight.

"Do you dispute my ownership?" snarled Garona, fire in her eyes and her muscles tensed to drive the blade through the leather armor.

There was silence for a moment. The Bleeding Hollow orc looked at Garona, looked at the sprawled Khadgar, and looked at Garona again. He snorted and said, "Go get something worth fighting for, first, half-breed!"

And with that the orc leader backed away. The others relaxed, and started to file out of the ruined common room.

One of his subordinates asked him as they left the building, "What duz she have a use for human slave anyway?"

The orc leader said something that Khadgar could not hear. The subordinate shouted from outside, "Dat's *disgusting!*"

Khadgar tried to stand, but Garona waved her hand for him to stay down. Despite himself, Khadgar flinched.

Garona moved to the empty window, watched for a moment, then returned to where Khadgar had propped himself up against the wall.

"I think they're gone," she said at last. "I was afraid they might double back to even the score. Their leader is probably going to be challenged tonight by his subordinates."

Khadgar touched the tender side of his face. "I'm fine, thanks for asking."

Garona shook her head. "You idiot of a paleskin! If I hadn't knocked you down, the orc leader would have killed you outright, and then turned on me because I couldn't keep you in line."

Khadgar sighed deeply. "Sorry. You're right."

"You're right I'm right," said Garona. "They kept you alive long enough for me to get back only because they thought you'd hidden something in the inn. That you wouldn't be dumb enough to be out in the middle of a war zone without equipment."

"Did you have to hit that hard?" asked Khadgar.

"To convince them? Yes. Not that I didn't enjoy it." She threw the hares at him. "Here, skin these and get the water boiling. There're still pots and some tubers left in the kitchen."

"Despite what you're telling your friends," said Khadgar, "I am not your slave."

Garona chuckled. "Of course. But I caught breakfast. You get to cook it!"

Breakfast was a hearty stew of rabbit and potato, seasoned with herbs Khadgar found in the remains of the kitchen garden and mushrooms Garona picked in the wilderness. Khadgar checked the mushrooms to see if any of them were poisonous. None of them were.

"Orcs use their young as taste-testers," said Garona. "If they survive, they know its good for the community."

They set out on the road again, heading for Stormwind. Once more, the woods were eerily quiet, and all they encountered was the remains of war.

About midday, they came upon the Bleeding Hollow orcs once more. They were in a wide clear space around a shattered watchtower, all facedown. Something large, heavy, and sharp had torn through their back armor, and several were missing their heads.

Garona quickly moved from body to body, pulling salvageable gear from them. Khadgar scanned the horizon.

Garona shouted over, "Are you going to help?"

"In a moment," said Khadgar. "I want to make sure that whatever killed our friends is not still around."

Garona scanned the edges of the clearing, then looked skyward. Nothing was overhead but low, ink-spattered clouds.

"Well?" she said. "I don't hear anything."

"Neither did the orcs, until it was too late," said Khadgar, joining her at the orc leader's body. "They were hit in the back, while running, and from an attacker taller than they were." He pointed at hoof prints in the dust. They were those of iron-shod, heavy horses. "Cavalry. Human cavalry."

Garona nodded. "So we're getting close, at least. Take what you can from them. We can use their rations—they're nasty but nutritious. And take a weapon, at least a knife."

Khadgar looked at Garona. "I've been thinking."

Garona laughed. "I wonder how many human disasters start with *that* line."

"We're within range of Stormwind patrols," said Khadgar. "I don't think Medivh is following us, at least not directly. So maybe we should split up."

"Thought of that," said Garona, rummaging through one of the orc's packs, and pulling out first a cloak, and then a small cloth-wrapped parcel. She opened the parcel to find a flint and steel and a vial of oily liquid. "Fire-starting kit," she explained. "Orcs love fire, and this is a quick starter."

"So you think we should split up," said Khadgar.

"No," said Garona. "I said I thought about it. The trouble is that no one is in control of this area, human or orc. You might walk fifty yards away and hit another patrol of the Bleeding Hollow clan, and I might get ambushed by your cavalry buddies. If the two of us are together, there's a better chance of survival. One is the other's slave."

"Prisoner," said Khadgar. "Humans don't take slaves."

"Sure you do," said Garona. "You just call them something else. So we should stay together."

"And that's it?" said Khadgar.

"Mostly," said Garona. "Plus there is the little fact that I haven't reported in to Gul'dan for some time. If and when we do run into him, I will explain that I was held prisoner at Karazhan, and he should have shown more wisdom than to send one of his followers into a trap."

"You think he'd believe that?" asked Khadgar.

"I am uncertain that he would," said Garona. "Which is another good reason to stay with you."

"You could buy yourself a lot of influence with what you've learned," said Khadgar.

Garona nodded. "Yeah. If I don't get an ax through my brain before I get to tell anyone. No, for the moment I'll take my chances with the paleskins. Now, I need one more thing."

"What's that?"

"I need to gather the bodies together, and heap some brush and tinder over them. We can cache what we don't need, but we need to burn the bodies. It's the least we can do."

Khadgar frowned. "If the heavy horse are still in the area, a plume of smoke will bring them at once."

"I know," said Garona, looking around at the fragments of the patrol. "But it's the right thing to do. If you found human soldiers killed in an ambush, wouldn't you want to bury them?"

Khadgar's mouth made a grim line, but he didn't say anything. Instead, he went to grab the farthest orc and drag him back to the remains of the watchtower. Within an hour, they had stripped the bodies and set the remains ablaze.

"Now we should go," said Khadgar, as Garona watched the smoke spiral upward.

"Won't this call the horsemen?" said Garona.

"Yes," said Khadgar. "And it will also send a message—

there are orcs here. Orcs who feel secure enough to burn the bodies of their comrades. I'd rather have a chance to explain ourselves at close range than facing a charging warhorse, thank you very much."

Garona nodded, and, stolen cloaks flapping behind them, they left the burning watchtower.

Garona spoke truly, in that the orc version of field rations were a nasty concoction of hardened syrup, nuts, and what Khadgar swore was boiled rat. Still, it kept them going, and they made good time.

A day and a day passed and the country opened up now into sprawling fields that rippled with growing crops. The land was no less desolate, though, the stables empty and the houses already collapsed in on themselves. They found several more burned spots of orc funerals, and an increasing number of hummocks marking the passing of human families and patrols.

Still, they kept to the brush and fence lines as much as possible. The more open terrain made it easier to see any other units, but left them more exposed. They holed up in a mostly intact farmhouse while a small army of orcs moved along the ridgeline.

Khadgar watched the line of units surge forward. Grunts, cavalry mounted on great wolves, and catapults done up in fanciful decorations of skulls and dragons. Beside him, Garona watched the procession and said, "Idiots."

Khadgar shot her a questioning glance.

"They could not be more exposed," she explained. "We can see them, and the paleskins can see them as well. This lot doesn't have an objective—they're just rolling through the countryside, looking for a fight. Looking for a noble death in battle." She shook her head.

"You don't think much of your people," said Khadgar.

"I don't think much of *any* people, right now," said Garona. "The orcs disown me, the humans will kill me. And the only human I really trusted turned out to be a demon."

"Well, there's me," said Khadgar, trying not to sound hurt.

Garona winced. "Yes, there is you. You are human, and I trust you. But I thought, I really thought, that Medivh was going to make a difference. Powerful, important, and willing to talk. Unprejudiced. But I deceived myself. He's just another madman. Maybe that's just my place—working for madmen. Maybe I'm just another pawn in the game. What did Medivh call it? The unforgiving clockwork of the universe?"

"Your role," said Khadgar, "is whatever you choose it to be. Medivh always wanted that as well."

"You think he was sane when he said that?" asked the half-orc.

Khadgar shrugged. "As sane as he ever was. I believe he was. And it sounds like you want to believe that as well."

"Ayep," drawled Garona. "It was all so simple, when I was working for Gul'dan. His little eyes and ears. Now I don't know who's right and who's wrong.

Which people are my people? Either of them? At least you don't have to worry about divided loyalties."

Khadgar didn't say anything, but looked out into the gathering dusk. Somewhere, over the horizon, the orc army had run into something. There was the low glow of a false dawn along the edge of the world in that direction, marked with the reflection of sudden flashes off the low clouds, and the echoes of war drums and death sounded like distant thunder.

Another day and a day passed. Now they moved through abandoned towns and marketplaces. The buildings were more whole now, but still abandoned. There were signs of recent inhabitation, both by human and orc troops, but now the only inhabitants were ghosts and memories.

Khadgar broke into a likely-looking shop, and while its shelves had been stripped bare, the hearth still had wood in the hopper and there were potatoes and onions in a small bin in the basement. Anything would be an improvement after the orc's iron rations.

Khadgar laid the fire and Garona took a cauldron to the nearby well. Khadgar thought about the next step. Medivh was a danger, perhaps a greater danger than the orcs. Could he be reasoned with, now? Convinced to shut the portal? Or was it too late?

Just the knowledge that there *was* a portal would be good news. If the humans could locate it, even shut it, it would strand the orcs on this world. Deny them reinforcements from Draenor.

The apprentice was pulled from his thoughts by the commotion outside. The clash of metal on metal. Human voices, bellowing.

"Garona," muttered Khadgar, and headed for the door.

He found them by the well. A patrol of about ten footmen, dressed in the blue livery of Azeroth, swords drawn. One of them was cradling a bleeding arm, but another pair had Garona in their grip, one restraining each arm. Her long-bladed dagger was on the ground. As Khadgar rounded the corner, the sergeant back-handed her across the face with a mailed glove.

"Where are the others?" he snarled. The half-orc's mouth leaked blackish-purple blood.

"Leave her alone!" shouted Khadgar. Without thinking, he pulled the energies into his mind and released a quick spell.

A brilliant light blossomed around Garona's head, a miniature sun that caught the humans unaware. The two footmen holding Garona let go of her, and she slid to the ground. The sergeant raised a hand to protect his eyes, and the remainder of the patrol was sufficiently surprised, so that Khadgar was among them and at Garona's side in a matter of moments.

"S'prised," muttered Garona through a split lip. "Lemme get my wind back."

"Stay down," said Khadgar softly. To the blinking sergeant he barked, "Are you in charge of this rabble?"

By now most of the footmen had recovered, and

had their swords level. The two next to Garona had backed up a pace, but they were watching her, not Khadgar.

The sergeant spat, "Who are *you* to interfere with the military? Get him out of the way, boys!"

"Hold!" said Khadgar, and the soldiers, having experienced his spells once, only advanced a single pace. "I am Khadgar, apprentice to Medivh the Magus, friend and ally to your King Llane. I have business with him. Take us at once to Stormwind."

The sergeant just chuckled. "Sure you are, and I am Lord Lothar. Medivh doesn't take apprentices. Even I know that. And who is your sweetheart, there, then?"

"She is . . ." Khadgar hesitated for a moment. "She is my prisoner. I am taking her to Stormwind for questioning."

"Huh," grunted the sergeant. "Well, boyo, we *found* your prisoner out here, armed, with you nowhere in sight. I'd say your prisoner escaped. Pity the orc would rather die than surrender."

"Don't touch her!" said Khadgar, and he raised his hand. Flames danced within his curled fingers.

"You're flirting with your own death," snarled the sergeant. In the distance, Khadgar could hear the heavy footfalls of horses. Reinforcements. But would they be any more willing to listen to a half-orc and a spellcaster than this lot were?

"You're making a horrible mistake, sir," said Khadgar, keeping his voice level.

"Stay out of this, boy," commanded the sergeant. "Take the orc. Kill her if she resists!"

The footmen took another step forward, those closest to Garona bending down to grab her again. She tried to squirm away and one kicked her with a heavy boot.

Khadgar bit back tears and unleashed the spell against the sergeant. The ball of flame slammed into his knee. The sergeant howled and dropped to the ground.

"Now stop this," hissed Khadgar.

"Kill them!" shouted the sergeant, his eyes wide in pain. "Kill them both!"

"Hold!" came another voice, darker and deeper, muffled by a great helm. The horsemen had arrived in the town square. About twenty riders, and Khadgar's heart sank. More here than even Garona could take care of. Their leader was in full armor, with a visored helm. Khadgar could not see his face.

The young apprentice rushed forward. "Sir," he said. "Call off these men. I am the apprentice to Magus Medivh."

"I know who you are," said the commander. "Stand down!" he ordered. "Keep the orc guarded, but let her go!"

Khadgar gulped and continued. "I have a prisoner and important information for King Llane. I need to see Lord Lothar, at once!"

The commander lifted his visor. "So you shall, lad," said Lothar. "So you shall."

FIFTEEN
Beneath Karazhan

The discussion at Stormwind Castle had not gone well, and now they were circling Medivh's Tower on gryphon-back. Beneath them, in the gathering dusk, Karazhan loomed large and empty. No lights shone from any of its windows, and the observatory atop the structure was dark. Beneath a now-moonless sky, even the pale stones of the tower were dark and brooding.

There had been a heated discussion in the King's Privy Quarters the previous evening. Khadgar and Garona were there, although the half-orc was asked to surrender her knife to Lothar in the presence of His Majesty. The King's Champion was there as well, and a gaggle of advisors and courtiers all hovering around King Llane. Khadgar could not smell a single spell-caster in the group, and surmised that any that had survived Medivh's poaching were either on the battlefield or squirreled away for safekeeping.

As for the King himself, the young man from the early visions had grown up. He had the broad shoulders and sharp features of his youth, only now starting to surrender to middle age. Of all present, he was resplendent, and his blue robes shone among the others. He kept an open-faced helm to one side of his seat, a great helm with white wings, as if he expected to be called onto the battlefield at any moment.

Khadgar wondered if such a call was not exactly what Llane desired, remembering the headstrong youth of the troll-vision. A direct conflict on an open and level field, with his forces' eventual triumph never in doubt. He wondered how much of the assuredness derived from the faith in the Magus's eventual support. Indeed, it seemed that one led naturally to the other—that the Magus will always support Stormwind, and Stormwind will always hold as a result of the Magus's support.

The healers had tended to Garona's split lip, but could do nothing for her temper. Several times Khadgar winced as she bluntly described the orcish opinions of the master mage's sanity, of the paleskins in general, and Llane's troops in particular.

"The orcs are relentless," she said. "And they will not let up. They will be back."

"They did not get within bowshot of the walls," countered Llane. To Khadgar, his majesty seemed more amused than alarmed by Garona's direct manner and blunt warnings.

"They did not get within bowshot of the walls," repeated Garona. "This time. Next time they will. And the time after that they will get over the walls. I don't think you are taking the orcs sufficiently seriously, sire."

"I assure you, I take this very seriously," said Llane. "But I am also aware of the strengths of Stormwind. Of its walls, of its armies, of its allies, and of its heart. Perhaps if you saw them, you too would be less confident in the power of the orcs."

Llane was similarly adamant about the Magus as well. Khadgar laid everything out before the privy council, with assurances and additions from Garona. The visions of the past, the erratic behavior, the visions that were not visions at all but rather true demonstrations of Sargeras's presence in Karazhan. Of Medivh's culpability in the present assault on Azeroth.

"If I had a silver groat for every man who has told me that Medivh is mad, I would be richer than I am today," said Llane. "He has a plan, young sir. It's as simple as that. More times than I can count he has gone off on some mad dash or another, and Lothar here had worried his beard to tatters. And each time he's proved to be right. The last time he was here did he not hare off to hunt a demon, and bring it back within a few hours? Hardly the action of one demon-possessed to decapitate one of his own."

"But it might be the action of one who was trying to

maintain his own innocence," put in Garona. "No one saw him kill this demon, in the heart of your city. Could he not have summoned it up, then killed and provided it as the one responsible?"

"Supposition," grumbled the king. "No. With respect to both of you, I do not deny that you saw what you saw. Not even these 'visions' of the past. But I think the Magus is crazy like a fox, and all this is part of some larger plan of his. He always speaks of larger plans and greater cycles."

"With all due respect," said Khadgar. "The Magus may have a larger plan, but the question is, does Stormwind and Azeroth truly have a place within that plan?"

So went most of the evening. King Llane was adamant on all points—that Azeroth could, with their allies, destroy or drive back the orc hordes to its home world, that Medivh was working on some plan that no one else could understand, and that Stormwind could withstand any assault "as long as men with stout hearts were manning the walls and the throne."

Lothar for his part was mostly silent, only breaking in to ask a relevant question, then shaking his head when Khadgar or Garona gave him a truthful answer. Finally, he spoke up.

"Llane, don't let your security blind you!" he said. "If we cannot count on Magus Medivh as an ally, we are weakened. If we discount the capabilities of the orcs, we are lost. Listen to what they are saying!"

"I am listening," said the King. "But I hear not only

with my head but with my heart. We spent many years with young Medivh, both before and during his long sleep. He remembers his friends. And once he reveals his thinking, I'm sure even you will appreciate what a friend we have in the Magus."

At last the King rose and dismissed all, promising to take the matters under proper consideration. Garona was muttering under her breath, and Lothar gave them rooms without windows and with guards on the doors, just to be sure.

Khadgar tried to sleep, but the frustration kept him pacing the floor for most of the night. Finally, when exhaustion had finally claimed him, there was a sound pounding on the door.

It was Lothar, in full armor, with a uniform draped over his arm. "Sleep like the dead, will you?" he said, holding out the livery with a smile. "Put this on and meet us at the top of the tower in fifteen minutes. And hurry, lad."

Khadgar struggled into the gear, which included trousers, heavy boots, blue livery marked with the lion of Azeroth, and heavy-bladed sword. He thought twice about the sword, but slung it onto his back. It might prove useful.

There were no less than six gryphons clustered on the towers, rustling their great wings in agitation. Lothar was there, and Garona as well. She was similarly dressed to Khadgar, with the blue tabard marked with the lion of Azeroth, and a heavy sword.

"Don't," she growled at him, "say a word."

"You look very good in it," he said. "It goes with your eyes."

Garona snorted. "Lothar said the same thing. He tried to convince me by saying that you were wearing the outfit, too. *And* that he wanted to make sure that none of the others shot me thinking I was someone else."

"Others?" said Khadgar, and looked around. In the morning light, it was clear that there were other flights of gryphons on other towers. Around six, including theirs, the gryphons' wings pink with the unrisen sun. He was unaware that there were this many trained gryphons in the world, much less Stormwind. Lothar must have gone to talk to the dwarves. The air was cold and sharp as a dagger thrust.

Lothar hurried up to them, and adjusted Khadgar's sword so he could ride gryphon-back with it.

"His Majesty," grumbled Lothar, "has an abiding faith in the strength of the people of Azeroth and the thickness of the walls of Stormwind. It doesn't hurt that he also has good people who take care of things when he's wrong."

"Like us," said Khadgar, grimly.

"Like us," repeated Lothar. He looked at Khadgar hard and added, "I had asked you how he was, you know."

"Yes," said Khadgar. "And I told you the truth, or as much of it as I understood it at the time. And I felt loyal to him."

"I understand," said Lothar. "And I feel loyal to him as well. I want to make sure what you say is true. But I also want you to be able to do what needs to be done, if we have to do it."

Khadgar nodded. "You believe me, don't you?"

Lothar nodded grimly. "Long ago, when I was your age, I was tending to Medivh. He was in his coma, then, that long sleep that denied him much of his youth. I thought it was a dream, but I swore there was another man opposite me, also watching over the Magus. He seemed to be made of burnished brass, and he had heavy horns on his brow, and his beard made of flames."

"Sargeras," said Khadgar.

Lothar let out a deep breath. "I thought I had fallen asleep, that it was a dream, that it could not be what I thought it was. You see, I too felt loyal to him. But I never forgot what I saw. And as the years passed I began to realize that I had seen a bit of the truth, and that it may come to this. We may yet save Medivh, but we might find that the darkness is too deeply rooted. Then we will have to do something sudden, horrible, and absolutely necessary. The question is—Are you up to it?"

Khadgar thought for a moment, then nodded. His stomach felt like ice. Lothar raised a hand. On his command, the other flights of gryphons strained aloft, springing to life as the first rays of the dawn crested the earth's rim, the new sunlight catching their wings and turning them golden.

The chill feeling in the pit of Khadgar's stomach did not ebb on the long flight to Karazhan. Garona rode behind him, but neither spoke as the land fled beneath their wings.

The land had changed beneath their wings. Great fields were little more than blackened wreckage, dotted by the remnants of toppled foundations. Forests were uprooted to feed the engines of war, creating huge scars in the landscape. Open pits yawned wide, the earth itself wounded and stripped to reach the metals beneath. Columns of smoke rose up along the horizon, though whether they were from battlefields or forges Khadgar could not say. They flew through the day and the sun was ebbing along the horizon now.

Karazhan rose like an ebon shadow at the center of its crater, sucking in the last dying rays of the day and giving nothing back. No lights shone from the tower nor from any of the hollow windows. The torches that flamed without consuming their source had been extinguished. Khadgar wondered if Medivh had fled.

Lothar kneed his gryphon down, and Khadgar followed, quickly setting down, and slipping from the back of the winged beast. As soon as he touched the ground, the gryphon shot aloft again, letting out a shrieking cry and heading north.

The Champion of Azeroth was already at the stairs, his huge shoulders tensed, his heavy frame moving with the quiet, agile grace of a cat, his blade drawn. Garona slunk forward as well, her hand dipping into her tabbard and coming up with her long-bladed dagger. The heavy blade from Stormwind clattered against Khadgar's hip, and he felt like a clumsy creature of stone compared to the other two. Behind him, more gryphons landed and discharged their warriors.

The observatory parapet was empty, and the upper level of the master mage's study deserted but not empty. There were still tools scattered about, and the smashed remnants of the golden device, an astrolabe, rested on the mantel. So if the tower was truly abandoned, it was done quickly.

Or it had not been abandoned at all.

Torches were fired and the party descended the myriad stairs, with Lothar, Garona, and Khadgar in the lead. Once these walls were familiar, were home, the many stairs a daily challenge. Now, the wall-mounted torches, with their cool, frozen flame, had been extinguished, and the moving torches of the invaders cast myriad armed shadows against the wall, giving the halls an alien, almost nightmarish cast. The very walls seemed to hold menace, and Khadgar expected every darkened doorway to hold a deadly ambush.

There was nothing. The galleries were empty, the banquet halls bare, the meeting rooms as devoid of life and furnishings as ever. The guest quarters were still furnished, but unoccupied. Khadgar checked his own quarters: Nothing had changed there.

Now the torchlight cast strange shadows on the walls of the library, twisting the iron frames and turning the bookcases into battlements. The books were untouched, and even Khadgar's most recent notes were still on the table. Had Medivh not thought enough of the library to take any of his volumes?

Tatters of paper caught Khadgar's eye, and he crossed to the shelves containing the epic poetry. This was new. Fragments of a scroll, now smashed and torn. Khadgar picked up a large piece, read a few words, then nodded.

"What is it?" said Lothar, looking like he expected the books to come to life at any moment and attack.

" 'The Song of Aegwynn,' " said Khadgar. "An epic poem about his mother."

Lothar grunted a note of understanding, but Khadgar wondered. Medivh had been here, after they had left. Yet only to destroy the scroll? Out of harsh memories of the Magus's conflict with his mother? Out of revenge for Sargeras's decisive loss to Aegwynn? Or did the act of destroying the scroll, the cipher used by the Guardians of Tirisfal, symbolize his resignation and final betrayal of the group?

Khadgar risked a simple spell—one used to divine magical presences—but came up with nothing more than the normal response when surrounded by magical tomes. If Medivh had cast a spell here, he had masked its presence sufficiently to beat anything Khadgar could manage.

Lothar noted the young mage tracing symbols into the air, and when he was done, said, "You'd best save your strength for when we find him."

Khadgar shook his head and wondered if they were going to find the Magus.

They found Moroes, instead, at the lowest level, near the entrance to the kitchen and larder. His crumpled form was splayed in the middle of the hallway, a bloody rainbow arcing along the floor to one side. His eyes were wide and open, but his face was surprisingly composed. Not even death seemed to surprise the castellan.

Garona dodged into the kitchen, and returned a moment later. Her face was a paler shade of green, and she held something up for Khadgar to see.

A set of rose-colored lenses, smashed. Cook. Khadgar nodded.

The bodies seemed to make the troops more alert now, and they moved to the great vault-like entranceway, and out into the courtyard itself. There had been no sign of Medivh, and only a few broken clues of his passing.

"Could he have another lair?" Lothar asked. "Another place he would hide?"

"He was often gone," said Khadgar. "Sometimes gone for days, then reappearing without warning." Something moved along the balcony overlooking the main entrance—just a slight wavering of the air. Khadgar started and stared at the location, but it looked normal.

"Perhaps he went to the orcs, to lead them," suggested the Champion.

Garona shook her head. "They would never accept a human leader."

"He couldn't vanish into thin air!" thundered Lothar. To the troops he shouted, "Form up! We're going to head back!"

Garona ignored the Champion, then said, "He didn't. Back into the tower." She parted the troops like a boat cutting through a choppy sea.

She disappeared once more in the open maw of the tower. Lothar looked at Khadgar, who shrugged and followed the half-orc.

Moroes had not moved, his blood smeared across the floor in a quarter circle, away from the wall. Garona touched that wall, as if trying to feel something along it. She frowned, cursed, and slapped the wall, which gave a very solid response.

"It should be here," she said.

"What should be?" asked Khadgar.

"A door," said the half-orc.

"There's never been a door here," said Khadgar.

"There's *always* been a door, probably," said Garona. "You've just never seen it. Look. Moroes died here," she stomped her foot next to the wall, "And then his body was moved, creating the smear of blood in the quarter-circle, to where we found it."

Lothar grunted assent, and started to run his hands along the wall as well.

Khadgar looked at the apparently blank wall. He had passed it five or six times a day. There should be nothing but earth and stone on the far side. Still . . .

"Stand away," the young mage said. "Let me try something."

The Champion and half-orc stood back, and Khadgar pulled the energies together for a spell. He has used it before, on real doors and locked books, but this was the first time he tried to work it on a door he could not see. He tried to envision the door, figuring how large it would have to be to move Moroes's body in the quarter circle, where the hinges would be, where the frame would be, and, if he wanted to keep it secure, where he would place the locks.

He envisioned the door, and flung a bit of magic into its unseen frame to unfasten those hidden locks. Half to his surprise, the wall shifted, and a seam appeared along one side. Not a lot, but enough to define the clear edges of a door that had not been there a moment before.

"Use your swords and pry it open," snarled Lothar, and the squad surged forward. The stone door resisted their attempts for a few moments, until some mechanism within it snapped loudly and the door swung outward, nuzzling Moroes's corpse as it did so, and revealed a stairway descending into the depths.

"He didn't vanish into thin air," said Garona grimly. "He stayed here, but went someplace no one else knew about."

Khadgar looked at Moroes's crumpled form. "Almost no one. But I wonder what else he has hidden."

They moved down the stairs, and a sense grew within Khadgar. While the upper levels felt spookily abandoned, the depths beneath the tower had a palpable aura of immediate menace and foreboding. The rough-hewn walls and floor were moist, and in the light of the torches seemed to undulate like living flesh.

It took a moment for Khadgar to realize that as the stairs continued to spiral down, they now had reversed their direction, moving opposite to the tower above, as if this descent was a mirror of that above.

Indeed, where an empty meeting room would be within the tower, here was a dungeon bedecked with unoccupied iron chains. Where a banquet hall stood unused above the surface was a room strewn with detritus and marked with mystic circles. The air felt heavy and oppressive here, as it had in the tower in Stormwind, where Huglar and Hugarin had been slain. Here was where the demon that attacked them had been summoned.

When they reached the level that mirrored the library, they found a set of iron-shod doors. The stairs continued to spiral down into the earth, but the company was brought up short here, regarding the mystic symbols carved deeply into the wood and dabbed with brownish blood. It seemed as if the wood itself was bleeding. Two huge rings of iron hung from the wounded doors.

"This would be the library," said Khadgar.

Lothar nodded. He had noted the similarities between the tower and this burrow as well. "See what he keeps here, if the books are all upstairs."

Garona said, "His study is at the top of the tower, with his observatory, so if he *is* here, he should be at the very bottom. We should press on."

But she was too late. As Khadgar touched the iron-shod doors, a spark leapt from his palm to the door, a signal, a magical trap. Khadgar had time to curse as the doors were flung open, back into the darkness of the library.

A kennel. Sargeras had no need for knowledge, so he turned the room over to his pets. The creatures lived within a darkness of their own making, and acrid smoke wafted out into the hallway.

There were eyes within. Eyes and flaming maws and bodies made of fire and shadow. They stalked forward, snarling.

Khadgar sketched runes in the air, pulling the energy together in his mind, to pull the doors closed again, as soldiers struggled with the great rings shut again. Neither spellcraft nor muscle could move the rings.

The beasts let out a harsh, choppy laugh, and crouched to spring.

Khadgar raised his hands to cast another spell, but Lothar batted them down.

"This is to waste your time and energy," he said. "It is to delay us. Head down and find Medivh."

"But they are . . ." started Khadgar, and the large demon-beast in the front leapt at them.

Lothar took two steps forward and brought up his blade to meet the leaping beast. As he pulled his blade upward, the runes etched deep into the metal blazed with a bright yellow light. For a half-second, Khadgar saw fear in the eyes of the demon-beast.

And then the arc of Lothar's cut intersected with the demon-beast's leap and the blade bit deep into the creature's flesh. Lothar's blade erupted from the creature's back, and he neatly bisected the forward portion of its torso in two. The beast had only a moment to squeal in pain as the blade pulled forward through its skull, completing the arch. The smoldering wreckage of the demon-beast, weeping fire and bleeding shadow, fell at Lothar's feet.

"Go!" thundered the Champion. "We'll take care of this and catch up."

Garona grabbed Khadgar, and pulled him down the stairs. Behind them, the soldiers had pulled their blades, as well, and the runes danced in brilliant flames as they drank deep of the shadows. The young mage and half-orc rounded the curve of the stairs, and behind them they heard the cries of the dying, from both human and inhuman throats.

They spiraled into the darkness, Garona holding a torch in one hand, dagger in the other. Now Khadgar noticed that the walls glowed with their own faint phosphorescence, a reddish hue like some nocturnal mushrooms deep within the forest. It was also growing warmer, and the sweat was beading along his forehead.

As they came to one of the dining halls, suddenly Khadgar's stomach wrenched and they were somewhere else. It moved suddenly upon them, like a leading edge of a summer storm.

They were atop one of the larger towers of Stormwind, and around them the city was in flames. Pillars of smoke rose from all sides, spreading into a black blanket above that snared the sun. A similar blanket of blackness surrounded the city walls, but this was made of orcish troops. From their viewpoint Khadgar and Garona could see the armies spread out like beetles on the verdant corpse that had been Stormwind's cropland. Now there were only siege towers and armed grunts, the colors of their banners a sickening rainbow.

The forests were gone as well, transformed into catapults that now rained fire down on the city itself. Most of the lower city was in flames, and as Khadgar watched, a section of the outer walls collapsed, and small dolls dressed in green and blue fought each other among the rubble.

"How did we get . . . ?" started Garona.

"Vision," said Khadgar bluntly, but he wondered if this was a random occurrence of the tower, or another delaying action by the Magus.

"I told the King. I told him, but he would not listen," she muttered. To Khadgar she said, "This is a vision of the future, then? How do we get out of the vision?"

The young mage shook his head. "We don't, at least for the moment. In the past these would come and go. Sometimes a good shock will break it."

A flaming piece of debris, a fiery missile from a catapult, passed within bowshot of the tower. Khadgar could feel the heat as it fell to earth.

Garona looked around. "At least it's just orc armies," she said grimly.

"That's good news?" said Khadgar, his eyes stinging as a column of smoke wafted over the tower.

"No demons in the orc armies," noted the half-orc. "If Medivh was with them, we would see much worse as well. Maybe we convinced him to help."

"I'm not seeing Medivh among our troops, either," said Khadgar, forgetting who he was speaking to for the moment. "Is he dead? Did he flee?"

"How far in the future are we?" asked Garona.

Behind them, there was a rise of voices in argument. The pair turned away from the parapet and saw that they were outside one of the royal audience halls, now converted into a coordination center against the assault. A small model of the city had been laid out on the table, and toy soldiers in the shapes of men and orcs were scattered around it. There was a constant flow of reports coming in as King Llane and his advisors hunched over the table.

"Breech along the Merchant's District Wall!"

"More fires in the lower city!"

"Large forces massing at the main gates again. It looks like spellcasters!"

Khadgar noted that none of the earlier courtiers were now present, replaced with grim-faced men in uniforms similar to their own. No sign of Lothar at the table, and Khadgar hoped he was on the front lines, carrying the battle to the foe.

Llane moved with a deft hand, as if his city was attacked on a regular basis. "Bring up the Fourth and Fifth Company to reinforce the breech. Get the militia to organize bucket brigades—take the water from the public baths. And bring up two squads of lancers to the main gate. When the orcs are about to attack, then launch a sortie against them. That will break the assault. Bring two mages over from the Goldsmith's street; are they done there?"

"That assault has been turned," came the report. "The mages are exhausted."

Llane nodded and said, "Have them stand down, then, pull back for an hour. Bring the younger mages from the academy instead. Send twice as many, but tell them to be careful. Commander Borton, I want your forces on the East wall. That's where I would hit next, if I were them."

To each commander in turn, Llane gave an assignment. There was no argument, no discussion, no suggestions. Each warrior in turn nodded and left. In the end, all that was left was King Llane and his small model of a city that was now in flames outside his window.

The king leaned forward, resting his knuckles on the table. His face looked worn and old. He looked up and said to the empty air, "You can make your report now."

The curtains opposite hissed against the floor as

Garona stepped out. The half-orc at Khadgar's side let out a gasp in surprise.

The future Garona was dressed in her customary black pants and black silk blouse, but wore a cloak marked with the lion's head of Azeroth. She had a wild look in her eyes. The present Garona gripped Khadgar's arm, and he could feel her nails dig into his arm.

"Bad news, sire," said Garona, approaching the King's side of the table. "The various clans are working together in this assault, unified under the Blackhand the Destroyer. None of them will betray the others until after Stormwind has fallen. Gul'dan is bringing up his warlocks by nightfall. Until then, the Blackrock clan will be trying to take the Eastern Wall." Khadgar heard a tremor in the half-orc's voice.

Llane let out a deep sigh, and said, "Expected and countered. We will throw this one back, just like the others. And we will hold until the reinforcements come. As long as men with stout hearts are manning the walls and the throne, Stormwind will hold."

The future-Garona nodded, and Khadgar now saw that large tears were pooling in the corners of her eyes. "The orc leaders agree with your assessment," she said, and her hand dipped into her black blouse.

Both Khadgar and the real Garona shouted as one as the future-Garona pulled her long-bladed dagger and shoved it upward beneath the King's left breast. She moved with a quickness and grace and left King Llane with nothing more than a puzzled expression on his face. His eyes were wide, and for a moment he hung there, suspended on her blade.

"The orc leaders agree with your assessment," she said again, and tears were running freely down the sides of her wide face. "And have enlisted an assassin to remove that strong heart on the throne. Someone you would let come close. Someone you would meet with alone."

Llane, King of Azeroth, Master of Stormwind, ally of wizard and warrior, slid to the floor.

"I'm sorry," said Garona.

"No!" shouted Garona, the present Garona, as she slipped to the floor herself. Suddenly they were back in the false dining hall. The wreckage of Stormwind was gone and the corpse of the king with it. The half-orc's tears remained, now in the eyes of the real Garona.

"I'm going to kill him," she said in a small voice. "I'm going to kill him. He treated me well, and listened when I talked, and I'm going to kill him. No."

Khadgar knelt down besides her. "It's okay. It may not be true. It may not happen. It's a vision."

"Its true," she said. "I saw it and I knew that it was true."

Khadgar was silent for a moment, reliving his own vision of the future, beneath a red-hued sky, battling Garona's people. He saw it and knew it was true as well. "We have to go," he said, but Garona just shook her head. "After all this, I thought I found someplace better than the orcs. But now I know, I'm going to destroy it all."

Khadgar looked up and down the stairs. No idea how Lothar's men were doing with the demons, no idea what lay at the base of the underground tower. His face formed a grim line, and he took a deep breath.

And slapped Garona hard across the face.

His own palm bled from striking a tusk, but the response on Garona was immediate. Her teary eyes widened and a mask of rage hardened on her expression.

"You idiot!" she shouted, and leapt on Khadgar bearing him over backward. "You never do that! You hear me! Do that again and I'll kill you!"

Khadgar was sprawled on his back, the half-orc on top of him. He didn't even see her draw the dagger, but now its blade was resting against the side of his neck.

"You can't," he managed with a harsh smile. "I had a vision of my own future. I think its true as well. If it is, then you can't kill me now. Same thing applies to you."

Garona blinked and rocked back on her haunches, suddenly in control again. "So if I am going to kill the King . . ."

"You're going to get out of here alive," said Khadgar. "So am I."

"But what if we're wrong," said Garona. "What if the vision is false?"

Khadgar pulled himself to his feet. "Then you die knowing that you'll never kill the King of Azeroth."

Garona sat for a moment, her mind working over

the possibilities. At length she said, "Give me a hand up. We have to move on."

They continued to spiral downward, through false analogs of the tower levels above. Finally they reached the level that would be the uppermost level, of Medivh's observatory and lair. Instead the stairs spilled out on a reddish plain. It seemed to be poured out of cooling obsidian, dark, reflective puzzle pieces floating on fire beneath their feet. Khadgar instinctively jumped back, but the footing seemed solid and the heat, while sweltering, was not oppressive.

In the center of the great cave was a simple collection of iron furniture. A work bench and stool, a few chairs, a gathering of cabinets. For a moment it looked oddly familiar, then Khadgar realized that it was set up in an exact duplicate to Medivh's tower room.

Standing among the iron furniture was the broad-shouldered form of the Magus. Khadgar strained to see something in his manner, in his bearing, that would betray him, that would reveal this figure to not be the Medivh he had come to know and trust, the older man who had shown his faith and encouraged his work. Something that would declare this to be an imposter.

There was nothing. This was the only Medivh he had ever known.

"Hello, Young Trust," said the Magus and flames ignited along his beard as he smiled. "Hello, Emissary. I've been expecting you both."

SIXTEEN

The Breaking of a Mage

"It was inspired, I must say," said the Medivh who was and was not Medivh. "Inspired to summon the shadow of my past, a piece that would stop me from pursuing you. Of course, while you were out gathering your strength, I was out gathering my own."

Khadgar looked at Garona and nodded. The half-orc moved a few steps to the right. They would surround the old man if they had to.

"Master, what happened to you?" said Khadgar, taking a step forward, trying to focus the Magus's attention on him.

The older mage laughed. "Happened to me? Nothing happened to me. This is who I am. I was tainted from birth, polluted from before my conception, a bad seed grown to bear bitter fruit. You have never seen the true Medivh."

"Magus, whatever has happened, I'm sure it can be fixed," said Khadgar, walking slowly toward him. Garona orbited out to the right, and her long-bladed dagger had vanished again—her hands were apparently empty.

"Why should I fix it?" said Medivh with an evil smile. "All goes as planned. The orcs will slay the humans and I will control them through warlock-chiefs like Gul'dan. I will lead these misshapened creations to the lost tomb where Sargeras's body is, protected against demon and human but not against orc, and my form will be free. And then I can shed this lumpish body and weakened spirit and burn this world as it so richly deserves."

Khadgar stepped to the left as he spoke. "You are Sargeras."

"Yes and no," said the Magus. "I am, for when Aegwynn killed my physical body I hid within her womb, and invested her very cells with my dark essence. When she finally chose to mate with a human mage, I was already there. Medivh's dark twin, completly subsumed within his form."

"Monstrous," said Khadgar.

Medivh grinned. "Little different than what Aegwynn had planned, for she placed the power of the *Tirisfalen* within the child as well. Small wonder that there was so little room for the young Medivh himself, with the demon and the light both fighting over his very soul. So when the power truly manifested within him, I shut him down for a while, until I could put my own plans into operation."

Khadgar continued to move left, trying not to watch as Garona crept up behind the older mage. Instead he said, "Is there anything of the real Medivh within you?"

"Some," said Medivh. "Enough to deal with you lesser creatures. Enough to fool the kings and wizards as to my intent. Medivh is a mask—I have left enough of him at the surface to display to others. And if in my workings I seem odd or even mad, they write it off to my position and responsibility, and to the power invested in me by my dear mother."

Medivh gave a predatory grin. "I was crafted first by Magna Aegwynn's politics to be her tool, and then shaped by demonic hands to be their tool. Even the Order saw me as little more than a weapon to be used against demons. And so it not surprising at all that I am nothing more that the sum of my parts."

Garona was behind the mage now, blade drawn, moving on the softest of steps on the obsidian floor. There were no tears in her eyes, but rather a steely determination. Khadgar kept himself focused on Medivh, not wanting to betray her with a single glance.

"You see," continued the mad mage, "I am nothing but one more component in the great machine, one that has been running since the Well of Eternity was first shattered. The one thing that the original bits of Medivh and myself agree on is that this cycle needs to be shattered. Of this, I assure you, we are of one mind."

Garona was within a step now, her dagger raised. She took the last step.

"Excuse me," said Medivh, and lashed out with a fist. Mystic energies danced along the older man's knuckles, and he caught the half-orc square in the face. She staggered backward under the blow.

Khadgar let loose a curse and raised his hands to cast a spell. Something to knock the mage off his balance. Something simple. Something quick.

Medivh was quicker, turning back to him and raising a claw-like hand. Immediately, Khadgar felt the air around him tighten into a restraining cloak, trapping his arms and legs and making it impossible for him to move. He shouted but his voice sounded muffled and coming from a great distance.

Medivh raised his other hand, and pain shot through Khadgar's body. The joints of his skeleton seemed to seethe with red-hot spikes that subsided quickly into dull, throbbing pains. His chest tightened, and his flesh felt like it dried out and crawled along his frame. He felt like the fluids were being pulled from his body, leaving a shriveled husk behind. And with it he felt his magic pulled away as well, his body drained of his ability to cast spells, to summon the requisite energies. He felt like a vessel being emptied.

As suddenly as the attack descended upon him, it

had passed, and Khadgar toppled to the floor, the wind knocked out of him. It hurt his chest to breath.

Garona had recovered at this point, and came in screaming this time, bringing her dagger-hand upward, to catch Medivh beneath the left breast. Instead of trying to back up, Medivh stepped toward the charging half-orc, inside the arc of her blow. He raised a hand and caught her forehead in his hand. She froze in mid-charge.

Mystic energy of a sickening yellow hue pulsed beneath his hand and the half-orc hung there, her body twitching helplessly, as the mage held her by the forehead.

"Poor, poor Garona," said Medivh. "I thought with your conflicting heritages, you of all people would understand what I'm going through. That you would understand the importance of making your own way. But you're just like the others, aren't you?"

The wide-eyed half-orc could only manage a spittle-drenched gurgle in response.

"Let me show you my world, Garona," said Medivh. "Let me drive my own divisions and doubts into you. You'll never know who you serve and why. You'll never find your peace."

Garona tried to scream, but it died in her throat as her face was bathed in a radiant sunburst issued from Medivh's palm.

Medivh laughed and let the half-orc collapse to the floor, sobbing. She tried to rise, but slumped again. Her eyes were wide and wild, and her breath was short and ragged, torn by tears.

Khadgar could breathe now, but the breath was short and tight. His joints burned, and his muscles ached. He saw his reflection in the obsidian floor. . . .

And it was the old man of the vision looking back at him. Heavy, tired eyes surrounded by wrinkles and gray hair. Even his beard had turned white.

And Khadgar's heart sank. Robbed of his youth, of his magic, he no longer felt like he would survive this battle.

"That was instructive," said Medivh, turning back to Khadgar. "One of the negative things about this humaniform cell I am trapped in is that the human part keeps reaching out. Making friends. Helping people. It makes it so difficult to destroy them later on. I almost wept when I killed Moroes and Cook, did you know? That's why I had to come down here. But it's like anything else. Once you get used to it, you can kill friends as easily as anyone else."

Now he stood a few paces in front of Khadgar, his shoulders straight, his eyes vibrant. Looking more like Medivh than at any time Khadgar had seen him. Looking confident. Looking at ease. Looking frighteningly, damnedly sane.

"And now you get to die, Young Trust," said the Magus. "It seems your trust was misplaced after all." Medivh raised a hand cupped with magical energy.

There was a throaty scream from the right. "Medivh!" bellowed Lothar, Champion of Azeroth.

Medivh looked up, and his face seemed to soften for a moment, though his hand still burned with the mystic power. "Anduin Lothar?" he said. "Old friend, why are you here?"

"Stop it now, Med," said Lothar, and Khadgar could hear the pain the Champion's voice. "Stop it before it is too late. I don't want to fight you."

"I don't want to fight you either, old friend," said Medivh raising his hand. "You have no idea what it's like to do the things I've done. Harsh things. Necessary things. I don't want to fight you. So lay down your weapon, friend, and let this be done."

Medivh opened his palm and the bits of magic droned toward the Champion, bathing him in stars.

"You want to help me, don't you, old friend," said Medivh, the harsh smile once more on his face. "You want to be my servant. Come help me dispose of this child. Then we can be friends again."

The spangling stars around Lothar faded, and the Champion took a slow, firm step forward, then another, then a third, and now Lothar charged forward. As he charged, the Champion raised his rune-carved blade high. He charged at Medivh, not at Khadgar. A curse rose in his voice, a curse backed by sorrow and tears.

Medivh was surprised, but just for a moment. He dodged backward and Lothar's first cut passed harmlessly through the space the Magus had occupied a half-second before. The Champion checked the swing and brought it back in a solid blocking motion, driving the mage another step back. Then an overhand chop, driving back another step.

Now Medivh had recovered himself, and the next blow landed squarely on a shield of bluish energy, the yellow fires of the sword spattering harmlessly like sparks. Lothar tried to cut upward, then thrust, then chop again. Each attack was met and countered by the shield.

Medivh snarled and raised a clawed hand, mystic energy dancing in his palm. Lothar screamed as his clothes suddenly burst into flames. Medivh smiled at his handiwork, then waved his hand, tossing the burning form of Lothar aside like a rag doll.

"Just. Gets. Easier," said Medivh, biting off the words and turning back to where Khadgar had been kneeling.

Except Khadgar had moved. Medivh turned to find the no-longer young mage right behind him, with the sword Lothar had provided drawn and pressed against the Magus's left breast. The runes along the blade glowed like miniature suns.

"Don't even blink," said Khadgar.

A moment paused, and a bead of sweat trickled down Medivh's cheek.

"So it comes to this," said the Magus. "I don't think you have the skill or the will to use that properly, Young Trust."

"I think," said Khadgar, and it seemed that his voice wheezed and burbled as he spoke, "that the human part of you, Medivh, kept others around despite your own plans. As a backup. As a plan for when you finally went mad. So your friends could put you down. So we could break the cycle where you cannot."

Medivh managed a small sigh, and his features softened. "I never meant to really harm anyone," he said. "I only wanted to have my own life." As he spoke, he jerked his hand upward, his palm glowing with mystic energy, seeking to scramble Khadgar's mind as he had Garona's.

Medivh never got the chance. At the first flinch, Khadgar lunged forward, driving the thin blade of the runesword between Medivh's ribs, into the heart.

Medivh looked surprised, even shocked, but his mouth still moved. He was trying to say something.

Khadgar drove the blade home to the hilt, the tip erupting from the back of the mage's robes. The mage sunk to his knees, and Khadgar dropped with him as well, keeping his hands firmly locked on the blade. The old mage gasped and struggled to say something.

"Thank you," he managed at last. "I fought it for as long as I could. . . ."

Then the master mage's face began to transform, the beard turning fully to flame, the horns sprouting from his brow. With the death of Medivh, Sargeras finally came fully to the surface. Khadgar felt the hilt of the runeblade grow warm, as the fires danced along Medivh's flesh, transforming him to a thing of shadow and flame.

Behind the kneeling, wounded Magus, Khadgar could see the smoldering form of Lothar rise once more. The Champion stumbled forward, his flesh and armor still smoking. He raised his runeblade once more, and brought it across in a hard, level swing.

The edge of the blade burst like a sun as it struck Medivh's neck, and severed the master mage's head from the neck in one smooth blow.

It was like unstoppering a bottle, for everything within Medivh rushed out at once through ragged remnants of his neck. A great torrent of energy and light, shadow and fire, smoke and rage, all spilling upward like a fountain, splashing against the ceiling of the underground vault, and dissipating away. Within the seething caldron of energies, Khadgar thought he could make out a horned face, crying in despair and rage.

And when it was over, all that was left was the skin and clothes of the Magus. All that was within him had been eaten away, and now that his human form had been ripped asunder, there was no way to contain it.

Lothar used the tip of his sword to stir aside the rags and flesh that had been Medivh and said, "We need to go."

Khadgar looked around. There was no sign of Garona. The Magus's head had boiled away all the flesh, leaving only a glistening red-white skull.

The former apprentice shook his head. "I need to stay here. Attend to a few things."

Lothar growled, "The greatest danger may be passed, but the obvious one is still there. We have to drive back the orcs and close the portal."

Khadgar thought of the vision, of Stormwind burning and Llane's death. He thought of his own vision, of his now-aged form in final battle with the orcs. Instead he said, "I must bury what's left of Medivh. I should find Garona. She couldn't have gone far."

Lothar grunted an assent and shambled toward the entrance. At last he turned and said, "It couldn't have been helped, you know. We tried to alter it, but it was all part of a larger scheme."

Khadgar nodded slowly, "I know. All part of a greater cycle. A cycle that now at last may be broken."

Lothar left the former apprentice beneath the citadel, and Khadgar gathered up what was left of the physical remains of the Magus. He found a shovel and a wooden box in the stable. He put the skull and the bits of skin in the box with the tattered remains of "The Song of Aegwynn," and buried them all deep in the courtyard in view of the tower. Perhaps later he would raise a monument, but for the time being it would be best to not let others know where the master mage's remains were. After he had finished burying the Magus, he dug two more graves, human-sized, and laid Moroes and Cook to rest to one side of Medivh.

He let out a deep sigh, and looked up at the tower. White-stoned Karazhan, home of the most mighty mage of Azeroth, the Last Guardian of the Order of Tirisfal loomed above him. Behind him the sky was lightening, and the sun threatened to touch the topmost level of the tower.

Something else caught his eye, above the empty, entrance hall, along the balcony overlooking the main entrance. A bit of movement, a fragment of a dream. Khadgar let out a deeper sigh and nodded at the ghostly trespasser that watched his every move.

"I can see you, now, you know," he said aloud.

EPILOGUE
Full Circle

The trespasser from the future looked down from the balcony at the no-longer young man of the past.

"How long have you been able to see me?" asked the trespasser.

"I have felt bits of you as long as I have been here," said Khadgar. "From my first day. How long have you been there?"

"Most of an evening," said the trespasser in his tattered red robes. "The dawn is coming up here."

"Here as well," said the former apprentice. "Perhaps that is why we can talk. You are a vision, but different than any I have seen before. We can see each other and converse. Are you future or past?"

"Future," said the trespasser. "Do you know who I am?"

"Your form is different than when I last saw you, you are younger, and calmer, but yes, I know," said Khadgar. He motioned toward the three heaps of turned earth—two large and one small. "I thought I just buried you."

"You did," said the trespasser. "At least you buried much of what was the worst about me."

"And now you're back. Or you will be back," said Khadgar. "Different, but the same."

The trespasser nodded. "In many ways, I was never here the first time around."

"More is the pity," said Khadgar. "So what are you in the future? Magus? Guardian? Demon?"

"Be reassured. I am a better being than I was," said the trespasser. "I am free of the taint of Sargeras thanks to your actions this day. Now I may deal directly with the Lord of the Burning Legion. Thank you. There cannot be success without sacrifice."

"Sacrifice," said Khadgar, the words bitter in his mouth. "Tell me this then, ghost of the future. Is all that we have seen true? Will Stormwind truly fall? Will Garona slay King Llane? Must I die, in this aged flesh, in some nether-spawned land?"

The being on the balcony paused for a long moment, and Khadgar feared that he would fade away. Instead he said, "As long as there are Guardians, there is Order. And as long as there is Order, the parts are there to be played. Decisions made millennia ago set both your path and mine. It is part of greater cycle, one that has held us all in its sway."

Khadgar craned his head upward. The sun was now touching the top half of the tower. "Perhaps there should not be Guardians then, if this has been the price."

"Agreed," said the trespasser, and as the strong light of day began to grow, he began to fade. "But for the moment, for your moment, we must all play our part. We all must pay this price. And then, when we have the chance, we will start anew."

And with that the trespasser was gone, the last fragments of his being swept back into the future by an errant wind of magic.

Khadgar shook his aged head and looked at the three newly-dug graves. Lothar's surviving men took their dead and wounded back with them to Stormwind. There was no sign of Garona, and though Khadgar would search the tower once more, he doubted that she was within. He would take what books he thought were valuable, what supplies he could, and set protective wards over the rest. Then he would leave as well, and follow Lothar into battle.

Hefting his shovel, he walked back into the now-abandoned keep of Karazhan, and wondered if he would ever return.

As the trespasser spoke a small breeze kicked up, a mere churning of the leaves, but it was enough to scatter the vision. The no-longer young man broke up and faded like dying fog, and the no-longer old man watched him go.

A single tear ran down the side of Medivh's face. So much sacrifice, so much pain. Both to keep the plan of the Guardians in place, and then so much sacrifice to break that plan, to break the world free of its lock-step. To bring about true peace.

And now, even that was at risk. Now one more sacrifice would have to be made. He would have to pull the power from this place if he would succeed in what was to come. In the final conflict with the Burning Legion.

The sun had risen farther now, and was almost to the level of his balcony. He would have to work quickly now.

He raised a hand, and the clouds began to swirl above the peak of the tower. Slowly first, then more quickly, until the upper ranges of the tower itself were encased within a hurricane.

Now he reached deep within himself, and released the words, words made up of equal parts regret and anger, words caught within him since the day that his life ended the first time. Words that laid claim to the whole of that previous life, for good and ill. Accepting its power, and in doing so, accepting the responsibility for what was done the last time he wore flesh.

The hurricane around the tower howled, and the tower itself resisted his claim. He stated it again, and then a third time, shouting to be heard over the winds that he himself had summoned. Slowly, almost grudgingly, the tower gave up its secrets.

The power burned from within the stones and mortars, and leached outward, channeled by the force of the winds toward the base, toward Medivh. All the visions began to bubble loose of its fabric, and stream downward. The fall of Sargeras, with its hundreds of screaming demons, fell in on him, as did the final conflict with Aegwynn and Khadgar's own battle beneath the dull red sun. Medivh's appearance before Gul'dan and the boyish battles of three young nobles and Moroes breaking Cook's favorite crystal, all were pulled into him. And with those visions came memories, and with those memories responsibilities. This must be avoided. This must never happen again. This must be corrected.

So too did the images and power leach upward from the hidden tower, from the pits beneath the tower itself. The fall of Stormwind flamed upward at him, and the death of Llane, and the myriad demons summoned in the middle of the night and unleashed against those in the Order too close to the truth. All of them fountained upward and were consumed within the form of the mage standing on the balcony.

All the shards, all the pieces of history, known and unrevealed, spiraled down the tower or rose from its dungeons and flowed into the man who had been the Last Guardian of Tirisfal. The pain was great, but Medivh grimaced and accepted it, taking the energy and the bittersweet memories it bore with equal measure.

The last image to fade was the one beneath the balcony itself, an image of a young man, a rucksack at his feet, a letter marked with the crimson seal of the Kirin

Tor, hope in his heart and butterflies in his stomach. That youth was the last to fade, as he moved slowly toward the entrance, the magic surrounding his vision, his shard of the past, spiraled upward, unraveling him and letting the energy pass into the former Magus. As the last bit of Khadgar fell into him, a tear pooled at the corner of Medivh's eye.

Medivh held both hands to his chest tightly, containing all that he had regained. The tower of Karazhan was just a tower now, a pile of stone in the remote reaches, far from the traveled paths. Now the power of the place was within him. And the responsibility to do better with it, this time.

"And so we start anew," says Medivh.

And with that, he transformed into a raven, and was gone.

ABOUT THE AUTHOR

Jeff Grubb is the author of Starcraft: Liberty's Crusade. He is also author or coauthor of books in the Forgotten Realms, Dragonlance, and Magic: The Gathering Lines. His job is building worlds, his hobby is explaining them to other people. He lives in Seattle with his wife and oft-times cowriter Kate Novak, and two cats.

Visit the Simon & Schuster Web site:

www.SimonSays.com

and sign up for our
mystery e-mail updates!

Keep up on the latest
new releases, author appearances,
news, chats, special offers, and more!
We'll deliver the information
right to your inbox — if it's new,
you'll know about it.

2350-01